48 STATES

EVETTE DAVIS

Cover Design by Rebecca Lown

Editing by Cassandra Dunn

Marketing and PR by Pacific and Court and Claire Mulcahy

❋ Created with Vellum

This book is dedicated to my father, Stephen Reiss, who died during the pandemic. "Writers write," he said, and he was right.

48 STATES

48 STATES

Those who have crossed
    With direct eyes, to death's other Kingdom
    Remember us—if at all—not as lost
    Violent souls, but only
    As the hollow men
    The stuffed men...

Is it like this
    In death's other kingdom
    Waking alone
    At the hour when we are
    Trembling with tenderness
    Lips that would kiss
    Form prayers to broken stone...

The eyes are not here
    There are no eyes here
    In this valley of dying stars
    In this hollow valley
    This broken jaw of our lost kingdoms

T.S. ELIOT

October 15, 2040
NOTICE TO EVACUATE
North Dakota

You are hereby notified that this area is now under the jurisdiction of the Department of Energy as directed by presidential executive order.

All civilians must evacuate the area within 30 days. Tune your radios to am 1040 or visit www.energyterritory/evacuation.gov for further instructions.

ONE

RIVER STRUGGLED to shut the bar's door against the howling wind. Winter was a bitch in the Territory, but at least her heavy gear kept her warm. Twenty pairs of eyes followed her as she entered the bar. She tracked the stares out of the corner of her eye as she walked towards an open seat, never acknowledging the scrutiny. She sighed with relief as she eased on to one of the barstools. She must have traveled up and down the highway a dozen times in her rig tonight, with nothing but natural gas flares for company. Up and back again until her arms ached from dragging the hoses in and out of the holding tanks. She could feel her back stiffening up. But it was another night without an injury, and more overtime pay in her bank account.

A bar back placed a bowl of freshly made popcorn in front of her. The buttery aroma transported her back to her childhood when jump ropes and sleepovers ruled the day...*Eeny, meeny, miny, moe, catch a tiger by the toe, if he hollers, let him go, eeny, meeny, miny, moe, my mother told me to pick the very best one...* A delivery from the bartender brought her back to the present.

"This is for you," he said, placing a glass of what was likely tequila —men always sent that, or Jägermeister—in front of her.

"Send it back, Bobby," River said, pushing the drink away.

"Sure thing," he said. "If I were you, I'd skip the drink and get out. Most of these guys just got back in town from their shifts."

"Thanks for the warning," River said. "I've had a long night myself, so please just bring me my usual?"

River watched Bobby walk away to make her drink. If she'd been looking for a lover, he would have been a good choice, with his tight black T-shirts and full sleeves of ink. His right arm was a multi-colored mix of peacocks with gleaming feathers, mermaids, and the rings of Saturn posted mid-bicep. An elaborately inked treasure map covered the other arm, but he never revealed what the prize was. A nose ring dangled from his septum, giving him a menacing air, but it was all a show. He'd come to nurse a broken heart. River wasn't sure of the particulars, only that he preferred being in the Territory to San Francisco. She reminded him how crazy it was to leave California for such a rotten, dangerous place, but he just laughed and told her "Anywhere can go rotten if you fuck it up bad enough." She nodded, knowing only too well that he was right.

"You're being stubborn, as usual," Bobby said as he returned with her rum and coke. "I'm going to say it again. Most of these guys just got off their twenty and are ready to party."

She knew what he meant. Williston, North Dakota served as the main outpost for the Territory. The state had been emptied by forced evacuation and then repopulated with a mix of workers, mostly veterans from the Caliphate War, working on rig crews in twenty-day shifts or hitches. As soon as the shifts ended, the crews came back into town ready to make up for lost time. If you wanted to have a drink and mind your own business, you patronized Outerlands. The other ten or so bars catered to a mix of preferences and price points. With a 20:5 ratio of men to women, Bobby was reminding River to be careful. Women were usually meant for one thing inside the Territory, and it wasn't for hauling.

Still, she was always glad to see the neon sign for Outerlands as she came around the bend in her rig on Highway 85. Its grey concrete floors were worn and pockmarked from years of use. The wood-paneled walls and lack of windows kept it dark inside. But the drinks were strong, and the management favored music from the 1970s. She chose Outerlands because she liked the name, and because they held a trivia night once a month. A voracious reader, she was good at collecting random bits of information, and usually managed to win a few rounds, especially if the topics involved history and literature. She wasn't in the mood to be chased out of her only source of entertainment.

"I can handle myself," River said.

"Maybe," he said. "But I feel compelled to ask for what must be the one hundredth time, why don't you get the hell out of here already?"

"And leave all this behind?" River mocked. "Compared to being stationed in France, this is paradise."

For nearly two years she'd managed to avoid telling him the truth. That her husband had killed himself and left her with a mound of debt and few options except to leave her daughter and work in this Godforsaken wasteland. That at eighty dollars an hour–more than one hundred if she worked overtime–she'd signed the contract to drive a haul truck inside the Territory as soon as they'd offered her a position.

"You know you don't belong here with all these *heathens*," Bobby said.

"*Heathens*...That's pretty good," River replied. "Your Berkeley roots are showing. Are you referring to their lack of godliness or just a general barbarous nature?"

"Both, and for the record, it was Berkeley undergrad. I studied creative writing at the University of San Francisco," Bobby said. "Until my scholarship ran out. The government cancelled student loans for MFA programs around the time they issued the first list of banned books."

"Here's to words and their meanings," River said, remembering that day. Her mother, a librarian, was outraged that the government ordered books it considered subversive to be pulled from the shelves.

River sensed someone standing behind her. The stench of body odor and solvents invaded her space as he leaned in to speak to her. She breathed through her mouth to avoid the smell.

"What's the matter?" he asked. "Don't you like my gift? Maybe I should've sent you what I'm having. Bartender! Bring over another 'Taste of a Woman.'"

"No thanks," River said, wanting nothing to do with the bourbon cocktail he was pushing. "I'm not drinking."

"That's a bunch of bullshit," he said, cutting her off. "I see your glass right there."

"You didn't let me finish," River said. "I was about to say I'm not drinking with other people."

"Well, that's too bad," he said. "Because I've decided you and I are going to have ourselves a little party tonight."

"That's not going to happen," River said, keeping her gaze straight ahead.

"Oh, come on," he said. "I can be a lot of fun."

"Actually, I was just leaving."

"We can walk out together then," he said. "Are we clear?"

The majority of the bar patrons, never candidates for charm school to begin with, sensed the promise of violence and turned to watch. Her unwanted visitor grinned, egged on by the spectators, revealing a mouth full of missing and half-broken teeth.

"I promise to be nice," he said, grabbing River's newly cropped brown hair. The pain was immediate as he dragged her closer to his rank breath. "Don't make this harder than it has to be. I don't want to have to hurt you."

River nodded as she rose from the barstool. She stomped on his foot, grabbed his other hand, and brought his arm in close, using it as a fulcrum to send him tumbling. The man let out a whimper as his bone snapped. He landed flat on his back with a thud. River snatched her Glock from the back of her jeans and pointed it straight at his chest.

"If you so much as raise a finger, I will put a bullet through your heart," River said. "Are we clear?"

Her attacker nodded, but remained otherwise motionless.

"Good," she said. "Because I don't want to have to hurt you."

River turned back to the bar, grabbed her glass, and finished her drink, catching Bobby's eye along the way.

"I'll pay you next time," she said, heading for the door.

She kept her gun out and did not let her guard down until she was inside the cab of her truck with the engine running. The snap of the man's forearm echoed in her head as she tried to catch her breath. Two tours of duty in the Army, and she still hadn't grown comfortable with her ability to inflict pain. It didn't compute with the images she carried of herself.

Her father's death, and the poverty it brought, forced her to enlist after high school. Although it had been a welcome distraction from the ache of bitter disappointment, she carried a lingering sense of shame over how easily she'd adapted to the Army, to the physical endurance and, eventually, the feel of a gun in her hand. The preparation for war, the rehearsal to kill, the military's rhythms and customs, hierarchy, division of labor–all of it brought a sense of organization and certainty that were comforting. Beyond the orderliness, it bore no resemblance to what she'd previously wanted or had known, back when she'd been a different person with a different trajectory. She'd mistakenly believed that her life would be pleasant and filled with possibilities, until it had all been irrevocably altered, like the landscape of the Territory.

River felt safer cooped up in the desert in the Middle East with twenty men and little more than a hole to shit in, than working in the Territory. For almost two years she'd been ignoring incessant offers to buy her a drink, and made sure to engage the flimsy chain on her motel door nightly. Her gun had been a constant companion since arriving.

River thought about switching bars as she drove home. She decided against it. If she saw the rig tech again, the semi-automatic would prove crucial; there would be no fumbling to reload, just a steady supply of bullets in the chamber. If he came for her, she would end it. There was no penalty for killing a man inside the Territory. For that you would need laws, and the government had signed them all away.

TWO

THE SKIN around Cooper's identification tag itched. It had since the day he'd gotten it. He suspected they'd put the damn chip in wrong, too hurried to get everyone tagged and bagged to identify the proper spot on his forearm. That was the government for you, always moving faster than their brains could carry them, but then they'd been in a rush to get under the skin of every American after the killings.

Normally the tag was just a mild annoyance. Cooper was a former soldier, after all. But today it stung as he scratched. He glanced at the angry patch of skin on his right forearm, then raised his eyes back to the road. He was barreling down Texas highways at speeds unsafe for most mortals, but if he didn't hurry, he was going to be late for what was certain to be an uncomfortable meeting and a very bad day.

He'd signed on with Universal Industries as head of security prior to the formation of the Energy Territories, and had accumulated enough zeros in his bank account to retire comfortably in a few years. It all seemed to be working so well. Unfortunately, today was the day the entire situation was going to explode and Cooper knew there was very little he could do except try to contain things. The same way the Russians contained Chernobyl, he thought, but what the hell.

Cooper gave himself a good slap in the face. He'd been burning the candle at both ends, flying to North Dakota, Wyoming, and then back to corporate headquarters in Houston every few days to review security reports and work with ground crews to clear away brush and debris inside the Territories, and the pace was beginning to catch up with him despite his ironman conditioning. The eyes in the sky had to be able to see clearly. More importantly, so did the guards on the ground. Territory One had a defendable space of twenty miles between its borders and production areas. Wyoming, now Territory Two, was more complicated, its terrain forcing them to focus their operations on the east side of the state. The city of Casper served as the main hub; he'd personally overseen the burning of the brush all the way to Cheyenne.

Cooper's thoughts drifted back to his grandparents' farm in Michigan, where he went to live when he was ten, after his parents died in a car crash. As a child, he loved to roam the grounds, exploring the goings-on between the stalks of corn and the cattails in the creek. There were beehives down by the river and snakes in the orchards. The raspberries were sweet and juicy straight off the bushes. Sometimes when he was stationed overseas, far away from the things he loved, he would try to remember the musty scent of his grandparents' root cellar, a magical cool, dark space that held row upon row of wooden baskets filled with the bounty of that year's crops. There were piles of pale-yellow onions and Macintosh apples, and jars of pickled vegetables and jams lined the shelves. There was a box of candles and a giant square-shaped flashlight with a beam that could shine halfway across the darkness when the dogs heard a noise. It was all there, everything they needed to survive a storm or some other kind of trouble.

His grandparents, it seemed to him as a child, were prepared for anything. The same desire for preparation and order drew him into the Marine Corps as a young man. It was the fuel that fed all of his ambitions. In Cooper's opinion, every good thing ever created came from folks like his grandparents: honest, hard-working people who took pride in the smallest of details, because in the end, the details were all you had. What you honed and shaped was what you got, and Cooper had made sure to see to his affairs with the same care his grandparents had lavished on their life and loved ones.

The Territories were a great distance from his childhood home, and

Cooper had been away for a long, long while. So long, in fact, that the farm was gone. Only his memories remained. After his grandparents died, the government took the land, demolishing the house to create a buffer for a new interstate. It was all a circle, Cooper thought as he scratched his arm and continued down the highway: creation, demolition, and creation again. Sometimes in the name of progress you had to destroy the things you loved.

THREE

It was midnight by the time River pulled her truck back onto the road, the full moon illuminating the pavement in front of her. She felt giddy with victory, but also slightly embarrassed at how easy it was to answer most of the trivia night questions. Lucky for her, she remembered her high school book report about daylight savings time being abolished. The reunification of the two Koreas had been big news; you almost didn't have to be a trivia nerd to remember that day in 2025. The question about the only state to not legalize marijuana stumped her, never having been that interested in the stuff, but someone on her team remembered it was Alabama. It was fun to win trivia night, but it was more fun being in a room with other people who liked to use their brains. She missed that part of her life. It was rare to find avid readers inside the Territory. Even the clerk at the Post Office seemed mystified by her habits.

"You sure do get a lot of mail," the woman had said earlier in the day when River had picked up a few packages. "What's inside all the boxes?"

When River said they were books, the postmaster replied, "Books! What do you need those for?"

"I read them," River said, her usual reply.

Her response always made the clerk giggle, like it was the funniest thing she ever heard. As with the bartender, though, she never told her the truth: that books were one of the few pleasures she allowed herself in the Territory. That they were her escape from a brutal but boring existence and provided solace for a broken heart.

After leaving the post office River had gone home, made coffee, and grabbed her laptop to call her mother. Ingrid Petersen picked up immediately. River could see her daughter, Ava, playing in the distance behind her mother.

"Hi, Mom," River said.

"Hi yourself," Ingrid said. "Hey, I know you and I need to catch up, but she's been asking about you all day. Can I put her on?"

"You bet!" River said in a voice reserved for small children and puppies. "Hey, Ava. How's my girl?"

"I miss you," Ava said, nestled squarely in her grandmother's lap. The three-year-old had her father's jet-black hair, but River's eyes. She was grateful to see a bit of herself when she looked at Ava. It somehow gave her less to regret. Still, she wondered if it had been fair to bring her daughter into a world with so much uncertainty, and into a home with so much upheaval. River and her mother were almost the same age when they'd had their daughters, although their circumstances were quite different. As a mother, Ingrid had always been warm and loving, the benefit of never having been a combat soldier. For River, it was difficult to reconcile the wide disparity between war and mother-hood. She often found it difficult to express tenderness, an emotion she'd hidden away in combat. Emotions don't turn on and off like a light switch she told herself, but she couldn't help worrying she was letting her daughter down.

"I miss you too, pumpkin," River said. "I promise I'll be home soon, and then you and I will be able to see more of each other."

"OK, Mama. Love you," Ava said, disappearing from the screen.

River scrutinized her mother, noting the deep creases at the folds of her eyelids, a hint of a shadow beneath. Raising a child took energy, more than a 55-year-old woman should have to muster after a day's work.

"You look tired, Mom," River said.

"I was about to say the same thing to you," Ingrid said.

"I took an extra shift," River said. "It paid double, so it was worth it."

"River, it's time to stop this nonsense and come back home," her mother scolded. "We have enough money to get by now. Marc's debt is paid off."

"Just a few more weeks and then I'll come home," River pleaded, hoping to get her off the phone. But a thought did nag at her.

What are you still doing here when your daughter needs you?

Before River could answer her own question, a man appeared in the road several feet in front of her. She blinked a few times to clear her sight, worried the two rum and Cokes had caught up with her. But then the specter raised his arms over his head in surrender. River's brain reverted to combat mode as she slammed on the brakes, forcing her truck to the side of the road. She pulled her Glock from beneath the driver's seat, her internal voice doing an assessment. *I have seventeen bullets in a new magazine, and he is one man with no weapon showing.*

She watched the reaction of the man as she climbed out of her truck. He was definitely surprised to see a woman. As the seconds whirled past, River scrutinized the figure in front of her, trying to get a sense of what she was dealing with. The stranger stood stock still, except for his chest, which rose and fell rapidly like a dog panting. In the light of the full moon, she noted a hint of red hair under a navy ski cap and a pale face marked by some nasty scrapes. His hands were also a mess, chewed up and bloody like he'd slid down a mountain on his fingers.

"Keep your hands up where I can see them," she said, her gun trained on him. "We don't get a lot of hitchhikers in this part of the world. Tell me what you're doing here."

"I had an accident," the man said.

"An accident?" River repeated.

"I was kayaking on the Missouri, collided with a boulder and got tossed out," he said. "I must have hit my head. When I woke up, I was miles downstream and pretty beat up."

River remained silent, her sixth sense telling her she was missing something.

"Can I put my hands down?" the man asked. "I'm exhausted."

"Not yet," she said. "Tell me again how you got here."

"I told you, I had an accident."

"Kayaking at night? Near the Territory?" River asked. "You're either stupid, crazy, or worse, you're one of those protesters looking for trouble. I'll tell you right now, trouble is not something I want any part of." She fished a small Maglite out of her coat pocket and ran the beam across the stranger's frame. She went back and forth twice, finally stopping when she caught something she'd missed before. "Did you also shoot yourself while you were kayaking?" River asked, eyeing what was clearly a bullet hole through the sleeve of his dry suit.

"I know it looks bad," the man said. "But I can explain."

"I doubt that very much," she said.

"Please, I need your help," he said. "One night, and then I'll be on my way. If you'll just let me sleep in your truck and get me a first aid kit, I'll patch myself up and be out at dawn. If anyone asks, you can tell them you had no idea I was there."

"You do know where you are?" she asked. "They'll shoot us both if they find out I've been harboring a fugitive, and it would be a totally legal kill."

"I know it," the man said, looking River straight in the eye. "I'm wounded. It's winter and freezing outside. I have no weapon or food, very few supplies, and no idea where I am. The truth is, you are my only chance for survival."

River had seconds to decide. At the moment, they were alone. It was possible a car or another tanker truck would appear on the highway, or maybe a patrol drone would pass overhead. If they were discovered, she would have no choice but to turn him in. What she was contemplating was against the rules. She'd just told him she didn't want trouble, but, really, a tiny part of her did. Maybe she was over-confident from a night of winning, of being in her element, but she wanted to know more about the stranger standing before her. How did this man with ginger hair manage to trespass into the Territory? She'd driven this stretch of road countless times and encountered nothing and gone home to more of the same. Maybe she could steal away a little time to learn his story, take a break from the monotony of her existence. One night, and then the mystery man would be gone. And if he tried anything, she reasoned, she would kill him without a second thought.

"OK," she said. "One night, and then you are dust in the wind. Got it?"

"Got it. I promise, I won't be any trouble," the man said, lowering his arms just seconds before he passed out.

LIBRARY OF CONGRESS
ONLINE RESOURCES DIVISION

POST IN A PUBLIC PLACE
NOTICE OF FEDERAL CURFEW

Please be advised that by executive order, the President of the United States has declared a curfew and ban on public assembly from dusk to dawn.

No business or place of entertainment shall stay open after dark.

Vehicles driving after dusk will be subject to search. Self-driving vehicles without minders will be impounded. Unregistered drones will be destroyed.

This order shall stay in place until it is deemed safe for individuals to congregate in public.

This notice must not be tampered with or removed.

United States Printing Office

FOUR

POST IN A PUBLIC PLACE

THE STRANGER'S body hit the asphalt. River had to get him into her
truck before someone discovered them. As she had dozens of times
before in the Army, she lifted his limp body and carried him to her
truck. River spread out some old papers and rags to keep his blood
from staining the upholstery. She was grateful he wasn't as heavy as
Marc had been. Her husband had been impossible to move after he'd
passed out.

As soon as River pulled into the parking lot of the motel, she realized the harder part was coming up: she had to get her wounded guest
into her room unseen. It was 12:45 a.m. She hoped the night manager
kept to his normal routine. This was around the time he usually
walked over to a nearby all-night diner for a cup of coffee and some
pie. He probably favored one of the waitresses. Even with the manager
gone, she made the trip down the corridor with her heart in her throat,
tucking the man's wounded arm under hers and dragging him along
like he'd had one too many. As she walked, she rehearsed her excuse.
If she encountered anyone, she'd say her date drank too much, got in a
fight, and then passed out, which in these parts would seem perfectly
normal.

Mercifully, she made it to her room without seeing a soul. Safely
inside, the curtains and blinds drawn, River dumped him on her bed

and inspected her unconscious house guest. She carefully removed his dry suit and the clothing underneath, to examine him for more wounds. Running her hands over his body, she felt alarmed, as if she'd broken a rule. Of course, there were none, she was a grown woman and a former soldier alone in an Energy Territory. She would have been crazy not to take a closer look and search his belongings. Miraculously, she found no other serious injuries except a wound that went straight through his arm and left a dime-size hole in his triceps. He was lucky the bullet went through so cleanly.

She cleaned him up using the first aid supplies she stockpiled to treat her own work injuries. Other than being scraped up from his wild ride down the river, he seemed healthy, albeit a little on the skinny side. His dry bag was a curious mix of clothing and research tools—test tubes, a box of pencils, and a notebook. The rest of his gear was expensive, but authentic, giving credence to his story that he'd been on the river. Whoever he was, his clothing made it clear he came from money. His skin, covered in freckles, was worn from the sun and wind—something she recognized from her own lifetime in the west.

Exhausted, her chores complete, River sat in a chair and half-watched, half-dozed as the stranger in her bed tossed and turned, murmuring to himself in the grip of a nightmare. His mumbles turned to screams, startling her, and she debated whether to wake him up before her neighbors complained. Before she finished her deliberations, he bolted upright, locking in on River.

"Where am I?" he asked, his eyes wide with fright.

"In my room," River said. "You've been asleep for a few hours."

"What time is it?" he asked.

"Four-thirty, maybe five in the morning," River said. "I took my watch off when I carried you in."

"You carried me in?"

"After you passed out in the middle of the road, it seemed like the polite thing to do," River said.

The man nodded. It was clear he was trying to piece events together. He closed his eyes and leaned his head back against the pillow.

"I flagged you down in the road," he said.

"Yes, and you said you'd be no trouble," River said gruffly. "You promised to sleep in my truck and be on your way."

"I'm sorry. Give me a minute and I'll get out of here," he said, starting to rise.

"I wouldn't do that if I were you," River said. "You're pretty beat up. As much as I hate to admit it, you could use a few more hours of rest."

The man turned a faint shade of green while trying to get out of bed.

"Are you going to be sick?" River asked.

"Maybe," he whispered.

River got up, grabbed a wastepaper basket, and set it next to the bed. "Use this," she said. "We can't call housekeeping to clean up your mess. You're a fugitive."

"I'll be fine. I just need a minute to get my bearings," the man said, opening his eyes. "Tell me your name."

"Why?"

"When I thank someone for saving my life, I usually like to use their name," he said.

"It's River," she said, worried about what divulging the information would cost her.

"I'm Finn," he said, his eyelids drooping. "You're right. I think I might need to close my eyes for a little while."

As she watched her mystery man fall back asleep, her stomach growled loudly. She'd missed a day's worth of meals. She looked over at Finn, wondering if she dared leave the room. Finally, hunger won out, and she slipped away for some supplies, tucking her gun into the waist of her jeans before pulling on a heavy coat.

FIVE

RIVER WALKED into the apartment ninety minutes later, just as Finn sat up to inspect the bandage around his arm.

"Are you bleeding through?" she asked, turning her back to him to set the food on a table.

"I don't think so," Finn replied. "You tied this nice and tight. Thank you."

Finn kept River in his gaze, his red hair out of its ponytail, cascading across his shoulders. She returned his stare, and felt her cheeks warm, suddenly remembering that he was naked as a jaybird in her bed.

"I assume you removed my clothing for *medical* reasons," Finn said, reading her discomfort. "If you give me my gear bag, I'll grab a change of clothes. I don't suppose you saved my ski hat?"

"I was checking for more gunshot wounds," River said, pulling his bag from the corner where she'd tossed it. "Funny enough, your hat did make it. I put it with your other stuff. Are you hungry?"

"Starving!" he said. "What's in the bag?"

"Oh, you know, the usual," she said. "*Steak frites* and a *salad verte.*"

"*Très agréable, mademoiselle,*" Finn said. "*Et pour le dessert?*"

River replied, "*Il n'y a pas de dessert pour les blessés,*" telling him there was no dessert for the wounded.

"I'm impressed," Finn said. "You don't come across too many French-speaking truckers."

Finn's remarks reminded River of another part of the conversation she'd had with her mother the day before. Her mom had been adamant that River restart her French language studies once she left the Territory. She loved her mother, but what was the use of speaking French, of wanting to see the world, when she lived six thousand feet above sea level in a small town in the middle of Idaho?

In the spring before sixth grade, the Community School, the fancy private place a few miles up the road from her home, offered River a scholarship. She stayed through high school, graduating at the top of her class. She made friends, joined the yearbook, and daydreamed about her first trip to France upon graduation, but could not shake the sensation of being, as they liked to say in her parts, a little too far out over her skis. The problem with wanting so much, River later realized, is that it was heartbreaking when it didn't work out.

"It's just a cheap parlor trick I use to keep rich Ivy Leaguers like you amused," River said. "Anyway, what I really have is some breakfast sandwiches. I hope you're not a vegetarian because everything around here comes with bacon."

"I'm so hungry that I would eat meat even if I was a vegetarian," Finn said. "Hey, I managed to insult you. I'm sorry. I was just surprised to hear you speak French, and with a good accent, too. You've obviously studied."

"That was a long time ago," she said. "As you can see, I've got a job now that doesn't require foreign language skills. OK, I'm going to step into the bathroom and reload my gun. Why don't you get dressed, and when I come out you can tell me what happened."

River came out of the bathroom and found Finn sitting on the edge of the bed, wearing a pair of faded chocolate brown cords and a navy-blue T-shirt. For a man on the run, he didn't seem very worried. He looked quite relaxed, in fact. He reminded River of some of the boys back home, the ones who always seemed to remain calm despite careening head first over the handlebars of their mountain bike or snowboard. She loved, and also hated, those boys. Loved them because they were beautiful and resilient, but hated them because they didn't seem to have any real problems.

River walked up to the small dining table in the kitchen and set her weapon down.

"You don't need that," Finn said. "I'm not going to hurt you."

"Maybe," River said, "but in my experience, you can never be too careful. After all, I did find you standing in the middle of the road with a bullet wound. You want to tell me again how you got there?"

Finn eased himself off the bed, wincing as he sat down in one of the chairs at the table. River, sitting across from him, inched herself back a bit and grabbed the gun, placing it on her lap. Then she pulled several bottles of water from the shopping bag and placed them on the table.

"If you need water, drink from one of these," she said. "The stuff from the tap tastes funny."

"Really?" Finn asked. "What does it taste like?"

"Like a chemical. Sort of like lighter fluid," she said. "It's been known to catch fire, although I haven't seen it happen. I've just heard the stories."

Finn nodded and reached for one of the sandwiches, bandages covering the tips of his fingers. Steam poured out as he unwrapped the paper and set it back down to cool. He looked around at her books, piles of them, arranged on every surface but the table they were eating on.

"Looks like you enjoy reading," Finn said, nodding towards the stacks.

"There isn't much to do around here," she said. "I'm just passing the time."

Finn's gaze wandered over the titles. "I'd have to be pretty bored to read *Moby Dick*."

"It's an American classic," she said, grabbing her breakfast. "The whale is a metaphor, you know."

"Next you're going to tell me there's a book club," Finn said.

"If there was, it would have to be for picture books," River said. "There aren't a lot of deep thinkers here. Although there are a few of us who...." River stopped herself.

"Who what?" Finn asked.

She'd just told a perfect stranger more than she'd uttered to the clerk at the post office in almost two years. She felt like one of those giddy girls who couldn't stop talking after the cute boy said hello. How long had it been since she'd spoken with someone so easily?

"I was going to say we have a trivia game we play once a month at a bar in town. I was heading home from there from when I found you standing in the road last night."

"Are you any good?" he asked.

"Yes," River said, wondering again what it was about Finn that made her so chatty. "Let's get back to you, though. Are you going to answer my question?"

Finn nodded. "I'm a scientist," he replied. "Hydrologist, actually."

"From some kind of privileged family," River said, unsure why she felt the need to take a dig.

"I work for the USGS in Montana," he said, ignoring her jibe.

"Yes, but how did you get inside the Territory?"

"I was collecting samples," he said. "They washed away when the guards opened fire. They must have hit my arm while I was paddling. I flipped my kayak over for cover. I'm lucky I didn't break my neck."

"Universal Industries doesn't like visitors near the Territories," River said. "Half the security detail is staffed by veterans from the Caliphate Wars. They're pretty devoted to the idea of never having to deal with the Middle East or terrorists again and would happily kill anyone they viewed as a threat."

"You included?" Finn asked.

"We're talking about *you* at the moment," River said. "What made you think you could float so close?"

"I thought I had permission," Finn said. "I guess I was mistaken."

River caught the slight hesitation in his response, but let it pass. She knew from her experience as a combat translator that everybody held a little something back.

"Why risk your life?" River asked. "What were you thinking you would accomplish?"

"It didn't occur to me that the government and Universal might not be on the same page," Finn said. "I asked for permission to test the waters close to the Territory. I'm just a scientist trying to collect information."

"Why is that so important?" River asked.

"Where are you from?" Finn asked.

"Why is that important?" River repeated.

Finn glared.

"Hailey, Idaho," River said.

"Thank you," he said. "The Big Wood River. Does it freeze in the winter?"

"Of course," she said.

"Imagine if it didn't," Finn said, fixing her with his hazel eyes. "None of it."

"I could see that happening when it stays too warm to snow...," River said.

Finn shook his head. "I've been out in the field for weeks taking samples in temperatures as low as sixteen degrees Fahrenheit, which anybody knows is well below freezing," Finn said. "In fact, it had been even colder the week before. But no matter how low the temperature dropped, the water did not freeze. Can you imagine? At first, I thought I was crazy, but test after test confirmed my findings.

"There are variables in which liquid would not freeze below thirty-two degrees Fahrenheit," Finn continued. "But none exist in the water-ways I've been observing."

"What do you think it means?" River asked.

"To be honest, I wasn't sure," Finn said. "But now that you've described the tap water tasting like butane, I have a good idea. All I have to do now is go back out and get new samples."

"Listen, no offense, but I don't want any part of this," River said, fidgeting in her seat. "My contract is up in a few weeks and I plan to collect my overtime pay and head home. I'm sure whatever you're trying to do is important, but..."

"I understand," Finn said before she could finish. "You've done too much already. I just need to find a way to get to my truck. If I can make it back to Montana, I can straighten this whole thing out."

"Your truck is probably blown to pieces by now, or impounded," River said. "Whatever you've discovered, it probably threatens Universal's plans. Do you know anything about the guy who runs the Territories? He'll never let you shut him down. Forget Montana, you should be thinking of Canada."

"No," Finn said.

"No?"

"I'm not skulking out of my own country," Finn said. "I just have to use my imagination and think of a way out of this. My...I mean, the government can't be sanctioning this kind of behavior. They need to know what's happening."

"You're something else, Ivy League. This isn't a game...the *President of the United States* is the one who gave them the power to be here," she said. "How can you trump that?"

"You'd be surprised," Finn replied. "What time do you have to go back to work? You haven't slept and I imagine you could use some rest. I hope you realize that I'm not going to hurt you. Let me stay until dusk. Come nightfall I'll make my way back to the border. I'll figure out a plan of escape while you sleep."

"I have today off, but I have an important errand to run. I'll be back in time for dinner," she said. "First, though, I'm going to catch forty winks, but I'll be sleeping with my weapon right next to me."

"Suit yourself," Finn said, rising slowly from the chair, as if it pained him.

"There's Advil in the medicine cabinet in the bathroom, and something stronger," River said.

"I'll stick with over-the-counter," Finn said. "A little pain is just what I need to stay sharp."

SIX

ELIZABETH CUNNINGHAM WAS PREPARING for a journey. A presidential train trip, code named Resurrection, was scheduled to depart from Washington in two weeks' time. The itinerary included Pennsylvania, Ohio, Indiana, and Iowa, with the final destination being Colorado, where she would speak at the Denver Convention Center to an audience of thousands. It was the first major public event since she'd gone into hiding, increasing the pressure she felt to make not a good speech, but a *great speech*. The kind of speech that could restore a nation's faith in democracy, remarks she knew should last well beyond her lifetime. In an effort to prepare, her chief of staff had sent a lovely but extremely green speechwriter to help her with her remarks, which were nowhere near ready for prime time. The young girl had been tasked with updating Elizabeth's initial draft. It had not been a productive effort and now the two were staring at each other awkwardly.

"You don't sound convincing," the assistant said, a faux black leather binder pressed up against her crisp white oxford. "Let's go through it again."

"Not convincing?" Elizabeth asked. "Perhaps it's because I'm having difficulty with what you've written *uhhh...*"

"It's Lauren," the aide said, straightening her spine. "Our job is to reassure the American people that things are back to normal. You have to behave confidently and tell them things are proceeding as planned."

"Lauren, I'm going to tell you something I shouldn't," Elizabeth said. "I have never been less confident that things are proceeding as planned. Surprisingly, I find my doubt comforting. It tells me that all my senses are functioning as a human being. Does that make sense?"

Before the aide could say anything further, the President's phone rang. She pulled it out of her pocket and smiled when she saw the caller.

"This is my son," she said. "Could you give me a minute?"

The aide nodded and walked out, her shoulders hunched in defeat.

"Hello, stranger," Elizabeth said. "How did your trip go?"

"I don't have much time, so please listen," Finn said. "Your friends at Universal tried to kill me. I managed to escape, but it was close."

"Where are you now?" she asked, turning her body away from the doorway for more privacy from nearby staff. The phone suddenly felt slippery in her hands as her palm grew damp from fear.

"I'm inside the Territory," he said. "I'm safe, but I have to get out of here."

"I'll send someone," Elizabeth said, knowing it might be a lie. She didn't want to risk an incident by sending in the FBI, but who was left on her very short list of people to trust? Her thoughts immediately went to her husband Richard. If only he were with her. There was no one she trusted more to keep her son safe. Unfortunately, he was not an option.

"No," Finn said. "It's too risky. But don't worry, I have a plan. Listen, I have to go. I'll try to call you again soon."

The line went dead and Elizabeth stared at the phone in frustration, worried it was too dangerous to call him back. What had happened to Finn? She had nothing, no sense of his injuries, his location, or his plans. She felt flush as a warm wave of shame made its way through her body.

This was her fault.

First her husband went missing, and now her son was in danger. There would be no Hallmark cards extolling her domestic virtues anytime soon. Oddly, her feelings ran more towards anger than worry.

If there was a way to survive, she knew Finn would find it. He was raised to endure nature's worst hardships, and he tolerated pain and discomfort with a stoicism that would have made his Protestant ancestors proud. But this was not his doing. It was hers. She was supposed to be the most powerful person on Earth, and yet it did not feel that way at all. She felt powerless. Worse, she was supposed to be the architect of the nation's resurrection, but as the days wore on, she felt more like a merchant of death. She blamed it on random selection and fate. She was the one that had lived, and therefore she was responsible for seeing to the accounting of the dead. It had all begun with a disembodied voice coming over the public announcement system.

"Attention, C32-A is now Air Force One."

"Copy that, Air Force One. Touchdown is at zero nine hundred hours."

Elizabeth heard the words, but thought it might be an auditory hallucination caused by thousands of miles of travel, over too few days, with little to no sleep. It wasn't her brain playing tricks; it was the universe playing a horrible joke. At approximately 3 p.m. on April 10, 2040 she became president of the United States. Her staff woke her up from a nap to tell her the news, their faces ashen with grief.

As a child she'd read about the idea in civics class, and of course she'd been cognizant of the protocol as Secretary of State, but in that moment the words from her schoolbooks seemed surreal. *In the Federal Government, the fourth in line for succession after the Vice President, Speaker of the House and President Pro Tem of the Senate, is the Secretary of State.* As the gravity of the situation sunk in, Elizabeth gnawed on her thumbnail until it tore it off at the quick, trying to grasp what had happened, and more importantly, what was about to come. While she'd been ricocheting around the globe like a pinball, much of the country's leadership was assassinated in a coordinated terrorist attack at the White House. It was supposed to be impossible and therefore not contemplated, and yet it did happen, while she'd been barreling through the atmosphere at almost 600 miles an hour towards Andrews Air Force Base.

News of the assassinations was like a thick blanket, smothering the cool comfortable air inside the plane's cabin. Time whirred past. Aides and senior staff began to scramble around her, grabbing binders and files. Before she knew it, her Air Force Boeing 747 was landing. Elizabeth's assistant grabbed her briefcase and coat, leaving her with nothing to occupy her hands as she descended the jet way, her knees ready to buckle. The Chief Justice was waiting on the tarmac along with her husband and Finn. That day, as she raised her right hand to swear to protect and defend the Constitution, she felt her pulse in her throat, and her tongue thicken in her mouth as the coppery taste of fear settled in. She'd been coming home to quit, to tell the president that she was worn out from the constant strife and conflict. That she wanted to return to academia, to a calmer, less demanding life.

Later, as she was driven to an undisclosed location, the White House an active crime scene under investigation, she came to understand that regret is pointless in times of crisis. There was never a moment in which she could have refused the job. There was no one to look in the eye to explain that while she was deeply honored, she nevertheless had to graciously decline so she could accept a comfortable teaching post. That night, as she boarded the submarine that was to become her temporary home, Elizabeth recalled her time spent as a Congresswoman, and as a member of the House Committee on Foreign Relations. She thought about her degree in international affairs and fluency in four languages and how those skills and experiences gave her the necessary qualifications to be Secretary of State. What prepared her for her new job? What should she draw on to become the leader of her country at time when it had been so brutally attacked? These were questions that eluded easy answers, but eventually, a sense of ruthless expediency settled in. That was *before*. Now, there was only *after*. She was obligated to move ahead, knowing full well that she was entering uncharted Territory and about to govern a country whose landscape was growing ever more unrecognizable by the hour.

The rise of the Second Islamic State forced the United States to deploy thousands of troops to Afghanistan, Libya, Iraq, Egypt, Syria, and finally France, which was compromised by civil war. It was almost impossible to believe that after all of the bloodshed Elizabeth had witnessed in the Middle East and Europe, the same fate would befall her own country. That the president of the United States and several members of his cabinet would be assassinated by ISIS, sending the government underground. Or that innocent civilians would be killed at a shopping mall in broad daylight. The upheaval of both events unmoored the country from its long-held traditions and expectations. Decisions that would have been unthinkable became acceptable in a heartbeat.

No decision had wrought more guilt, though, than the one she made to create the Territories. Universal Industries had arrived on her doorstep after the killings at the mall with a proposal to "leave the Middle East, abandoning the region." Universal's founder, Redmond "Red" Pierce had urged her to act quickly. The United States would buy no foreign oil; instead, it would maintain its own supply of oil and gas and become a power unto itself. That part had been easy to agree to.

The more difficult tasks had been introducing a national identification program to a public reared on privacy laws and ordering the mass deportations of anyone who posed a threat to national security. There were horrible moments of doubt as she signed the stack of executive orders. She tried to soothe herself with the knowledge that there were few remedies available to a storied civilization that had ceased to exist in its most familiar form. She also came to know another terrible truth: that there was no need to annihilate a population to render life unrecognizable, to throw a country's destiny off course. Even a few degrees of variation from the original terminus could be a grand departure with unforeseen consequences. Restoring a proud nation's equilibrium was not easy, but it could be done. Elizabeth had seen to it, one painstaking detail after another.

It was Universal Industries, though, that figured out how to accomplish the unthinkable: relocate 1.3 million people in exchange for an *endless* supply of oil and gas. A surcharge on the delivery of the fuel would cover the cost of their efforts. And just like that, with the stroke of her pen, a migration began as the populations of North Dakota and

Wyoming were evacuated. On paper, it seemed foolproof. But Elizabeth was beginning to understand there were hidden costs, penalties that hadn't been spelled out. She began to fear that what she'd lost so far had merely been a prepayment to a much larger bill about to come due. First her husband and now Finn. She might be President of the United States, but for all the tools at her command, she was rather powerless when it came to finding her husband or saving her son.

SEVEN

Finn hated that he hung up on his mother. That was the story of his life: interrupted conversations. One of these days he was going to get the two people he loved in one room to talk.

He adjusted his body in the faux leather recliner which turned out to be the only comfortable piece of furniture in the room besides the bed. Finn looked around, taking in the popcorn ceiling, industrial grey carpet, and drab walls, wondering why anyone would voluntarily live here. Was River a fugitive? He'd heard stories of people wanted for crimes signing up for jobs. The thought made him laugh softly. Yes, she was tough as nails, but she didn't seem dangerous.

Finn scanned his temporary lodgings for more clues about his mystery host. Incongruous was the only word that came to mind. In some respects, the shabby, book-laden space looked more like a well-worn corner of a library than a studio apartment. Half of her collection he'd already read, and the other half were certainly books he might put on his list, if he thought about it. There were no photographs. Did she have family or friends? If she brought other men back to her bed—a thought that made Finn unaccountably uncomfortable—they would learn very little about her. Did she tell them how she came to have a near-perfect French accent while driving a truck in the middle of a desolate fracking Territory?

The one detail he was certain about was that she'd been in the military. She had the bearing of a soldier, especially when she held her gun in her lap. The story of how all of those seemingly random pieces came to be a part of the woman who'd saved his life was likely worth a beer or two. It was too bad he'd never hear the tale since he was leaving shortly.

As odd as the circumstances were, she intrigued him. Maybe it was her toughness. Maybe it was her beauty. It was probably both. He didn't encounter that many females that interested him. Truthfully, he didn't encounter many women, period. Finn wasn't much of a lady's man. On a scale of one to ten, ten being a complete recluse, Finn ranked himself an eleven, which is why he remained unmarried at an age when most men already had a family. There had been one Forest Ranger, but she'd opted to become a fire spotter in the wilderness, a choice he tried not to take personally. His family was a pack of recluses, that was their problem. They didn't know how to integrate with people.

As bad as he was, his father held the prize at the moment: missing in action for two years, having walked out on his family after his mother agreed to create the energy Territories.

Finn could still remember his father's anger: "There are fifty stars on our flag," he'd said. "Are you planning to commission a new version?"

"Don't be flippant," his mother had replied. "I wouldn't even be president if it weren't for the assassination. And now this new event. You visited the site with me. You saw the bodies. We can't become a country where every public gathering is a potential deathtrap. Look at France. There are American troops stationed on their soil trying to help quell a civil war. People expect their government to do something to make sure these kinds of terrorist attacks don't happen."

"I agree," Richard said. "But not this. *Anything* but this. You're wiping out several national parks, not to mention the existence of two states and their history. It's part of our country's history. It's our history, Elizabeth; my family, *our family*, has maintained a home in Wyoming for generations."

"History will live on," she'd replied. "We'll make sure people remember. More than half of the country has never even been to North Dakota. No one will even notice its absence."

"Lewis and Clarke were there," he'd said, using the lecturing voice he'd developed as an American history professor at Yale. "You can walk in their footsteps."

"Not anymore," she'd said. "The United States can't afford to be sentimental. There are too many lives at stake."

The argument at the White House was one of the last times Finn had seen his father. The very last time was in Wyoming when they were preparing to evacuate their home. As they packed up the boxes, his father made it clear he wasn't going back to Washington. While they were together, Finn couldn't stop thinking about the fact that his father was about to walk away. The person who had taken him into the wilderness and taught him how to become a man was now about to perpetrate a terrible act of cowardice. There had been moments in the last two years when Finn wondered why he hadn't confronted his father; demanded he go back to Washington and be a husband to his wife, honor his wedding vows and help his mother get through what was obviously the worst moments of the country's existence. But Finn was more likely to camp on the narrow edge of a mountainside, in billowing winds, with an ice ax as his only companion, than tell his father he was a selfish bastard.

Two years passed without a word of communication. Sometimes when he was out in the field, hundreds of miles from civilization, Finn would quiet his mind and try to let his intuition speak to him. A few days before he'd left for the Territories, he'd been out in the far north of Montana taking samples when he'd come face to face with an elk, his piercing gaze fixed on Finn, a set of antlers only inches away. The massive bull stayed stock still, droplets of moisture from its breath ringing its nostrils, creating an air of exasperation as if it was waiting for Finn to comprehend a message. Days later, Finn continued to think about the encounter, wondering if it had been a sign. Maybe death had been staring him in the face, or maybe his father was right in front of his nose, and he just couldn't see him. Of course, there was also the possibility that the encounter meant nothing. Somehow though, he'd managed to avoid being gored to death by an elk. Now he had to find a way to escape the Territories without being shot again and without bringing harm to River. Finn knew if he didn't find a way out of this mess, his mother would be alone.

EIGHT

THE SUN WAS high in the sky as River pulled into the gas station. She'd almost missed the exit, her mind stuck back at the motel, wondering what her fugitive guest was doing to amuse himself. For better or worse, the red-haired stranger from the road had captured her attention. His arrival was a gut-punch reminder of her loneliness.

River opened the door of her truck as an icy wind whipped past. She pulled her ski hat down tighter against her skull. As she headed for the cashier inside, she passed an older man sitting on a bench. He did not look up at her as she opened the door.

The truck had been a gift to herself. She'd seen the old Chevy parked with a for sale sign in the parking lot of the bar one night when she pulled in with her tanker truck. She'd arrived in the Territory driving a beat-up sedan that belonged to her mom, which was functional, but not much fun to drive in bad weather. As soon as she spotted the truck, she decided to splurge and buy it for herself. She always said if things got dire, she could sell it and make her money back, but she doubted she'd ever be able to make that choice.

River's truck was full of small throw blankets, shawls, and scarves she'd knitted to distribute at a donation center on the border between North and South Dakota. When she first started coming, she would pull up in a parking lot, open up her tailgate, and wait for people to find her so she could hand her wares out for free. After several trips, the locals began to anticipate her arrival, waiting patiently on the third Saturday of every month between noon and three. She often came with special requests that had been made during her visit the month before.

She was a prodigious creator. The Territories were not a place for socializing. Other than trivia night and a few drinks now and then at the end of her shift, she did not go out alone. That was a recipe for more of what she'd gotten a few weeks back at Outerlands. She preferred to stay inside her motel room, but that kind of enforced isolation—even if she knew it was temporary—required an antidote. Hers was to stay busy. She wasn't going to smother herself in food or drink. In a few weeks she would go home to Ava, and her daughter didn't deserve a drunk for a mother. So she read like a fiend and made blankets for the less fortunate. There were no knit stores in the Territory. Just the idea of one, with all of its brightly colored yarn in the midst of the cold gray landscape, made River laugh. Everything she needed came by mail. She didn't splurge on expensive fibers—no one was getting cashmere—but she did order light shades of blue and pink for baby blankets and lovely dark grey and navy colored yarn for shawls. It all had to be washable. It gave her such a thrill to see the look on people's faces when they were able to have something soft and warm to call their own. It was the same feeling she experienced when she picked up a book. Not quite as soft, but just as satisfying, and something that belonged to her.

The station and its service bay looked like they hadn't changed much since the 1950s. The remnants of an old faded mural with the Mobile Gas winged horse remained on a wall on one side of the main building. As soon as she stepped inside the store, River made a beeline for the refrigerators in the back. She grabbed a diet soda and picked up a premade turkey sandwich before heading to the register. River figured the clerk behind the counter was seventeen, eighteen at the most, considering he didn't have a single whisker on his face. There was an upside-down cross dangling from his ear, and he was wearing what looked to be a very old and worn-out Rolling Stones T-shirt.

"Cool shirt," River said.

"Thanks," he said. "I got it at Goodwill. You gonna buy a full tank today?"

River nodded and put forty-five dollars on the counter. "That ought to cover my gas and the food," she said, grabbing her things. This time as she passed the man sitting on the bench, he looked up at her. His face was a series of hard lines and craggy channels. River guessed he was on his way to eighty, give or take. He was dressed in a threadbare red flannel shirt and jeans tucked into a pair of worn cowboy boots, which hardly seemed sufficient against the day's frigid temperatures. The nub of a cigarette sat between his thumb and forefinger, the end wet with spittle.

"I'll have you know I have visited all fifty states, and even a few more you've probably never even heard of," he said.

Normally River didn't speak to strangers. But as she looked over at the tattered old man braving the elements, she saw a kindred soul, another survivor moving along the highway.

"All fifty, you don't say," River said, smiling. "That's a lot more than me."

"Aren't you going to ask me about the others?" he asked, a mischievous grin on his face. "About where else I've been?"

"OK," she said. "Where else have you been?"

The man leaned back on the bench and crossed his legs at the ankle. He tossed the old butt aside and took out a bag of tobacco and some rolling papers and slowly began to prepare another cigarette. "Now let's see," he said, as little brown bits blew away. "I've also been to the state of confusion, the state of denial, and even the state of unconsciousness. And maybe a few others I can't recall at the moment."

"That's pretty good," she said. "I think I might've visited one or two of those places myself."

"I know," the man said. "I could tell right away. That's why I decided to talk to you. I could tell you're a fellow traveler like myself. There are a few of us out on the road today. You best keep an eye out."

"I'll do that," she said.

River walked back to her truck. As she pumped her gas, a black Range Rover pulled up on the opposite side. A tall man with closely cropped red hair got out. He nodded curtly at her as he went inside to pay. She'd only seen cars like his with blue United Nations flags attached when stationed overseas. They were a fancy ride for diplomats and millionaires. She used his absence as an opportunity to peer into the cargo area, which was packed with cases of bottled water, canned goods, and dry food. The clanging of the bell on the store's entrance door sent her scurrying back towards her truck, trying to look extremely busy. Not a word passed between them as the stranger pumped his gas. When he was finished, he looked over at River, offered another curt nod, got in his car, and drove away.

"He's another one like you," the man yelled from his bench, catching River's eye. "Just wait. You'll see."

River smiled and waved as she got into her truck. "Crazy old man," she muttered under her breath as she started her engine.

NINE

REDMOND PIERCE WAS JOLTED awake as his car hit one of the speed bumps in the secure parking lot in front of his office. An urgent morning call with Washington dictated his driver come at five-thirty, and as a result, he hadn't been able to do his regular thirty laps in his salt-water pool. Despite the chaos of the past few years, he'd kept himself remarkably fit, his stylist managing to keep his short, deep brown hair from showing any traces of the encroaching gray. Without his regular morning stimulation though, his sixty-year-old body had immediately dozed off in the car. As he stepped out to the curb, Red directed his driver to return at four. He had tickets for the Symphony with his wife, and wanted to change prior to the performance. The city had just begun to enjoy public assemblies again, something he liked to think he'd helped make possible. The board of the symphony seemed to agree, providing him with a box for the new season. Red had a new suit made for the occasion, and was looking forward to taking his wife out for the evening. She was actually his second wife. and much, much younger. The national curfew had been difficult for someone her age to tolerate.

Standing in the shadows, Cooper Smith eyed his boss as he entered through the front door of Universal's Houston-based complex amid a sea of crisply dressed young professionals. Cooper watched as one by one they stopped what they were doing to shake Red's hand and thank him for their job. Red smiled warmly.

"They love me," Red said, glancing up at Cooper before he walked up to the scanner and leaned in, allowing the machine to map his cornea. Red waved his right wrist over a second reader that beeped as it acknowledged the identification tag embedded under his skin. More employees followed behind Red, the machine confirming their identities as they passed through. Cooper thought it sounded like the checkout counter at a grocery store as the clerk rang up each item. Once Red cleared security, he handed his briefcase to a young aide and strode off at full speed toward his office, from which he was scheduled to have an early morning video call with the President of the United States and her cabinet. Cooper followed, scratching ferociously at the small, growing rash on his wrist near the tag.

Red took a seat at his desk. Never one for subtleties, corporate legend was that the table was an exact replica of the one used by President Harry Truman when he made the decision to drop an atomic bomb on Hiroshima. Cooper watched from his perch against a wall as Red read the report detailing the security team's encounter with Finn Cunningham, the CEO's lips set in a grim line as he reviewed the details. On paper, Cooper had made sure his team looked like a bunch of bumbling idiots, but Cooper had asked them to shoot to injure, not to kill. His men reported wounding Finn. He hoped the scientist had managed to survive the night.

"I'm still not sure why it took you the better half of the morning to report him missing," Red said. "Tell me this, do we think the man is dead or just injured and wandering around inside the Territory?"

"Hard to know," Cooper replied. "My boys got a shot off, but Finn proved to be more capable than we thought. He managed to float away without a trace in the darkness."

"Really?" Red said. "More capable than an Army sharpshooter? I find that very difficult to believe. I think a more plausible story is that you didn't *want* to find him. That you're losing your nerve to see this thing through, maybe feeling too sympathetic towards that ugly hag in the White House. If you think you can slow me down, you are very much mistaken. It's too late."

Cooper took a deep breath, summoning his restraint. Red possessed an inflated sense of himself and his destiny. That was nothing out of the ordinary for the CEO of an oil company, or for many CEOs in general, but Cooper had assumed that once Red got the Territories he would calm down. Clearly, he'd misread the situation, which was now blossoming into a full-blown emergency.

"Take it easy, Red. It's not as easy as it looks, trying to hit a moving target floating down a river," Cooper said. "We initiated a manhunt and discovered what looks to be a trail of blood on the highway, about a half-mile from where the river bends near the holding ponds. The trail goes on a few feet and then it disappears. He may have been picked up by a driver."

"What do the cameras show?" Red asked.

"It's being reviewed now," Cooper said. "Most quadrants show nothing but the usual drunken fights in parking lots and a few prostitutes visiting the worker barracks."

"Keep looking," Red said. "If he's alive, he's somewhere close by."

"And if we find him?" Cooper asked.

"I have no patience for stupid questions like that," Red said. "You know the scientist has to be disposed of."

"I'm not so sure," Cooper said.

"Jesus H. Christ. You've been mewing like a little pussy about killing him since we started this conversation a few weeks ago," Red said. "If you don't have what it takes to make this country great again, then you should move aside and let me finish the job myself."

Cooper felt an icy chill run up his spine at Red's easy merging of two very different concepts. "Be sensible," Cooper said, looking around to make sure the door to Red's office was closed. "Murdering the President's son is not going to get you what you're after. I'm just trying to make sure you think things through."

Red rose from his chair and locked eyes with Cooper. "I am crystal clear about what needs to be done," he said. "Your job is to find Finn Cunningham before some sympathetic soul inside the Territory decides to help him."

"I'll take care of things," Cooper said. "What about this morning? Are you still going to ask her?"

"You know I am," Red said. "Are you afraid I'm going to hurt that bull dyke's feelings?"

"No," Cooper said. "That's not what I'm afraid of."

The door opened and Red's young assistant walked in. "You have ten minutes," she said, and began inspecting the video conferencing equipment mounted on a wall across from Red's desk. "Drilling reports are on the table in front of you, as well as crude shipments and a freight schedule."

"Well, at least someone here knows how to do their job," Red said, glaring at his security director. Cooper, fortunately, was blessed with an infinite well of patience. During his twenty years in the Marine Corps, he'd encountered just about every kind of nightmare recruit, megalomaniac superior officer, and horrific combat situation imaginable. Red was going to use this morning's call to make his request for Pennsylvania, something the President was *never* going to agree to. Cooper knew that "no" would not be an acceptable answer.

"I think you should wait," Cooper continued as soon as they were alone again. "Let me arrange a meeting in Washington."

"Wait?" Red asked. "Should I wait until the country is on its knees again begging for mercy? Should I wait until this menopausal bitch is out of the White House and someone who knows what the hell he's doing is installed? I shouldn't even have to ask. I mean, who knows this shit better than me? If she were smart, she would just let me do what's necessary and not force me to check in with her like this. I don't work for her, after all."

"Technically, *you do*," Cooper said. "We all do. The Territories belong to the government."

"Technically?" he said. "I'm the reason we're here today. I'm the reason we have the Territories. Without me there would be nothing. We'd all be wandering around in the dark while our enemies cut our balls off."

Cooper understood why Red was pushing so hard. His boss coveted the Marcellus Play: thirty-four million acres of proven reserves, stretching from Alabama to New York with eight states in between. Pennsylvania was the star of the show. If Red got his way, it would be the biggest Territory of them all, with enough resources to ensure the country became the dominant exporter of oil to world markets, and guarantee the United States never ran a national debt again. Red had considered asking for Alabama or West Virginia, but dismissed the idea. Yes, the populations were smaller, less educated and the states politically insignificant, but their probable reserves were vastly deeper in the ground, making drilling all the more expensive. In Red's estimation, evacuating Wyoming and North Dakota had been relatively easy; everything that came after should be even easier.

What Red did not consider were the downsides. Like all self-absorbed leaders, he was unconcerned with the logistics. That was Cooper's job, and he knew evacuating Pennsylvania would be more difficult, regardless of what they'd learned from their first forays. Using the same tools the United States had employed to intern the Japanese during World War Two, the government had managed to forcibly relocate millions. Although relocation plans and programs—as well as millions in assistance funds—had been established and allocated, thousands remained in refugee cities in Utah, South Dakota, Nebraska, Colorado, and Idaho. Red liked to say they simply lacked the gumption to make a go of it, but it was more complicated than that. When you pull a tree out by its roots, you can't expect it to live once it's been replanted.

Pennsylvania was the same exercise, but at a magnitude several times greater than previous efforts. The population was larger and closer to other major cities. And as if all of that was not enough, there was also the thorny issue of its historic value as an *original* thirteenth colony. In short, it wasn't going to be pretty.

Cooper enjoyed a cordial relationship with almost every member of Elizabeth Cunningham's cabinet and understood long ago that the President was not inclined to ask millions of people to relocate again. Becoming forty-eight states had been a shock to the nation's system, one that was only now diminishing. You didn't have to be a battle-tested veteran to know Red's ambitions were going to collide with the government's. Before Cooper could further encourage Red to hold his temper, a red light began to flash on the large flat screen and the aide's voice came over the intercom.

"Stand by for the President in 5-4-3-2-1."

Elizabeth Cunningham and her cabinet appeared. "Good morning, gentlemen," she said.

"Let's skip the pleasantries. We don't much like each other anyway," Red said, cutting her off. "I think the time is right to annex Pennsylvania. We simply can't wait for you to dither around on this any longer."

At the sound of Red's voice, the President sprang from her chair as if shaking off a large insect. Cooper knew from speaking with her chief of staff that the first two evacuations remained distressing memories. Elizabeth Cunningham had insisted on being one of the first to tour Williston after the residents of North Dakota had been evacuated. Cooper had also been there as she'd peered into the abandoned houses, the doors ajar—exposing long dark hallways to nowhere. Empty swing sets and play yards dotted neighborhoods. Small-town businesses that had probably survived the advent of the railway, or the highway system, or even the Internet were now empty shells, their founders and customers carted off to parts unknown. Main streets had been transformed into ghost towns, but unlike popular fiction, there had been no zombie plague, no deadly influenza epidemic, or mass killings. Instead, the government and Universal had made everyone disappear to make room for a massive oil and natural gas extraction operation. Wyoming was done in the same fashion, only the President had declined to attend the evacuation.

In the conference room, Cooper stayed out of the camera's view, so he could watch and not be seen. Did she know her son was trapped inside the Territory? He hadn't thought to review the intercept phone records before joining Red this morning. There had been too many other loose ends to clean up. He followed the gaze of the cabinet members as they eyed the President who was chewing on what was left of her fingernails.

Cooper felt sorry for her. If it weren't for bad luck, she'd have no luck at all. She was sworn in and not long after faced another domestic terrorism event so horrific, it changed the course of the country. When there is a flood, you help people dry out their homes and rebuild. When there is a fire, you clear the ashes and start again. When there is a tornado, you remove the debris and plan anew. What do you do when a country is knocked off its axis? Unhinged from its moorings by radicalism, which by its very nature arrives as the cold breath of death against your neck. Cooper knew from experience that there was very little for Elizabeth to do but assess the pending threats and make a plan of action. Every decision was going to have negative consequences, she was not going to please everyone, and there would be no time to build consensus or debate. The situation felt a lot more akin to being a soldier than a politician.

An uncomfortable silence enveloped the room after Red made his request. Elizabeth turned her back to the camera, deep in thought. It was obvious that she was trying to maintain her composure. It was a double-edged situation. No one wanted to speak before the President, but there was also palpable dread at having to be present for the discussion that was pending. Human nature dictated someone start the ball rolling to get the group through what was certain to be an awkward thirty minutes. "What do you think, Madam President?" a member of the cabinet finally asked.

"*Impossible*," she said, turning back to face Red. "There's no way we can initiate another evacuation. First, we're about to restart congressional elections after a two-year hiatus. Pennsylvania is a huge state, a *swing state*. We'll be accused of interfering. Two, it's a massive undertaking and would require moving more people than the two previous relocations, and for what reason? We have enough oil to run as an independent nation. That was the goal and it's been met."

"Exporting more oil would give us greater leverage over the Russians and their new Federation," Red said. "That has got to be worth something."

"Make up your mind. Is the oil going to help the country remain independent or tweak a foe?" she asked. "It doesn't really matter because it's not that simple. Do I need to remind all of you that in the last two years, in addition to forcibly relocating families from their homes, the government imposed a nationwide curfew, implemented a national identification program and DNA registry, and closed its borders and deported almost three million people? There are still thousands living in temporary refugee cities, with no means to leave. What our country needs is a return to some sense of normalcy, not more upheaval."

Red's veneer of civility was disintegrating. Cooper thought about pulling the plug on the call, but Red began to speak before he could intervene. "Don't be such a coward," he said. "The refugee cities are a crisis of your own making. You simply lack the will to do what is needed. It's not that complicated. If I were in charge, those freeloaders would be cut off. Once the subsidized food stops showing up on their dinner tables, they will move on. As for Pennsylvania, the world must operate on a simple maxim: the good of the many at the expense of the few. Yes, people will be inconvenienced, but it's nothing compared to how they would feel if we sent their sons and daughters to war. We must stay one step ahead of our enemies, show the world we are capable of dominating the playing field."

"This is the United States. We do not forgo one group of people for another," Elizabeth said. "There are children living in those cities. We cannot just cut off food and water."

"You're just making excuses to avoid doing difficult things," Red said. "You don't like the Territories because your husband left you over their formation. You need to separate out your emotions. In time you'll see that adding another Territory is the right thing to do. There are a lot of people out there who agree with me. They understand we have to make sacrifices to protect our freedom."

Cooper winced. The CEO had never been one for niceties. At one time his directness had probably been an asset to the President. Now, it was salt in a very deep wound. Few brought it up directly, but it was common knowledge among those in the intelligence and security communities that Richard Cunningham had left his wife sometime in the days after she'd signed the executive orders. He'd relinquished his Secret Service detail and disappeared. Some said he, an accomplished outdoorsman, had retreated into the wilderness. Others speculated he'd traveled abroad. What was clear though, in Cooper's opinion, was that he'd abandoned his wife, forcing her to endure alone one of the country's greatest upheavals since the Civil War, Pearl Harbor, and 9-11.

"Red, this government has put up with your coarse behavior

because you did the country a great service in helping establish the Territories," the President said. "While we appreciate your assistance, your request has been denied. We have what we need at the moment. I'll expect you to provide a full report about production inside the Territories to my Energy Secretary before the end of the day.

"And one more thing," she continued. "You are not the absolute power here. I am. You would do well to remember that." The screen abruptly turned black. Cooper sincerely hoped it was not a harbinger of things to come.

TEN

As soon as the screen went dark, Red jumped up from his seat and began to pace.

"That bitch," he said. "Can you believe her, dismissing me like that?"

"What did you expect?" Cooper asked. "I'm going to tell you again, even though it makes you angry: I think you should let this idea go, and focus on our existing portfolio. We've got plenty of operational issues on our plate now. I was just in Territory One last week doing a security check. I understand our holding ponds are nearing capacity."

"Why should that matter?" Red asked. "Look, this is all *very simple*. The President created the Energy Territories by Executive Order, and in doing so, suspended all local, state and federal laws. There are no environmental regulations to adhere to."

"Subject to the whims of the President and her government," Cooper said.

"That is precisely why I asked you to kill her son," Red said. "Finn Cunningham is a Yale-educated hydrologist with a master's degree in public policy from Columbia. She obviously sent him to find something she can use to shut me down."

"Why would she do that?" Cooper asked. "The Territories supply this country with the energy it needs to operate. That doesn't make any sense."

Red resumed pacing the room, muttering. "She can't do this to me. I came up with the idea for the Territories in the first place. I helped save this country from ruin. I am a goddamned patriot!" Red said. "Coop, let me tell you. When I lay my head down at night, I am at *peace* with my maker. I've helped spare thousands of people from the horrors of war. Whatever the long-term costs, it's worth it to press on."

The hair on the back of Cooper's neck rose. "What exactly are you trying to say?" he asked.

"I'm saying the holding ponds in Territory One have been at capacity for months," Red said. "I formed a secret team to manage the overflow...using the river. I assumed the Missouri could withstand a little abuse."

Cooper was no tree hugger, far from it. In college he'd despised the hippies and viewed recycling as a joke, but even he knew what Red was saying was momentous. It had been almost eighty years since industry disposed of its toxic chemicals in the country's main waterways. The Great Lakes, Erie Canal–they were text book cases of pollution that started political movements. People like their drinking water, and they don't take kindly to it being polluted.

"Why the hell did you do that?" Cooper asked. "We could have just called the DOE to help us haul it away."

"And give that woman leverage over me? Never. You and I both know the White House isn't going to agree to more Territories. I'm going to have to take matters into my own hands and plan the next evacuation myself," Red said. "We've got to get our hands on that oil, Cooper. The United States can't be held hostage by weak leaders that don't understand the bigger picture."

Well-schooled in feigning interest and obedience during moments of extreme duress, Cooper nodded sympathetically. "Why don't you let me arrange another meeting with the President?" Cooper asked. "See if we can convince her to reconsider?"

"Fine. Arrange a visit. In the meantime, I'm going to get started on my plans," Red said. "It's regrettable but inevitable that blood has to be shed in the service of a greater good. You need to find Finn Cunningham and take care of things."

"Take care?" Cooper repeated.

"Do I need to spell things out for you?" Red said. "You are the head of security after all. Make him dis-ah-peer, PRONTO!"

"Make him disappear," Cooper repeated. "That is exactly what I will do."

ELEVEN

THE PRESIDENT EYED her Cabinet warily. "Well?" she asked. "Am I crazy, or is he?"

Silence filled the air until finally a brave soul spoke up. "Pennsylvania is *full* of shallow reserves," the Secretary of Energy said sheepishly. "It was a prime resource area even prior to the...*incident*."

"Brian, it's been two years," the President said. "At least call it by one of the nicknames the cable TV anchors gave it that day: the mall massacre or the mall murders."

Brian Hagerman, a former Senator from Texas, shook his head. "I know what they call it, Elizabeth. It's just difficult to discuss, even now."

Elizabeth loathed these discussions. Why was she the one that had to prod people to face the difficulties of the situation? She had a room full of men and none of them seemed inclined to lift their heads out of the sand. "Is it easier to discuss forcing the entire population of Pennsylvania to walk away from their homes and jobs?" she asked. "And let's not forget the thirty thousand Amish or the major universities. I'm sure Carnegie Mellon would love to relocate; it's only been in existence since 1900. And go where? We still have thousands living in the refugee cities. I don't want to continue to be the hand that erases history, *our history*, as a nation."

"We find it *all* difficult to discuss, Elizabeth," Brian said, wondering how he'd managed to become the focus of the President's ire. "This is not what I signed up for...none of us did."

The President watched the other members of her cabinet nod in agreement, and stifled an urge to laugh. Not a happy guffaw, but an ear-splitting banshee screech that no doubt would cause the White House medics to rush in to sedate her. It went without saying that none of them had signed up for this kind of life; they were all victims of the short end of the stick of history and destiny. At the moment though, they were all the country had, and they were one hundred percent in charge.

The argument was made and accepted that politics had no place in the aftermath of a tragedy of such epic proportions, which is how the United States Congress came to be suspended for two years. What the country needed were professionals to run the place, not individuals who would vote against a policy for the sake of winning a future election. There was no time for debate, and more importantly, no desire. There was only the need to act: to deport, to evacuate, to impose a national curfew, and to establish the Territories. At the end of the day, there wasn't a single elected official inside the Beltway who wanted to go on record one way or the other about the subcutaneous installation of identification tags in every legal citizen of the United States. You were either voting to spy on your fellow man, or the one who let the terrorists get away. In a world of 24-hour media scrutiny, the appetite for lofty decisions disappeared. So here they were, public servants who'd signed on for careers of an entirely different sort, expecting terms of service that would eventually result in book deals, lucrative speaking fees, or offers of employment at prestigious universities. Instead, they were the lone branch of government functioning at the moment. Although some had probably fantasized about what it would be like to have absolute power, at the moment it felt suffocating.

Elizabeth returned to her seat at the conference table, inserting herself next to the Secretary of the Interior—a former congressman from California whose biggest problem once upon a time involved a millionaire with a beach house blocking access to a beloved surfing spot. She looked down at her hands. One of her fingers was bleeding. She'd unknowingly chewed the nail off, exposing the raw skin underneath.

"I know none of us anticipated being in this position, but what choice did we have?" she asked. "Thanks to the National Pause and the suspension of Congress, we are all this country has at the moment, and no matter what we do, someone will object. On one side they're already accusing me of getting ready to soften on immigration, and on the other I'm a fascist that ordered the government to spy on its own people."

"Do you regret implementing Red's plan?"

"No," she said, glancing at the wedding band she still wore on her finger. "But that doesn't mean I'll agree to another Energy Territory. Thank you, gentlemen," she continued. "I think we're done for the day."

One by one her cabinet members left the room. Elizabeth breathed deeply to maintain her composure. It would not do to reveal her emotions in front of them. When she was certain she was alone, she let out the gut wrenching sob that had been festering in her chest. She hated that Red had the power to hurt her; he possessed an uncanny ability to find his opponent's most vulnerable spot. It was an open secret that her husband had walked out, something people whispered about but didn't bring up directly, which was fine with her. Announcing it to her entire cabinet was sheer genius on Red's part. What better way to humiliate her? She might grieve in private, but she would never let Red see he'd made a direct hit. Her privacy, as usual, was short-lived. Her back to the door, she briskly wiped the tears from her eyes and assumed the cheery soulless façade of a public figure as the secret service agents walked in.

"Good morning, gentleman," she said. "What can I do for you?"

Elizabeth could tell from the look on their faces that this was about Richard, her allegedly Houdini-like husband whom everyone assumed had somehow found a way to elude the Secret Service.

But everyone was wrong.

Elizabeth knew Richard's general whereabout most of the time and had within a few days of his leaving. There was very little she didn't know about the comings and goings of the American public, but knowing where someone was and doing something about it were different things.

"He's been back at the camps bringing baby formula and medicines," the agent said. "He's beginning to draw crowds and ...."

"And what?" Elizabeth asked.

"Well, he's become a bit of a folk hero," the agent said, studiously avoiding the president's gaze. "Posters–wild art really–portraying him as a kind of guardian angel are popping up all over the settlements."

Elizabeth closed her eyes and exhaled again, hoping the breath she was releasing would lessen the confusion and anger she felt at her husband. Why did a man who desperately wanted to disappear also draw attention to himself in the worst possible way? Was he trying to embarrass her, or assuage his own guilt? Either way, she was forced to deal with the mess. It wasn't that she didn't admire his work.

He was bringing much-needed gifts to the inhabitants of the refugee cities. On a blistering hot day, he might arrive with several gallons of ice cream for the children. On a rainy day, it might be cans of soups and stews for the families. Richard seemed to relish showering the camp's inhabitants with the creature comforts they might have enjoyed before the relocations.

For months she'd avoided an investigation into his activities, for the same reason she pretended not to know where her husband was because it was easier. But admiring his activities did not ease the sting of knowing he preferred playing Robin Hood to being first spouse of the United States. Luckily the press seemed to have moved on from the settlements and rarely reported on the inhabitants. This new art could be their undoing if anyone recognized him.

In the darkest moments of her longest nights, she told herself Richard would come home when he was ready and not before. She didn't know what she wanted to do about him or their relationship, so she did nothing. She forced the Secret Service to do the same. The worst part was lying to Finn. It pained her to keep her son in the dark, but if she told him the truth, he would go looking for his father and attempt a reconciliation, something she was at best ambivalent about. But Elizabeth did know one thing for certain, only something truly momentous would cause Richard to surface. She wondered if Finn's predicament was enough to finally draw him home.

TWELVE

RIVER PULLED into the motel parking lot, a bag of groceries on the passenger seat beside her. Food was nothing special inside the Territory. The potatoes looked like golf balls and the bananas were green sticks more suitable for throwing to a dog than eating. The survivalists drank protein shakes with a side of farmed beetles or crickets–a common food source in the refugee camps. Most people ate fast food, so the shopkeepers knew to limit their stock. Still, she'd found a nice head of lettuce, a frozen loaf of garlic bread, and a red wine actually bottled in Idaho.

When Marc was alive, they ate simply. On Fridays, they would drive up to Ketchum to listen to music on the deck of one of the hamburger joints, Bald Mountain standing proud in the distance. In the winter they would stay closer to home, grabbing a seat at the bar at Mahoney's to watch football. When Ava was a baby, she could come along for the ride and sleep through just about anything. Later they asked River's mother to keep an eye on her. They only visited local watering holes, not the fancy places the tourists came to eat at after skiing or hiking all day that served truffled pasta and racks of Idaho lamb for forty dollars a plate.

Her marriage was nothing like the one her parents had. When her father was alive, her mother brought home cookbooks from the library and they would take turns making dishes. Her parents' tastes ran towards Mexican and Italian. River's tastes grew as she did, from simple recipes for macaroni and cheese to more complicated French dishes like crepes and *coq au vin*.

That was light years away from where she was now, trying to feed one person in a dingy motel room. Her stove was electric, but it did have an oven and a broiler. Tonight's menu, although nothing fancy— spaghetti with meat sauce and the garlic bread—was confirmation of a hunger for more than food. It was a yearning for companionship, a desire that existed even when Marc had been alive. Sometimes she thought the yearning was worse because of him. Certainly, when she first joined the Army, she missed her father. She missed her life. She longed for her past, her youth, the person she'd hoped to become.

Sequestered inside the Territory, though, she'd become a loner with no connection to anyone. Why the man hiding out in her apartment spurred her to change her circumstances—even for one night—she couldn't say. River learned early on to manage her emotions. Self-control at that scale slowed time and made her feel older than her years. Tonight, though, her key just inches away from the deadbolt, she felt as nervous as a seventeen-year-old on the way to homecoming.

What she saw when she opened the door almost didn't register. Finn was sitting in a chair reading. The apartment was spotless.

"Well, well, Ivy League," she said, eyeing the neatly arranged book-shelves. "Somebody kept themselves busy."

"You've got an amazing collection of books," Finn said with a grin. "It was a little tough with my fingers still tender, but I managed, although I may have gone overboard. I tend to organize when I'm cooped up."

"Nerd alert!" River said, smiling.

"It takes one to know one," Finn said. "Your library is a dead giveaway."

River dropped the bag of groceries on the kitchen table. "I brought some things to make dinner," she said. "You need a good meal before you hit the road tonight. It's nothing fancy, but it should give you the energy to try to get back across."

"I appreciate it," Finn said. "What can I do to help?"

"You could set the table and open the wine," she said.

Finn did as he was told and poured two glasses of Syrah. River put a pot of water on the stove for the pasta and set to browning the ground beef in a skillet.

"Will you tell me where you were today?" Finn asked as he set the table.

"I knit," River said, her back to Finn. "Mostly scarves and blankets, and I donate them to people living in the refugee cities. There's a donation center a few hours from here. I drive there once a month and drop things off for people."

"So, you read books and knit," Finn said. "You're a real party animal."

"Yep," she said. "Now you know my secret."

Twenty minutes later, they sat down to dinner. Finn ate quickly and returned to the stove. River watched as he heaped more noodles and sauce on his plate, wondering how he managed to stay so slim with an appetite like a bear. A pleasant silence fell between them as River rose to set the plates in the sink. Finn got up too, and grabbed his phone from a nearby table.

"Mind if I put on some music?" he asked.

"Sure," River said.

Billie Holiday came belting out of the phone's speaker.

"I thought we might dance," Finn said.

"I can't," River replied. "Two left feet."

"You've just never had the right partner," Finn said, gesturing for her to come to him.

River crossed the room, a distance that felt like the Grand Canyon, and walked into Finn's arms.

"Just let me lead," he said. "We'll go slow and you'll see in no time that a patient partner makes all the difference in the world."

She leaned into him and felt his hand on her back, guiding her. Soon they were moving gingerly across the sliver of open floor in the room. Funny, she thought, I don't feel so awkward tonight. Then she realized it was because she wasn't being dragged around by a man twice her size.

"Why do you listen to such old music?" she asked.

"Because it's romantic," he said. "You know, you're doing just fine. Why did you say you were clumsy?"

River was about to reply when someone banged on her front door. Finn released River and grabbed his phone to silence the music.

"Security!" a voice yelled from the corridor. "We're conducting a search."

River locked eyes with Finn and signaled with one finger against her lips for him to stay silent, and then with her other hand gestured for him to hide under the bed.

Another set of rapid knocks sent River's blood pressure soaring.

"Open the door, or we'll kick it in!"

"Hold on a minute," River yelled. "I'm putting on some clothes."

Finn moved quickly, scanning the room for his gear bag. He grabbed it, biting back the pain from his injured fingertips as he slid under the bed, just barely fitting beneath the sagging mattress. Once Finn was out of sight, River walked to the door and peered through the peephole at two well-armed guards. One of them was larger than the other and looked to be former special operations. His partner was smaller in build, but still telegraphed a lethalness that was apparent through the viewfinder. She turned around one more time to make sure Finn was out of view, swallowed hard, and opened the door.

"What can I do for you gentlemen?" she asked, hoping her face was not as flushed as it felt.

"We're conducting a search for a fugitive," the smaller guard said, his hand resting confidently on an assault rifle. "Step into the hallway please."

"By all means," River said.

"Our security footage indicates you brought a guest home with you last evening," the guard continued. "Where is he now?"

River thought about the table set for two, along with the half-drunk wine glasses and recognized this was the moment when she should point to under the bed and tell the guards, *There he is! The man that coerced me into giving him a place to stay,* before she put herself in serious jeopardy.

But that was not what she did.

"Guest is kind of a *formal* word," River said. "We met at a bar and spent a little time together. He was a bit too drunk to perform, if you get my meaning. I kicked him out a while later. Don't actually recall his name, but I'm not one for long-term relationships."

"What bar?" the same smallish guard asked.

"Prairie Dog, the one behind the discount store," River said.

"There's no footage of anyone leaving the room but you," he replied.

"Must be a glitch in the system," River said, shrugging her shoulders.

"What about the music?" the guard asked. "We heard music playing."

"Nope, not from in here," she said. "You must have been mistaken."

"We're going to search your room," the guard said, as his larger, completely silent partner stepped inside.

River nodded, somehow managing to maintain an air of indifference that was in direct conflict with her mental state. Her entire body had grown clammy at the realization that Universal had the place under surveillance. She did her best to surreptitiously glance down the hall to identify where the cameras were located, but it wasn't at all obvious. She'd known the work sites and holding ponds had cameras–a precaution against slackers and terrorism, but the bars and motels where people lived? That she hadn't factored in. What an idiot she'd been. She should have known Universal would spy on its employees. *There is no way to get out of this alive,* she thought to herself. *Thanks to my foolishness, we are going to be lined up against the wall and shot, and I will never see my daughter again.*

Finn had been listening to the entire conversation, waiting for the moment when she would tip them off to his existence. He hadn't expected her to lie to save him. He couldn't see River, but he wondered if she was scared, perhaps contemplating her own death. He didn't want to be responsible for that.

"Don't shoot," he yelled loud enough for both guards to hear him. "I'm under the bed."

"Are you armed?" the larger guard barked, breaking his silence. "Slide your weapon out first so we can see it."

"I'm not armed," Finn yelled back. "There is no weapon."

"Ok, move s-l-o-w-l-y and keep your hands where I can see them," the guard said. "Failure to obey will result in in your immediate execution."

Finn slid out from under the bed and lay still, waiting for directions.

"Stand up and place your hands on top of your head," the guard ordered. Finn did as he was told, wondering if he should offer any information to exonerate River, or maybe reveal his identity. Surely they wouldn't kill the son of the President of the United States without considering the ramifications. The larger guard remained silent, mechanically patting Finn down. Once he finished, he marched Finn toward the door.

River grew chilled, her T-shirt wet with perspiration as she stood in the hallway awaiting their fate. She wanted to peer into the room, but knew better than to display any interest. After what felt like an eternity, the two of them came walking out. They paused at the doorway, Finn looking grim. She read his eyes, saw something that looked like gratitude or maybe remorse, but neither spoke as he was led away. River's breath caught in her throat as she waited, wondering what would happen next. To her surprise, the more slightly built patrolman escorted Finn toward the exit of the motel. The other lingered in the doorway, turning to face her. His body was so large she disappeared in his shadow.

"You have ten minutes to get out of here before the cleanup squad arrives," he said in a low voice. "Don't ask questions. You can thank your friends from Syria for the heads up. Now go, the cameras on the roads to the minor checkpoints have been disabled."

River remained stock still, knowing the slightest twitch recorded on video could be her death sentence. Once the second guard departed, she walked back into her room, fighting to maintain her composure. As soon as the door closed, she collapsed against it, giving herself only milliseconds to collect to her wits. For all of its intolerable moments, serving in the Army had just saved her life. With lightning speed, she threw a few supplies into a backpack, including her gun and all of her spare ammunition, before walking out of her apartment and into the darkness.

THIRTEEN

FINN WAS PUT in the back seat of a massive black SUV. He glanced at the shaved heads of the two guards who'd hauled him away wondering if they were going to kill him before the night was over. They hadn't beat him to a pulp or confined him with restraints, but he had no idea if the light touch was a sign of their intentions or a way to mess with his head. He thought about trying to jump from the car as it was moving but didn't like the odds of his surviving. Instead, he remained quiet and calm, hoping that his fortitude would help him survive.

He was resting his hands atop his gear bag, which was perched on his lap. The fact that they hadn't confiscated his bag was also puzzling, but he knew very little about how the Territories were governed. It hadn't seemed important to know those details before, but now his ignorance felt foolish. To keep himself occupied, Finn rummaged around in his bag, his fingers grasping his father's hat.

So much had happened since he'd left his house in Billings with his belongings. Finn had eyed the overstuffed bag before leaving. It was a lot of gear, too much really, but he tended to overpack. In his experience, every expedition had its unexpected twists and turns, an extra T-shirt or logbook might come in handy. Despite his already heavy haul, he'd stuffed the green felt hat into the bag, too; in much the same way his father had shoved his lucky fishing totem into his son's hands at the last moment.

"Keep this for me, will you?" he'd asked, except it hadn't really been a question. It was one of many orders issued by his father over the years that arrived camouflaged as a question. Finn accepted them all without protest.

For his father, a deeply respected educator who dealt with life based on its certainties, it was a destabilizing time. Until that day, there had been right and there had been wrong. And then afterwards, Finn knew his father's place in the world must have seemed smaller; he was adrift in a universe where the people who should make the decisions didn't, and men with no credentials suddenly emerged as leaders.

"I don't recognize this country anymore," he'd said to Finn during their last dinner together at their home in Wyoming. Finn spent a few days at the house at the mouth of the Tetons with his father, packing up before the evacuation. Richard Cunningham remained non-committal about his next steps to the end. He'd refused secret service protection and only reluctantly agreed to an identification tag. "I'm going to visit friends," was the most he'd been willing to offer. Finn flew out the next day, one of the last flights before the airport in Jackson Hole was decommissioned for civilian use. His father sent a few emails in the beginning, and then nothing, answering neither his phone nor email. His father's initial silence didn't register as serious. They had been on countless backpacking trips where they spoke no more than a few words to one another. By the time Finn resurfaced from his work, his father was nowhere to be found. Finn had done his best to comfort his mother, but their communications were sporadic at best while she was in hiding. Silence, it seemed, had become the family's official insignia.

The hat, meanwhile, hand sewn in Austria, had traveled with Finn to Montana from Wyoming. It was one of the few mementos he'd taken with him from their family home. Sitting in the back of the SUV, feeling far away from his family and the life he once knew, Finn pulled the hat out of the bag and ran his fingers over its worn edges, the crown covered with flies and small souvenir pins marking specific journeys. Chamonix was perched next to a silver dragon from Slovenia. Fastened nearby was a Hot Head Leech from Wyoming, and above it sat a Montana Stonefly.

He let out a long sigh, stuffing his good luck charm back into his bag. At the moment, it seemed more like a Jonah, bringing all of his family's bad luck with him to the river, but he tried to hold on to his faith. Somehow, he would get out of this. When they arrived at their destination, he would have to decide whether to reveal his identity. At this point, he didn't know if being the son of the president saved his life or sealed his death. He was also plagued by another terrible thought: he might have just sent a woman to her death. He hoped not. As a scientist, he was trained to recognize unusual variables, and River had them in spades: a French-speaking truck driver sporting a voracious reading habit, a love of knitting and automatic weapons. That kind of combination didn't come along often. It was too bad they would not see each other again, he thought. She was someone he would remember for the rest of his life, no matter how long it lasted.

An explosion interrupted his thoughts as the SUV swerved across the highway. Finn heard the unmistakable slap of a flat tire against the pavement. When the car came to a stop, the guard in the passenger seat opened the door and warned Finn: "Stay seated and silent," as he stepped outside. Finn watched him pass his window and bend down to examine the tire, releasing a string of expletives into the darkness. At the sound of his partner's exasperation, the driver also exited, leaving Finn alone in the back seat.

Finn looked out the window, wondering how they were going to get help stranded in the middle of nowhere, when something caught his eye. A lone figure was walking out of the darkness, the guards unable to see because they were on the other side of the car. He recognized River immediately as they locked eyes. As she had in her apartment, River pressed her finger to her lips, admonishing him to remain silent. Then she disappeared from view and the sounds of a major brawl filled the air. Finn almost jumped out of his skin when the car door opened abruptly and River–a large gash on one of her hands and what looked to be the beginning of fabulous shiner around her left eye–stood before him.

"Come on," she said, extending her uninjured hand.

Finn looked at her dumbly, trying to process how the woman he'd been daydreaming about a few minutes ago was standing in front of him. Before he could utter a word, she shut him down. "Save it, there's no time, Ivy League," she said. "We've got to get out of here."

Finn nodded and jumped out of the car. River took off in a fast jog slightly ahead of him. He followed, trying to figure out where they were going. His question was answered moments later when they arrived at an old pick-up truck parked behind a berm of prairie grass and snow.

"Get in," River said.

The engine turned over and the vehicle started to move before he'd even closed the door. He struggled to stay inside, his bruised body, sore fingers, and wounded arm not the best line of defense against gravity or velocity. Finally, he slammed the door shut with a grunt, his eyes wide with surprise as he turned to face his getaway driver.

"We need to leave the Territory," River said. "They were taking you east on the road to Minot. Universal keeps a large supply depot, post office and a few holding cells there. I made a lucky guess they intended to lock you in there for the night until they figured out what to do next. For now, my plan is to take us south through the grasslands and enter Montana at a less-guarded security crossing. I have it on good authority the cameras are turned off there."

"Can we hike over?" Finn asked.

"We'd freeze to death," River said. "And I don't want to risk trying to steal gear. It would only draw more attention to us."

"Good point," Finn said, pausing briefly before adding, "I thought they were going to kill you back at the motel. That's why I gave myself up."

"It turns out I have a guardian angel," River said. "Somebody on the security team is connected to my platoon in Syria. They gave me a ten-minute head start to leave town."

"But you didn't leave," Finn said. "Why?"

"I'll let you know when I understand myself, Ivy League," River said, keeping her gaze firmly fixed on the road ahead.

FOURTEEN

THE ARAPAHO GARDEN Apartments near Fort Collins were a product of another era. The three one-hundred-unit buildings were named back when real estate developers wanted to give residents the feeling they were paying tribute to some important cultural milestone, when in fact nothing could be further from the truth. The word garden was also misleading, as there was not a shred of green to be found as far as the eye could see. The apartments had been converted into refugee housing. Every blade of grass, shrub, and tree on the property had either been trampled or turned into kindling. Normally it would have all been hidden under a blanket of snow, but it had been unseasonably warm in Colorado the last few weeks, the temperatures hovering in the high fifties.

The weather-beaten wood and stucco structures had seen better days, but then again, so had Richard Cunningham. Like the housing, he was a mere specter of the man he used to be, wandering aimlessly across the plains. Technically he had a purpose in life, but it was counterfeit, ginned up to appease a guilty conscience. The beneficiaries of his penance were unaware. They had no idea he'd been a professor at a major university, or that he used to publish a non-fiction book every three years. They were also unaware that he'd abandoned his family, avoiding all contact for the last two years.

Self-righteous anger initially brought him to the refugee cities. He had an appetite to feed his own worst suspicions about what had happened. In time, though, as he traveled through Colorado, Idaho, Nebraska, South Dakota, and Utah, his motivations changed. Richard was not religious, but he nevertheless knew he had sinned, and quite spectacularly. Making matters worse, he had nothing but time on his hands, ribbons of unaccounted hours unfurling before him. Rather than face his digressions, he turned his energies to filling the time. And fill it he did, with food and first aid supplies, diapers, games, and coloring books. In the rear of his car, he carried dozens of little things and a few very large items that most people took for granted until the safety net was ripped out from underneath them.

They were called refugee "cities," but were nothing of the sort. They were a hodgepodge of rundown apartment complexes, old motels, and lakeside homes commandeered by the Energy Department. They'd managed to confine thousands into space for hundreds with the promise that it was temporary. Regardless of the country, the outcome from the arrival of hordes of refugees was the same. Conditions quickly became squalid, and diseases long eradicated like whooping cough and measles returned with a vengeance. Schools were overwhelmed and infrastructure buckled. Those who could move away from the government's garbage dumps did. The fact that these miseries took place on US soil with an American flag overhead did not seem to register as ironic to anyone. The media labeled the long-term inhabitants of these outposts many things. They were losers and aimless grifters intent on stealing from the government. Some said they lacked fortitude or were just plain lazy.

The truth was more complicated. The stories Richard heard pointed mostly to bad luck, the congenital kind. They lacked the friends or connections necessary to relocate. Some drank away their relocation payments. Others failed to qualify for government assistance because of criminal records. Richard had spent a lifetime studying nations and their ability to transform landscapes, but he also knew about their difficulty managing the human condition, which is how he found a way to forgive Elizabeth for being the ringleader of such stunning dysfunction and injustice. This was the fundamental Achilles heel of government because there was no way to compel human beings to act in their best interests through legislation. It was simply not possible. The result was a group of people making permanent homes out of temporary shelters.

The plan for this supply run was to make two stops. The first was Arapahoe, where he'd unloaded several boxes of bottled water, baby formula, fleece blankets, and some over-the-counter medicines. From there he drove ten hours towards Bear Lake, Utah, so he could deliver more of the same, along with a crib for a woman with a new baby. He'd pitched a one-man tent in Logan–the ground cold, but mostly free of snow–and then drove the last stretch of Route 89 early the next morning to reach the former lakeside resort. A few neighbors helped him carry the crib's box into the single-family cinder block house on Lake Cottage Drive. He was just closing up his car when he noticed the motorcade of SUVs heading in his direction.

"It's the President," one of the children playing on the sidewalk exclaimed. "They said she would be coming today."

Richard looked at one of the men who'd helped lug in the box. "The President?" he asked.

"Yes," the man explained. "She often comes unannounced. The rumor is that she doesn't want anyone to try to sugar-coat things, so she keeps her visits a secret."

That sounded like Elizabeth, Richard thought. She was no show-boater.

"Well, I've got a long drive ahead of me," Richard said. "I better get going."

"You should stay," the man said. "She should know about the good work you do."

"No," Richard said. "I prefer to stay out of the limelight."

"Suit yourself," the man said. "We'll see you in a few weeks."

Richard nodded and pulled his baseball cap lower on his head as he hopped in the driver's seat. Lake Cottage Drive was located inside a classic 1950s housing tract, which meant that he could avoid his wife's motorcade by using one of the other roads that looped around the subdivision.

He was more than three hours away from a warm bed and a meal, which was plenty of time for the feelings of relief and shame coursing through his system to battle it out. Richard made three or four trips a month to the ten different refugee camps without a single hiccup until today. In between trips, he returned home and arranged for supplies. Sometimes he called on old friends, who dutifully maintained the charade and did not ask about Elizabeth. Their unwillingness to air dirty laundry spared Richard the awkwardness of a confession. He didn't have to look anyone in the eye and admit that it took only a few days for the smug warmth of self-congratulation to wear off before he realized the gravity of his mistake. Or that the longer he stayed away, the more difficult it became for him to imagine an apology sufficient to make amends. Not once in thirty-plus years of marriage had he and Elizabeth walked out on one another. They'd debated, argued at the top of their lungs, but they usually settled their differences before turning off the light. Something about that fateful day, the creation of the Territories, had caused him to break down and breach their compact, and after a lifetime of compromise and communication, he'd abandoned his marriage and his son.

It was too close for comfort, their near meeting. Richard took it as a sign that his grace period was running out. He assumed Elizabeth could find him if she wanted to. She was the most powerful woman in the world. She granted him anonymity because she could. He and Elizabeth had not spoken for two years. That was a long time, and yet he was certain that if their paths had crossed out in front of that house, she would have embraced him. That was what made his miserable existence even more painful: knowing that the woman who had carried his only child and stayed married to him for more than three decades would likely forgive him. Not because she wasn't angry, he was certain she was. Or because she thought he was right; he knew she didn't. She would forgive him because she understood his pain better than he did. That was the most difficult of the truths he'd come to understand. Difficult because how on earth could he accept her forgiveness when he had yet to forgive himself?

His pulse was racing as he pulled away from the street. After a few seconds he got up the nerve to look in his rear-view mirror. There was

nothing to see but emptiness as he looped his way through the neigh-
borhood and back out to the highway.

FIFTEEN

ELIZABETH WATCHED her husband pull away and disappear into the distance. His driving was measured, not too fast as to draw attention, but with a certain rapidity of purpose. His car was covered in dust, the rear license plate missing. Leave it to Richard to take on the trappings of a messiah and a fugitive. How was it that the local police hadn't stopped him? Maybe he put the plate back on after his deliveries. Or maybe, as she knew too well, the police had more important things to worry about.

"Do you want us to detain him, Madam President?" the head of her security detail asked.

Elizabeth hesitated before replying, wondering if she should chase after Richard and tell him that their son was in danger. Maybe it was worth all of the awkwardness to band together to find a way to rescue Finn. Then she remembered that Finn was trapped inside the Territory, and that would probably dredge up old transgressions. Would Richard blame her for their son's misfortune? She didn't want to find out.

"No," she said. "Let him go."

"Are you sure?" he asked.

"Today is not the day," she said. She would have to deal with Finn's predicament on her own.

"Understood," her bodyguard said, having asked and received the same answer several times. "Please stay in the car until we can secure the perimeter."

Bear Lake was the first stop in what was certain to be a long day. After meeting with a few families, she would be heading back to the airport in Salt Lake City for a quick trip to Denver, where the elections team had arranged for focus groups. She intended to stay for most of them, and perhaps make unannounced visits to some of the other nearby refugee cities. She visited all of the camps in an unmarked charter–something previously unthinkable, but now a necessity if she was to protect herself and the inhabitants. She visited to bear witness to her actions and to make herself accountable.

With the swipe of a pen, she'd begun the chain of events that allowed people to arrive at this place. Not quite homeless, but not at home. President Franklin D. Roosevelt signed Executive Order 9066 in 1942, sending 100,000 Japanese to internment camps. It turned out the exalted FDR had nothing on her when it came to moving the masses, but he had intended to *confine* people. She'd had no such intention, and yet here she was with a group of individuals who'd failed to move on. They were trapped with no known method for dislodgement. Her advisors were urging her to close down the camp cities as soon as possible, to put an end to the millions in aid the government was providing, and to eliminate election issues for her party. Elizabeth had no stomach for interjecting politics into her decision-making when it came to the refugees, but she knew that her reluctance, like Richard's anonymity, could not last. Elections were on the horizon and everything she'd done or more precisely *not done* would be fodder for political operatives intent on blaming her, the candidates, or her party. She'd hardly thought about her political affiliation since the tragedies began. What did it matter? They'd all been in the same boat when the tide turned against them.

Elizabeth's guards gave her the all-clear sign and she stepped out of the car. On the sidewalk was a young boy. He looked to be about six or seven, but was terribly small for his age. His sweater and jeans hung off his slight frame, likely hand-me-downs from someone else in his family or the camp.

"Hello," Elizabeth said. "How are you?"

"My mother said not to talk to strangers," the boy said.

"That's just what I told my son when he was your age," Elizabeth replied, noticing the boy held something. "What's that in your hand?"

The boy unclasped his fingers, revealing a small metal airplane in his palm. It was an inexpensive replica of a commercial airliner. "It's a plane," the boy said. "One day I'm going to be a pilot."

"Is that so?" Elizabeth asked. "I came on a plane today to see you."

"I want to learn to fly so I can leave this place," the boy said. "Mom is always saying that if she had one wish, it would be to get on an airplane and fly away from here. So, I'm going to help her."

"What a good boy you are," Elizabeth said. "I'm sure you will make a very fine aviator one day. Is your mother at home now? Do you think I could meet her?"

The boy nodded and led her into the one-story house he'd been standing in front of. It had once been someone's vacation home before the government took possession. There was nothing but a brown patch of dirt for a yard. The front door was ajar, but not wide open. As the boy stepped inside, he called out, "Mom, there's a lady here to see you."

"What on earth, Toby," the boy's mother said. "What did I say about speaking to strangers?"

"This one is different," the boy replied. "She came...in a big car."

A young woman came into view, clutching a newborn baby. She was in her late twenties and clearly the source of the children's raven-colored hair. They all seemed too small and Elizabeth suspected their slenderness had more to do with lack of food than genetics. There was not a winter coat among them.

"I'm sorry to barge in," Elizabeth said. "Do you know who I am?"

The woman's eyes were wide with fright as she nodded. "You're the President. I've seen you on TV. Did we do something wrong?" she asked.

Now it was Elizabeth who felt small. "No, not at all," she said. "I came here to see how you and your neighbors are doing. Tell me your name, please."

"It's Patricia," she said. "But folks call me Patty."

"Nice to meet you, Patty," Elizabeth said. "I see you just had a baby. Are you feeling OK?"

"I'm better today," Patty said. "The angel came and brought me a crib and some baby formula. I can't seem to make any milk to feed him. The doctor says I don't eat enough, but how can I when I need to feed Toby?"

Elizabeth looked at the boy and signaled to one of the members of her security detail. "Toby, in the back of my car is a box of toys. Would you like to go outside and pick out one or two for yourself? One of my friends here will help you."

There was no reply, only the whirr of a small boy running away. "An angel you say?" Elizabeth asked Patty. "Have you seen him before?"

"Only once," she said. "He noticed I was expecting and asked me what he could do to help. I told him about my ex and how he ran off during the evacuations with another woman and took most of our stuff. Today he showed up with a brand-new crib, baby formula, and some food for the pantry. He wouldn't tell me his name, said he was just glad to help. I get the same rations as everyone else, but with me being pregnant and having a growing boy, it didn't seem to go very far. I don't have any family nearby and I can't work with Toby around. The school here at the camp is only part time. There aren't enough teachers."

"Toby says you would like to leave and go somewhere else," Elizabeth said.

"I have family in California," she said. "A sister. She said I could come live with her. Our car would probably make it, but I don't have enough money to drive there and stay in motels with a baby."

"If you could fly there in the next few days, would you go?" Elizabeth asked. "You would have to leave everything but your clothing behind, but I could arrange it."

Patty stood still, tears beginning to leak out of the corners of her eyes. "I don't have to do anything bad do I?" she asked. "I mean, I am a woman with two kids and no father. I know what you must think of me. I'm not proud of myself, but…"

Elizabeth walked over to the woman and placed her arm around her. "You don't have to do anything except pack," she said. "This is a second chance. All you have to do is be ready to go in two days."

Patty wiped her sleeve across her nose and smiled. "Two angels in one day," she said. "It's a miracle."

Elizabeth stayed at the house for a while longer, making sure the woman's sister existed and was really able to take her in. Then she arranged for the same charter that ferried her around secretly to make a quick trip to San Diego and deliver Patty, Toby, and baby Taylor to their new home near the ocean. She knew she couldn't replicate her generosity more than a few times. It was a drop in the bucket for the misery she'd caused, but what else could she do but try to repair things when she saw an opening? Was that what Richard was doing, she wondered. Were they both atoning for their sins?

She felt elated as she said her goodbyes, knowing the feeling was fleeting. The fate of the nation, and the survival of her son, weighed more than a few kind gestures, but generosity and compassion were the only things she could give freely at the moment. For now, the battle to even the scale of suffering—hers and others'—would be won in dribs and drabs, a few dozen Patties sent off to the embrace of their families, one at a time.

SIXTEEN

FINN LOOKED over at River sleeping, her head resting against the drivers' side window, and thought about how luck was a funny, fickle thing. As a boy, he'd often pretend to be invisible or protected by a force field, running through imaginary barriers as he blasted his enemies into the next galaxy. He felt the same invincibility tonight as he and River sailed through the empty guard post—beneficiaries of some omnipotent being removing obstacles in their path.

Safe for the moment, Finn tried to process all that had happened. He'd been shot and nearly drowned on the mighty Missouri. A mystery woman had saved his life not once, but twice. Why? Why did she come back? And why had the hand of fate thrown him into her path? He could have stumbled into the road and found a car full of ex-soldiers like the ones who'd detained him. Instead, he found her. Although he could not explain it, he knew it meant something.

Finn watched River the way one observes a tiger when it's sleeping. It's only then that you can get in close enough to admire their beauty. From afar she seemed dangerous, if not lethal, and yet he found her lovely, even with the whopper of a black eye she'd gotten saving him, or maybe because if it. She was slender, but muscular. Her hair cut short out of what looked more like utility than fashion. He thought about the hazardous, demanding work she carried out day after day, her life as a soldier, and realized that she was as tough or tougher than most of the men he knew. No one had ever rescued him from anything, let alone searched for him in the middle of the night while he was a prisoner in an unmarked car with two armed guards. He wasn't sure he would have done the same thing, and it made him question the veracity of his moral compass. Whatever he thought his lofty intentions were for himself in this world, he'd never risked his life for *anybody* intentionally or accidentally. He'd never been the person who happened to notice someone drowning at the beach or choking on their dinner. He wasn't a hero or predisposed to being one. Sitting in the darkness, Finn wondered if his desire for solitude was a form of selfishness.

"I can hear you thinking, Ivy League," River said, opening her eyes.

"You can?" Finn asked, startled out of his thoughts. "I haven't said a word."

"You don't have to," she said.

"Are you saying you have ESP?"

"No, something better," River said. "Two tours in the Army, the last one in Syria. Crazy place, a lot of dangerous people…it pays to learn to listen to the silence."

"OK, what am I thinking?" he asked.

"You want to know why there was no guard at the post," she said. "You're wondering how we got through so easily."

"That's exactly what I was thinking," Finn said, grateful her guess landed on the first half of his ponderings.

"I think it's *you*," she said. "Something about you has them doing things differently. They didn't put out an alert. They didn't set up any roadblocks."

"I don't know about that," Finn said. "You're the one who got a ten-minute warning. I was being driven off towards a firing squad."

"Maybe," River said. "Or maybe they don't want anyone to know you're missing."

"I *am* a government employee," Finn said. "They should be worried about killing me. I had permission…to be there." Finn was about to say permission from the company, but he stopped himself. He couldn't discuss his arrangements. River would abandon him the first chance she got if he revealed who he was. Unlike other children who'd been subjected to the campaign trail, his mother had been sworn in under duress. Popular magazines had not come calling for a photo spread of the commander-in-chief and her family, allowing him to remain relatively anonymous. Maybe there was an official press photo floating around on the Internet, but you would have to know his last name to make the connection. River hadn't asked and he wasn't going to tell.

"I didn't kill those guards," she said. "In case you're wondering."

"I wasn't going to ask," Finn said.

"I couldn't," she said. "Not after they'd tipped me off."

"You did the right thing," he said. "It will come back in our favor later that no one was killed."

"I agree," River said. "But what now? What next?"

"Now we go and get my camping gear and some supplies and hide out in the wilderness until we can sort things out."

"Too dangerous," she said. "They could be waiting for you at your house."

"I agree," Finn said. "But I don't keep my gear at my house. I keep it somewhere else, and there is no way the security guys at Universal know anything about it."

SEVENTEEN

THE PRESIDENT FIDGETED in her seat, anxious for the process to begin. Only hours after leaving Bear Lake, Elizabeth found herself in Denver, sitting in a nondescript strip mall conference room re-reading a memo, while her staff made final arrangements for a series of focus groups. She arrived just in time for a group made up solely of women. Other sessions would be just men and a few groups would be mixed.

In politics, focus groups are the holy grail of elections. More substantial than a yes or no answer taken during a telephone or online survey, focus groups offer a glimpse into the electorate's psyche. A chance for unvarnished voter sentiment. Wondering how women over fifty respond to a certain female presidential candidate? Want to know if one million dollars is too much money for a CEO to make in a year? Go ahead and ask. The groups she was attending had been arranged specifically for her benefit so she could hear first-hand what voters thought about the last two years since the massacre. While she knew the feedback was necessary, it was also intimidating. Alone in the dark, eavesdropping on her fellow citizens, she felt vulnerable to criticism. The room was full of mostly rookie staff who were too green to be jaded, but also too fresh to understand the magnitude of the changes she'd ushered in.

"Good evening," the focus group host said to the attendees. "I'm going to be taking you through a series of questions this evening. There is no wrong or right answer. I'm interested in your views and those of your fellow participants. The only thing I ask is that you remain respectful of people's opinions and raise your hand to speak."

A few more ground rules were issued, and then the moderator got to the heart of the matter. "Is the country better off than it was two years ago?"

"I think so," a woman said. "At first I couldn't get the images out of my mind. We stopped watching the news for a while. But now, things feel like they're getting back to normal. Our town had its Christmas parade this past year, and my husband's company has started hiring new employees. We've even been talking about taking a trip, to California to see the ocean."

Another woman raised her hand; this one according to Elizabeth's guide had a son graduating from high school. "I agree," she said. "We just let John drive to the mall alone for the first time. I mean, can you imagine? He's almost eighteen and we refused to let him out of our sight. But now, since the security cameras were installed downtown, we feel safe again."

Elizabeth watched most of the group nod their heads in agreement. All accept one person, a woman in her late-twenties, with two toddlers at home, according to the participant list. The moderator also noticed her demeanor and called on her. "And you? What do you think?"

"I'm not sure," she said. "I used to be an artist living near Cody, Wyoming."

The team of advisors surrounding the President jumped out of their seats. "What the hell," the main consultant said. "There aren't supposed to be relocation participants in this group, it will taint the results. We need to pull her out."

"No," Elizabeth said.

"Madam President, if we could just…"

"You may *not*," she replied sharply. "Sit down and listen. We won't be able to avoid unpleasant truths on the campaign trail. We might as well see what happens when you throw her opinions into the mix." The consultants sat down in unison, turning their dejected gazes towards the glass. The moderator encouraged the woman to continue.

"We were relocated, *obviously*… I suppose that has gone fairly well. My husband found a new job in Denver right away as a teacher, and we used the relocation money to purchase a new house. I had my second child not long after we arrived. It's just that things feel different now."

"How so?" the moderator asked.

"Well, for one thing I have an electronic chip in my arm that the government is using to track my movements. There are daily drone flights over the center of town. When I walk around, it seems like almost everyone in our city is white, and of course there are no immigrants at all since we closed our borders."

"Those are *good things*," another participant replied. "If you're living your life right, the government has no interest in you or your whereabouts. It's because of these changes that we're safe now. There haven't been any more bombings, no more wars in the Middle East. A few years ago, it seemed like everyone I knew had a son or daughter coming home from Syria or Egypt missing an arm or a leg, or worse… And now look. We have peace. We have prosperity again. Who cares if a drone flies over our city? They're not looking for us."

"But there are wars in the Middle East," the artist replied. "We just don't send our soldiers. As for the rest, well, I have nothing to hide, but that doesn't mean I like giving away my privacy. This is the United States of America. It used to be a place of expression, of vastness. Now? I don't know. I love my county, but as I said it feels *different*, as if we lost *something*, only I can't say exactly what it is."

"I think the Territories were a good idea," said another participant. "It's hard…these changes, but I would gladly trade some of my privacy to prevent terrorism. I don't see how we can avoid it; besides, I feel like all those technology companies knew as much or more about me before all of this happened. It was just less obvious."

"OK, good points," the moderator said, reclaiming the discussion before it could slip away from him. "Let's take an informal poll by a show of hands. All of those who think the current security measures have been a good thing raise your hand."

The President watched all but the artist raise their hands. She wondered how the group would react if they knew there were moments when she sided with the artist and other times when she worried she hadn't gone far enough to protect people. That uncertainty often gave her comfort, hoping that in not having satisfied herself, she might well have created a state of balance. Elizabeth knew the dilemma well: what was the value of privacy if your child could be crucified at the hands of a terrorist at a shopping mall and used as reality TV fodder on feeds beamed to the Middle East and Africa? In moments of great clarity, the choice seemed simple to Elizabeth: either the terrorists spied on you as they plotted to kill you, or the government watched over its citizens to protect them. It came down to a matter of lesser evils, and she was relieved to see that most of the women in the room maintained the same reluctant acceptance she did.

EIGHTEEN

COOPER WAS DREAMING. He was back in some Godforsaken shithole and couldn't find his gun. Orders were being issued, members of his unit were running out the door, but Cooper was there, frozen with horror at not being able to locate his weapon. He was just about to tell his CO when the ringing of the phone penetrated his troubled sleep.

"Cooper!" he yelled into the phone, still half at attention from his nightmare.

"Sir, we lost the package," said a voice on the other end of the line.

"Come again," Cooper said.

"We were ambushed and he was taken from the vehicle on the way to the safe house," the voice continued.

Cooper sat up in bed, fully awake now, his attention focused on every word and their implications for his survival and the country's. "Who the hell came to help him? He was alone in there. He doesn't know a living soul," Cooper said.

There was a long pause before the man on the line spoke again. "It was the woman," he said.

There was no going back to sleep after that. Cooper got up and sat in the dark of his living room, a whisky in his hand. He'd sent two of his best men to the motel to fish the scientist out and keep him safe until he could figure out what to do next, keeping him out of sight until he got Red under control. What were the odds that the President's son would actually find a sympathetic person to help him inside the Territory, and that she'd beat his guards to hell and steal his bargaining chip? You just can't make stuff like that up, he thought as his phone rang for the second time that evening. This time, Cooper thought grimly, it was his turn to explain his epic failure to a man who was already frustrated at his lack of results.

"How does a privileged little shit like this kid keep out-maneuvering you?" Red asked. "Do you at least have surveillance in place?"

"Yes, but...."

"But what?" Red asked.

"Red, it's three in the morning," Cooper said. "Can we finish this later?"

"I'm not concerned with the time," Red said. "I'm concerned with finding Finn Cunningham before he can tell his mother I tried to have him killed."

"I have two of my best teams staking out their homes," Cooper replied. That at least was the truth. His elite forces were fanned out across Montana and Idaho looking for them. So far, though, they were ghosts who had disappeared into the night without a trace.

"Tell me again about the woman," Red said.

"Her name is Jennifer Petersen," Cooper said. "She goes by the nickname River. I was going to email you her file in the morning."

"Do it now," Red said.

Cooper rose from his worn leather library chair and walked to his desk. He opened up his laptop and sent the file. The information would send Red further over the edge. He hoped he could keep his job long enough to stop his boss from executing any of his plans. It was just Cooper's luck that instead of a dumb lug of a waste haul driver, Finn had run into a war widow fluent in French and Arabic, who'd been a lead interpreter and guide for her platoon. Reading her personnel file was like reading a star pupil's report card: perfect attendance, no requests for sick leave or additional time off, and no disciplinary actions. She was a model employee, right up until the time she ambushed his guards and helped Finn escape.

"Jesus H. Christ with a cherry on top," Red said. "What was she even doing in the Territory?"

"Same as the others," Cooper said. "She's ex-army, a widow, and according to her credit report, dead broke. Her supervisor said she was the best member of his crew. He's sorry she's gone, as she was one of the few that showed up every day, and sober to boot."

"Did she and the boy know each other before?" Red asked.

"No," Cooper said. "As far as we can tell they have no connection to one another."

"Well, something made her decide to stick her neck out to save him," Red said. "Did they sleep together? Maybe she's a sex maniac. You know, she did choose to come up to the Territory and work. Maybe she likes things rough."

Cooper rolled his eyes. Red seemed to hate women, especially the tough, smart ones. He tended to lump women into only a handful of categories: feckless leader, sex maniac, or lesbian. Cooper wondered what had happened to cause Red to have such a low opinion of the opposite sex. Was it his mother? Did some girl crush his soul when he was young? In the end, it didn't matter, but still, it would have been nice to know.

"We have no way of knowing," Cooper said, keeping his tone light. "Nothing came up in our interviews. As far as we can tell, she basically lived like a hermit. We're going to need some more time to understand how this all happened."

"Understand? We don't need to understand jack shit," Red said. "As far as I'm concerned, the two of them are fugitives. You have two days to locate them before I send my own team out to kill them."

"Your own team?" Cooper asked. "I'm the head of security. Who else do you have working on this?"

There was no reply. Red hung up.

NINETEEN

THE ROLL-UP DOOR to the self-storage unit slammed shut with a loud *thunk*. "We're safe in here," Finn said, gesturing with his hand at the interior of the shed. It was a space so large they'd been able to park River's truck inside.

"You've got a lot of equipment here," River said, scanning the walls. "Most people would store this kind of stuff in their garage."

"I'm not *most* people," Finn said. "When I'm in the field, I don't like to stop my work. The USGS District Office and my house are in Billings, but I travel through the entire state, so I picked Helena as a very *non-scientific* middle point for keeping supplies. There's even a refrigerator to store water samples, which means I don't have to return to the lab after every trip."

"So, basically, you don't like going home," River said. "Why is that?"

Finn wondered how truthful he should be. So far, he'd been riding the line between omitting key details and outright lying, pretty successfully. Being on the run meant conversation was kept to a minimum. For the moment though, they were safe and well hidden, which meant more banter, and questions about his personal life and family were bound to come up. He didn't want to lie to River. He knew when the whole story came out, he would be better off having stuck mostly to the truth.

"There's not much to go home to," he said.

"Family?"

"Relocated," he said. "It broke up my parent's marriage."

River raised her right eyebrow slightly, but said nothing.

"What?" he asked.

"I'm trying to figure you out, Ivy League," she said. "You're obviously a bit of a recluse, certainly a science geek, but there's something else...I just can't put my finger on it."

"You've been cooped up in the Territory for God knows how long. But you told me you're from Idaho," Finn said, feeling nervous and defensive. "What's your excuse for not going home? You can't possibly have liked living in those conditions. You sat around reading the classics and knitting to pass the time. I didn't see much beyond your motel room, but the place looked like a hellhole, and of course there is the part about your drinking water catching on fire."

"I have my reasons," she said.

"I guess that makes us even," Finn said. "Shall we move on to other topics?"

"By all means," River said, but she wasn't finished, she was only pausing their conversation. As a soldier, she had honed her gut instincts. Maybe it was *mumbo-jumbo, hocus-pocus* to some, but she came home with all her fingers and toes and put a lot of the stock in her ability to sense and see what others either couldn't or wouldn't. As she gazed around at the walls of the storage unit, she noticed two things. First, the man she was with was meticulous. There wasn't so much as a roll of tape out of place. Second, he was serious about his gear, or more precisely, he was serious about being outside. Which made his arrival in the Territory all the more puzzling. How did a man so organized and prepared end up on the run with her? She knew she was going to find out eventually, she just hoped she could deal with the answer.

"What else do you have in here that could be of use to us?" she asked, breaking her silence.

"Food, mostly dry goods, a stove, camping gear, first aid supplies and some clothing," Finn said.

"Do you think any of the clothing would fit me?" River asked.

Finn nodded. "Probably. We're not exactly the same size, but I'm not all that big."

River had noticed the same thing back at the motel when she'd inspected him for injuries. There'd been an unavoidable comparison to Marc, whose hulking frame made most men look small. She wondered if she would always think of him first. "I'll give it a shot," River said. "But first, we should check your arm."

Finn disappeared behind a large baker's rack, returning with an enormous first aid kit. River settled down at an old card table and began picking her way through the green canvas bag, pulling out hospital grade sutures and rolls of gauze. "I know some Army medics who would've loved a bag like this," she said.

"Is that what you did?" Finn asked, pulling off his fleece.

River removed the original dressing from Finn's arm. "No. I was an interpreter and translator," she said. "But I also filled in as medic. I was first in at the checkpoints. I'm not formally trained, but I learned how to sew up a wound."

"Did you use your French?" Finn asked, wincing slightly as she swabbed his wound with antiseptic.

"No. If I'd been in Lebanon, maybe, but I also speak Arabic," River said, preparing her supplies. "Now that I can, I'm going to stich up your wound so it will heal faster. Do you want me to use some topical anesthesia?"

"It's ok," Finn said. "I've had to close myself up a few times. I can sit still. What about your hand?"

"Superglue," she said looking down at the open skin around her knuckles. "I'll seal it and wrap it in some gauze," River said.

True to his word, Finn hardly moved while she stitched the wound closed and bandaged the area again.

"Thanks, that should help," Finn said, rising from the chair. "I think it's time for dinner. Let me look at what we've got to work with."

Thirty minutes later, the two were seated at the card table spooning beef stew over ramen noodles. River had changed into a fresh fleece and down vest and borrowed a black wool ski hat. Finn wore the identical model only in navy, his hair pulled back in a ponytail, and he'd donned a grey wool sweater and a fresh pair of jeans.

"This is the kind of meal I used to eat when I went backpacking," River said. "It's not glamorous, but it fills you up."

"Exactly," Finn said. "Who did you camp with?"

"My dad mostly, but sometimes my mom would join us," River said. "He's dead now. He had a heart attack one day at work. After that I didn't go into the backcountry again."

"How come?" Finn asked, reaching for some Tabasco.

River didn't reply.

Finn looked up from his meal. "I'll be the first one to admit this is strange," he said. "But we already share a pretty complicated set of circumstances, so how about we just talk? I don't know what's going to happen next, but you can be certain I'll keep your secrets, whatever they are. You saved my life, and I won't forget it."

Bare her soul? Not likely. Who didn't have a sob story in the Army? Nothing about her situation made her special, so she'd never brought it up. Marc never asked, because he was trapped inside his own head, too sick to offer sympathy and comfort to anyone else. Inside the Territory, nobody asked personal questions, because you might not want to hear the answer. That left her mother, whose eyes begged for the truth, but River couldn't open up like that, afraid all of the bitterness and grief would come spilling out and drown her only remaining family member. There was something about Finn, though, something about his presence that made it OK to express her thoughts, to take them beyond just a whisper in her head.

"My dad's sudden death left us with a lot of debt and not enough money to pay the mortgage," she said. "I'd been accepted to Yale on a scholarship, Global Studies, but I had to decline. I joined the Army because it was the quickest way to help pay our bills. You can't earn much with only a high school diploma. The Army said they would pay for college, but of course that didn't happen. I married Marc instead and got pregnant. He's dead now, but I think you probably guessed that."

Finn was listening, but the buzzing in his head was slowing his response time. The random *almost* proximity of their lives was unnerving. She could have been someone he'd met years ago, walking through the Yale campus, maybe sipping a beer at a party. Instead, she'd been hurled into another universe and yet their paths had still crossed. He took it as another sign.

"I'm a Yalie," he said.

"I knew it was something like that," River said. "You have the look."

"The look?" Finn asked. "I'm not the slightest bit preppy or clean cut."

"No," she said. "It's not that, it's something else."

"What?"

"I don't know how to describe it exactly," she said. "I've noticed it all my life, being around rich kids. You always look like you know where you're going, like you have everything under control."

Finn snorted. "I think I know what you mean, but you're mistaken, about me at least," he said. "I'm not certain about very much, but maybe I have a good poker face. And I know a lot of kids who came from wealthy families that were uncertain about their place in the world when they were younger. It sounds like you knew what you wanted, but had some bad luck that knocked you off course. And it turns out you almost went to Yale, which means you're Ivy League, too…in a manner of speaking."

"But I didn't attend Yale," she said.

"Yes, but that doesn't take away from the fact that they *accepted you*," he said. "You are *de facto* Ivy League."

River laughed. "Maybe," she said. "I'll have to think about that."

"What would you have done if you hadn't joined the Army?" Finn asked.

River felt the corners of her eyes moisten. "Attend college with guys like you," she said. "Speak French, drink beer at parties, and see the world. I guess I *did* get to see the world, but only the *horrible* parts of it."

"*Il est pas trop tard pour voir le monde*," Finn said. "Really, it isn't too late to see the world. You have a lifetime ahead of you."

"*Romantisme français ne paie pas les factures,*" River replied, reminding Finn that romanticism didn't put money in the bank.

"Life can't all be about paying your bills," Finn said, scraping the last of his meal from the bowl.

"Spoken like someone who's never been in debt," she said. "This is what I was trying to describe, this certainty that you can just do what you want and everything else will fall into place."

"I would call that optimism," Finn said. "It's a critical survival trait. I have to be able to imagine a time when things will be better, a time when the things I want will come true."

"Now I know why you stay out here in the wilderness," River said. "It's so no one can pop your bubble."

Finn tried not to flinch, although she'd made a direct hit. "I assure you, my so-called bubble has a hole in it," he said. "My father is missing and I have no idea where he is. He was so angry about Wyoming's conversion to an Energy Territory that he walked out on my mother and me and disappeared."

"That's rough," she said. "You really have no idea where your father is?"

"I saw him just before he left our house when the evacuations began," he said. "But since then, there's been nothing."

"And your mom?" she asked.

"She's working. She has a very demanding job in another state," Finn said, catching her gaze. "There's a lot of security. It's difficult to visit her."

"*Jeeze,* you make her sound like the President of the United States," River said.

Finn held her gaze, saying nothing to correct her.

"Yeah, right," River said. "Like I said before, you have one hell of an imagination."

Still smarting from her jab earlier, Finn decided maybe honesty was the better policy and rose from his seat. He fished his phone from his bag and dialed his mother's number, putting the call on speaker so River could hear the ringing.

"What are you doing?" she asked.

Before he could reply, a woman's voice came over the speaker.

"Finn?" Elizabeth asked. "Is that you? Where are you? Are you safe?"

"I am," he said. "Where are you?"

"I'm back at the White House," she said. "Let me send the Secret Service to come and get you."

"I'm not alone," Finn said. "I escaped thanks to the help of a friend."

"Is he there with you?" she asked.

"It's a she," Finn said.

"Then put her on," Elizabeth said.

Finn handed the phone to River, who looked at the device with a mixture of shock and trepidation. "Hello," she said.

"This is Elizabeth Cunningham," she said. "Thank you for helping my son. Please convince him to let me send some agents to escort you back to Washington."

River set the phone on the table and abruptly stood up and walked away. Finn picked it up and turned off the speaker to talk directly with his mother. "Don't send anyone," he said. "We're fine. Look, I know this is going to sound crazy, but I think I know where Dad is. I'm going to look for him and then the three of us will come to you."

Out of the frying pan into the fire Elizabeth thought, trying to tamp down her rising nausea at her son's bad judgment. "Finn, your father doesn't want to be found," she said. "How can you be so certain you know where he is?"

"I just am," he said. "Trust me, I'll stay out of sight. They'll expect me to go straight to you."

"I'm leaving tomorrow," Elizabeth said. "Congressional elections are restarting. They've got me on a train traveling across the country to drum up interest. It ends with a televised speech in Denver. Meet me there in ten days whether you have your father or not. If I don't hear from you by that time, I'm sending the Air Force and the Marines."

"That won't be necessary," he said. "We'll see you in ten days."

After he hung up, Finn looked up to find River glaring at him from a corner. "My name is William Finn Cunningham," he said. "My mother is Elizabeth Cunningham, *President of the United States*."

Anger and pleasure simultaneously coursed through River's veins.

Her instincts had proven to be correct, he did have a secret, but the truth was much different than she'd allowed herself to imagine. She thought maybe he'd turn out to be a rogue employee who exceeded his authority, or was fleeing a breakup and tight-lipped about his home life. Instead, she was on the run with the son of the President.

"You bastard! *I knew it*," River said. "That's why Universal is being so cautious. They don't want to draw attention to themselves while they look for you."

"Look for *us*," Finn said. "They have to know by now that you were the one who sprung me."

"Why didn't you tell me sooner?" River asked.

"Why do you think?" Finn asked.

"No, Ivy League," she said. "Sarcasm is not an option. You've been caught lying."

"I didn't lie," Finn said. "I just wasn't totally forthcoming."

"Why should I believe anything you've told me?"

"I didn't lie to you," Finn said. "The story I told you in the motel is true. The water in the Missouri river and its tributaries is too warm. I visited the Territory to see if the conditions were the same there or worse, and they tried to kill me. Everything I told you about my father walking out is true. I swear."

River covered her eyes with the heels of her hands. "I was weeks away from getting out, free and clear," she said. "I don't need this trouble."

"I know you think you're better off without me," Finn said. "But before you decide, just hear me out. I think you're safer with me than alone. If you show up at home, they can say anything they want, accuse you of any crime, and the only person who can clear your name is me. We're better off staying together until we can get to my mother."

"And how do you propose we do that?" River asked. "You told your mom you know where your father is. What's that about?"

"I think we should look for my father and ask for his help," Finn said. "I have an idea of where to find him."

"Chasing after a ghost is not a tactical plan to clear our names," she said. "We need to choose a route to the White House."

"No, that's too far and too obvious. Besides, my mother is coming to us, sort of. She's leading a train trip through the United States to restart congressional elections. She'll be in Denver in ten days. We can meet her and resolve this with her help. All we have to do is stay out of the path of Universal. They won't look for us where I want to go."

River closed her eyes before blurting out: "I have a daughter. My mother is watching her in Idaho. We need to warn them."

"I don't think we can," Finn said. "Universal probably has people looking for us. They'll watch our homes, but since I'm involved, I don't think they'll try anything too aggressive. It's one thing to kill me inside the Territory where there are no laws, but outside they would be criminals. I think your family is safer staying in the dark."

River paced in circles. Finn watched her, her shoulders hunched as she deliberated, fully aware that she could leave and he'd be on his own to solve this mess. He was astonished at how much that troubled him. His attraction to her seemed incongruous, and of course ill-timed, but that was just the way of things, Finn thought. You never get what you want when you want it.

River, for her part, was far away, remembering the day her father died. The high school principal pulling her out of class, the blur of coming home, her mother sobbing, the funeral and then the cold hard reality of one less paycheck. Head down, she'd plowed through every obstacle, determined to keep control of the situation. But that wasn't what had happened; instead, she'd plunged into war, which was anything but controlled. Then marriage, and then a child, each experience less orderly than the previous one. The ugly truth was she liked being in the Territories, because while it was far from safe, it was mostly predictable. And she'd built up in her mind an idyllic exit, where she took her check and arrived home victorious. As usual, her plans were subject to the whims of fate, but this time things felt different. Finn was different. Despite his deception, she trusted him. Her relentless sarcasm and ribbing were camouflage to mask a growing sensation that they were connected somehow. That she didn't have to be in control of everything around him. It made her relax. Even standing there in a storage locker in the middle of nowhere, she knew he was right that they were better off together.

"Ok, I'll stay, but I want to know if there's anything else you're hiding from me," River said.

"No," he said, relieved. "I've told you everything."

"And where is this place you want to go to find your father?" she asked. "This place Universal will never think to find us?"

"Wyoming," Finn said. "Just outside Jackson Hole. I know it sounds crazy, and I'll tell you more, but I have reason to believe my father is hiding there."

"You want to go into another Territory?" River asked. "That's crazy."

"As you already pointed out, I have an overactive imagination," Finn said. "But think about it: it's the last place on earth they'd expect us to go."

TWENTY

COOPER WATCHED his boss from afar as he sat inside one of Universal's secure conference rooms. The Red he knew was an exacting leader with an almost fanatical personal grooming habit, but that was not the man he saw behind the bulletproof glass. The person occupying the chair this morning was unshaven, a fugitive's length of stubble casting a shadow across his face. It also seemed that Red's skin had taken on a sickly color, a sallow tinge. There were faint reddish rings around his eyes at the socket. Just for one moment, from Cooper's angle, Red seemed ghoulish, like poor Gollum of Middle Earth who was poisoned by the evil of the all-encompassing ring, but then the light changed, or Cooper blinked, and the illusion passed.

Red was sitting at a large conference table inside one of two "clean" rooms they used; both were swept twice a day for listening devices. Cooper walked in and took the chair next to his boss.

"I assume Finn is still missing or I would've heard from you already," Red said as Cooper turned off the ringer on his phone.

"We've got all available security personnel looking for them both," he said.

"It doesn't matter," Red said. "They're meaningless to me now."

"I haven't slept for days and have men scouring the country and all of a sudden you're saying it doesn't matter?" Cooper said. "What does that mean exactly?"

"It means you should shut up and listen closely," Red said. "I'm about to make my intentions crystal clear."

Red was feeling buoyant. After days of depressing news from his pathetic security chief, not to mention being marginalized and ignored by the Chief Witch of the White House, he was finally ready to break free and work on his own terms. The idea for a private army had come to him in a recent dream. In it, he was sitting with the founding fathers lamenting the fate of the country. James Madison was at his side listening sympathetically, and just before the vision ended, he urged Red to read the Bill of Rights. Red awakened ecstatic, grateful his ancestors had given him a sign of how to move forward. *A well-regulated Militia, being necessary to the security of a free State!* It was his destiny to save the United States. After all, he'd created the plan that brought the country this far. Now was the time to take it a step further. There were others like him, who knew the government was weak and could not be counted on in times of crisis. All he had to do was reach out and a new order would be formed. Red got up and walked over to an intercom by the door and pressed a button to speak.

"You can send them in now," he said.

A minute later, two dozen men and women walked into the room and took seats around the table. Red, who'd remained standing, walked over to the windows of the conference room and closed the blinds. Then he turned to face his audience, smirking at Cooper as he began to speak.

"You're in this room because you're the best of the best, recruited away from the FBI, CIA, and NSA," Red said. "But more importantly, you're here today because you've shown unwavering loyalty to me. In recognition, you're being rewarded with the opportunity of a lifetime— a chance to prove your loyalty and save this country from its savage future.

"Immediately following this meeting, you will be divided into teams," Red continued, taking his seat. "Team one will draft an evacuation plan for the great state of Pennsylvania. I want to know if it's possible to remove every man, woman and child from the state in one hundred and twenty days and..."

"Has the White House granted us permission?" one of the analysts interrupted.

Cooper watched Red scrutinize the young man, certain he would be fired before the day was done.

"Given the national interest, it may be that Universal acts out of necessity and seeks consensus later," Red said.

"How would we do that?" the same young man asked.

Clearly outraged by his impertinence, Red signaled for Cooper to have him removed. "I'm afraid that is no longer your concern," he said.

Cooper obliged, using the intercom to alert two guards, who escorted the overeager young aide out of the building.

"Now, is there anyone else who'd like to interrupt me?" Red asked.

Twenty-three faces stared back with not so much as a blink of an eye.

"That's better," Red said. "The simple fact of the matter is that the United States is due for a change in leadership. Until that happens, we're going to have to take matters into our own hands. I need both teams to get busy. As I started to explain, team one will be responsible for developing an evacuation plan. Team two will create a blueprint for building a private army. We can approach our existing security personnel inside the Territories, but we'll need a psychological screen to determine who's up to the task. I assume some kind of basic training will be necessary, so include the development of a secure instruction facility as part of your analysis."

"Screen for what?" a young woman asked.

"What we're doing will be considered treason," Red answered. "We know, of course, that it's quite the opposite, but we have to be certain the folks we choose will be up to the task."

"How many militia members are we talking about?" another team member asked.

"Enough to repel local law enforcement and the military in an initial battle, and then guard the Territory. Assume the necessary infrastructure, equipment and supplies will be available, but I need an army prepared to use those weapons when the time comes. You have two weeks to develop preliminary plans for my review. Now, go home and pack a bag. Given the nature of your work, you'll be restricted to our staff quarters for the next fourteen days."

Red watched the group file out, hopeful they were up to the task. He was on the verge of making history. All he had to do was build his army.

"Do you see now?" Red asked. "Do you see our path?"

"I do," Cooper said. "Red, it's one thing to guard the Territories, but to assemble an army to overtake the government? Are you prepared for the cost if you fail?"

"I won't fail. When have I ever failed?" Red asked.

"No, Red. This is something altogether different," Cooper said. "This is changing the course of history. This is tearing a hole in the fabric of our country."

"What choice do I have?" Red asked. "You know that bitch will never agree to any of this. She's old and tired. This whole thing has worn her out, what with her husband walking out on her. I bet he found himself a girlfriend in one of the refugee cities. All those young women stuck in those shitholes with no place to go. I bet he slid right in."

Cooper looked closely again at Red, noticing the yellow tinge was back. All the bile was bubbling up to the surface.

"I think you're underestimating her," Cooper said. "She's not a lightweight and she won't hesitate to put up a fight."

"You're wrong," Red said. "It's up to me to fix things. Luckily, I have a great group of people, and they're going to execute this plan, and we'll begin evacuations and establish a new Territory."

"Let's at least be on the record as having asked the President one more time to consider another Territory," Cooper said. "It costs you nothing and you can use it to your advantage."

"It costs me time I need to complete my plans and build my army," Red said.

"You just told me these whiz kids will have it all locked down for you," Cooper said. "Given your advantage, surely you can spare a little more time to see if she'll listen to your idea."

"Very well," Red said. "Set up the meeting."

Cooper nodded, but his head was spinning. He'd seen acts of insubordination in his day, antics that skirted protocol but generally kept to the spirit of the idea, which was to win the war. But this was something else entirely. This was all-out treason. Cooper knew great military leaders were by necessity audacious, but they executed their plans with enough skill or vision to succeed. Overthrow the US government? That was the provenance of the foolhardy and they were *always* the ones who got you killed. Cooper was not sure how this would all end, but he knew for certain he wanted to be on the right side of history.

TWENTY ONE

FOR THE REMAINDER of the day, Cooper's phone was a whirling dervish in his pocket, Red calling frequently. The man's impatience was excruciating, but Cooper was a good soldier, responding to his queries with his usual attentiveness. So, when the phone rang yet again, flashing an unlisted number, Cooper assumed it was his boss with another request.

"This is Cooper," he said.

"This is Elizabeth Cunningham," the President replied.

"Interesting," he said. "How do I know this is not some kind of joke?"

"Because I am the only one who can tell you my son is alive and well," she said. "And no thanks to you."

"Are we on a secure line?" he asked.

"What do you think?"

"Listen, I had a plan to get him out of the Territory safely," Cooper said. "I didn't expect to him to make a friend so quickly. Once I realized what had happened, I arranged for the checkpoints to be empty when they passed through."

"I don't remember having to stage my son's murder as a condition of his entry into the Territory," she said. "What the hell is going on?"

Dead silence filled the air while Cooper deliberated whether this moment signified the end, the instant when the last threads that held him to Red were torn away. He decided it did. "Red's lost his mind," Cooper said. "He's convinced that more Territories are the country's destiny."

"That's not news," Elizabeth said.

"True, but this is," Cooper said. "You're just weeks away from a succession movement that will make the Oklahoma City bombing look like child's play."

"I see," the President said. "This is all because I wouldn't agree to Pennsylvania?"

"This is not a temper tantrum, Madam President. This is treason," Cooper said. "Red is forming his own militia in an attempt to start a movement. He must be stopped before his plans reach critical mass."

"Isn't that your job?" the President asked.

"There is only so much I can do at this point," Cooper said. "He already suspects I helped your son escape. Red is building his own garrison. A separate team has been assigned to evaluate and plan the evacuation of Pennsylvania in one hundred and twenty days, with oil production coming on line three months later."

"That's crazy," she said. "We've got military bases strategically placed near every major city across the country. He won't get more than a hundred feet into the state."

"He's building a private army he believes will be able to hold off US troops long enough for him to bring the crude to the market," Cooper said. "Once the government sees the value of the product, he believes you'll come around."

"As someone sworn to uphold the Constitution, I can tell you with certainty that I will not *come around*," the President said. "Are you aware that we're about to restart elections? I'm embarking on a national train trip to reassure the American public that the worst is over and they can get back to living their lives. Meanwhile, there is an out-of-control CEO hell bent on revolution. How do you think that is going to go over with American voters?"

"With all due respect, that is why I stay out of politics," Cooper said. "I'm just here to deliver the message."

"Are you helping him?" she asked.

"We wouldn't be having this conversation if I were," Cooper said.

"Is he getting any help from inside the White House?" she asked.

"No," he said. "None that I know of."

"One more question," she said. "Is he going to try to kill me?"

"Not if I can help it," Cooper said.

"Well, that is reassuring," she said. "Just like you protected my son?"

"Just hear me out. I think I have a way to end all of this, but I have to be able to keep Red's confidence, or things will get ugly," he said. "Understand, though, that nothing can be guaranteed. If I were you, I'd buckle up for a bumpy ride. And while you're at it, have the FBI review the entire security plan for your trip."

Cooper ended the call hoping the President would take his advice seriously. Although he felt better for having told someone of Red's plans, he was also terrified. He knew better than anyone that Red only got more obstinate in the face of opposition. He didn't back down and he never apologized, even when he knew things would end badly. That meant Cooper would have to either outsmart him, or be more brutal.

TWENTY TWO

THEY CROSSED into Yellowstone at Roosevelt Arch, which had been the northern entrance to the park for more than one hundred years. River noticed that the stone still bore the original inscription "for the benefit and enjoyment of the people." The idea of enjoyment forced a bitter chuckle from her throat, which she swallowed before Finn could hear. Who had time for that, she wondered? How did you have fun when the world was falling apart, and people expected you to help hold it up? River shook her maudlin thoughts away as she prepared herself for the two thousand vertical feet Finn warned they would gain and lose. They set out on the trail to Jackson.

Finn cleaned both rifles and fastened one to each backpack, stuffing a box of shells in each of the outside pockets. They hadn't had to kill anyone yet, but they both knew it was possible that the day was coming. Under ideal conditions, Finn figured it would take the two of them ninety-plus hours to hike to Jackson. But they had no idea if his estimate would hold since their maps were outdated and photography inside the former state was forbidden. Normally Yellowstone was lousy with snow in the winter, its roads impassable. There was little snow on the ground where they were now, but they would be gaining altitude and surely hit powder as they climbed. After her nasty surprise at her apartment, River worried beyond the weather conditions about what kind of security and surveillance systems awaited them inside Universal's second Territory.

Prior to joining the trail, they'd stopped to buy dry goods, a pair of boots for River, and other supplies. Finn paid cash, another spare thing he kept in his storage locker. They'd left the truck at the trailhead, its license plates stashed in River's backpack, the vehicle ID scratched out with Finn's pocketknife.

On the way to the Montana border, River stole glances at Finn, wishing for the kind of X-ray vision superheroes enjoyed. Yes, she'd decided to come along with him, agreeing that they were safer together, but she still longed for a sign from the universe. Was he telling the truth, or was he just another mess she would be forced to clean up after? She watched him closely, but he continued to display the calm certainty she'd encountered that first night on the highway. In combat, she'd experienced many forms of fearlessness, especially the overt, brutal kind, but now she realized she was witnessing a quieter, nimbler version. In Finn, it came from his certainty that he had the skills to survive any situation. She fervently hoped his confidence was contagious as they powered to the top of the summit, her legs straining under the weight of her pack.

Back home in Sun Valley, she'd hiked to the top of Bald Mountain many times in the summer; with an elevation of 9100 feet, the peak afforded the determined with a striking view of the valley below. Somehow this felt steeper. Her back wet with perspiration, calf muscles throbbing, she stopped ostensibly to admire the grey, gauzy clouds haphazardly wrapped around the mountain tops. As she caught her breath, she watched the last light of the day hover in the spaces between sky and rock, wondering if the clouds meant snow overnight.

Before she could answer her own question, a loud screeching filled the air, and something grazed her forehead. The shock of the encounter sent her tumbling. The last thing River saw as she went down was the sky above her turning black.

Finn barely avoided the colony of bats as it came pouring out of a cave near the trail. He turned around to warn River, but was not able to say anything before one of them clipped her. Time stopped as he watched her tumble backward onto a set of boulders. He ran over just as she opened her eyes, a look of panic on her face.

"Bats," he said. "We must have startled them. Stay still and let me check you for injuries."

River nodded, happy to lay still until she could get her heart rate under control. She'd never seen bats before and it was downright creepy watching them spiral out into the dusk, squeaking to one another as they flew by. Finn slowly ran his hands along her back, which was mostly covered by her enormous pack. What had been an overloaded nuisance that morning had probably saved her from having a horrendous head injury, she realized.

"I think I'm OK," she said. "My pack blunted my fall. I'll probably be a little sore, but I'll manage. I've done worse to myself in the Army."

Finn continued his search for injuries despite her protests, taking an interest in a small cut on her forehead. "Yellowstone is home to the largest concentration of mammals in the lower 46 states, including 13 species of bats," he said, using his thumb to wipe away a trickle of blood.

"Now you tell me," River said, laughing.

Finn frowned and set down his pack, surveying the area around them. "I think we should make camp so I can clean that cut. You should probably get a rabies shot, but that will have to wait. It's getting dark. Do me a favor. Grab your rifle and keep it close while we set up. Yellowstone is a wild kingdom and bats are the smallest of the creatures we could encounter. Keep an eye out while we set up."

"You have a rifle, too," River said.

"Yes, but I'm betting you're a better shot than me," he replied.

They worked in amicable silence. River's body ached from the fall, but she'd been serious when she'd said she'd endured worse in the Army. Whatever discomfort she felt was easy to ignore. Finn pitched the tent while River put together the stove and chose a few supplies for dinner. It took two of them to set up the camouflage netting they'd purchased to hide their small campsite from drone patrols. There would be no open fire, only a small camp stove. They both carried flashlights but agreed they would use them sparingly to avoid drawing attention.

After some chili and crackers, they quickly cleaned their dishes to avoid being out in the frigid darkness. Finn dug a hole and washed their two bowls and spoons with water he'd warmed on the stove. River dried the dishes and set them back inside her pack, glancing at some of their supplies. Breakfast tomorrow and for the foreseeable future was oatmeal with raisins and cinnamon. Lunch was a mix of ramen and other instant soups. Choosing food for a backpacking trip was an unusually intimate act. There was only so much room and only so much weight that could be carried by two people. The menu required compromise and luck that there was a common set of tastes—she and Finn had done well on that score, generally favoring the same foods and flavors.

She'd never gone backpacking with her husband. She and Marc had camped in the desert courtesy of the United States government, and they'd eaten what was available. In Idaho, despite living on the edge of some of the most beautiful wilderness in the country, they had not taken a single trip. Ava had never been stuffed into a backpack as a toddler and carried into the forest to see the sun rise over the Sawtooth Mountains. What the hell had they done with all their time? It was difficult for River to remember now.

She thought about her earlier observation that there was never time for fun in her world. But there had been before her father died. Her life had been shockingly normal up to then. She wanted that for Ava. She wanted her daughter to know the blissful ignorance of an ordinary life, free of strife and tragedy. A life where your home is a sanctuary, full of laughter and love and maybe, if you're lucky, freshly baked treats straight out of the oven. Her father's death snuffed that life out right before her eyes, leaving war and death in its place.

Finn studied River as she stared off into space. They were inside the tent and he was changing the bandage on her forehead with a new one from their first aid kit.

"What are you thinking about?" he asked.

"It's so quiet," she said. "There are no drones, no AV-rovers—nothing, At some point we have to run into security for the Territory."

"Even with so little snow, I doubt a rover could manage this terrain without a handler. This area is so remote, I don't know if they'd bother to send a team," Finn said. "I know it sounds crazy, but after the last few days, I'm glad for the quiet."

"This is almost too quiet," she said. "In the Territory, all you hear is the beeps and blips of the equipment, the whine of a truck engine, even the bar fights have a familiar sound...you know what's happening by the noises around you."

"It must have been quiet at home in Idaho," Finn said.

"I can understand how a hermit like you would think that," River said, smiling. "Life, in fact, is actually *noisy*. Our house was very loud. Marc had the television on constantly. Later, when we had Ava, her crying added to the mix. We fought...there was yelling. I don't remember it ever being quiet, but I know that can't be true."

"Where did you live?"

"In my family's home. My mother let us move in with her," River said. "It was pretty much like you would imagine: cramped and awkward, but also very comforting. My mom is patient and kind. She's not one to complain. It was good to have someone to talk to when things got tough, to confirm I wasn't the one who'd gone crazy." River grimaced. "That was awful. I shouldn't have said that..."

"I think you should stop apologizing," Finn said. "I know you didn't mean anything. But even if you did, don't you think you have a right to say those things after all this time? You've given up an awful lot of your life for other people. First your father, then your husband. When was the last time someone asked you about you? *How are you, River?* What was it like to go to war? Why did you choose Marc? Did he do anything to make you happy? That's what I want to know about. I want to know about you, and I don't want you to apologize anymore for trying to survive."

River's heart was racing. She was scared, slightly embarrassed, and thrilled. No one had ever spoken to her like that.

"You really want to know?" she asked.

"I wouldn't have asked if I didn't want to know," Finn said. "You can tell me anything."

River wrapped her arms around herself in preparation for the unraveling, an image appearing in her mind's eye of her frightened eighteen-year-old self-leaving to report to basic training. "Once we understood we couldn't afford to keep the house, it just seemed so simple," she said. "The recruiters were right there in town. We'd been at war in the Middle East for so long, and the government didn't reinstate the draft, so the Army was anxious to get new troops overseas. They made it seem as if you could just serve and come right back home and go to college. You have an image in your mind of like 1-2-3…and then you get there and it's so much worse than you can imagine. Loud, filthy, scary…so much suffering and fear."

"You met Marc there?" he asked.

"I did," she said. "He was in my unit. Marc was a loner who joined the Army to get away from a miserable life. Then he realized what he'd abandoned was paradise compared to Syria, but it was too late. He was a lot of fun until the accident."

"What happened?" Finn asked.

"Marc had one more tour than me and was eligible for leave a few months after we met. When you arrive back in country after being on leave, the Army sends a bus to the airport to pick you up to return to base. Sometimes there is body armor and a weapon on the bus for you when you arrive, sometimes nothing. On *that* day, there was nothing for Marc and his buddies–no armor, no weapons, and their convoy hit a landmine. After he recovered from his injuries, he went straight back in for another tour. It destroyed him."

"How did he die?" Finn asked.

River had been expecting the question. "He shot himself in the mouth," she said, amazed at how liberating it felt to say the words aloud. She'd said very little about Marc's suicide, except to her mother, and even then, she'd been guarded. The military had offered her counseling, but she'd stopped going after a few times. "I've never told anyone this, but as horrible as it was to find him, I was also relieved."

"I can imagine," Finn said. "It must have been difficult to live with him."

"I know you mean well, but there is no way you could even begin to fathom the actual situation," River said. "Your family doesn't know what it's like to worry about whether you'll be able to pay your bills or whether you'll lose your home because you can't pay the mortgage. From the moment my father died, it seemed like things went from bad to worse, from worse to terrible, and then from terrible to horrible. I kept thinking, the whole time, *I can make this better*. Only it wasn't true. The only good thing to come out of it was my daughter Ava."

"You must have loved him," Finn said.

"No," she said, expressing yet another long-suppressed secret. "I didn't. Not in the way people really want to be loved. But I was married by the time I figured that out and decided to see it through."

"How do people want to be loved?" Finn asked.

"I have no idea, Ivy League," River said, reverting to his nickname out of a sense of self-preservation. "Why don't you tell me?"

A nervous laugh escaped Finn's mouth before he could stop himself. "I'm the wrong person to answer that question," he said. "As you've already figured out, I'm a bit of a loner. Most people find it odd, the way I like to disappear into the wild. It doesn't bother me. All I've ever wanted was to be in places like this, where I could be alone with my thoughts."

"That's not an answer," River said, feeling an odd quiver in her belly. "Tell me, how do people want to be loved?"

Finn straightened up and turned to face River, taking her hand in his. "I've never been in love before," he said. "I think I've been waiting for the right woman to come along and catch my attention. When I do meet her, I will love her the way I want to be loved: entirely, the good with the bad. I will tell her to go easy and forgive herself. Because to me that is what love is about: learning how to forgive one another."

Suddenly a ball of nervousness, River began to fidget. The insistent thumping of her pulse in her ears made it impossible to think straight. Although she'd issued the challenge, his words cut closer to bone than she'd been prepared for.

"This is silly," she said. "Maybe you're the one who hit his head back there on the rocks. You're only doing this because you feel sorry for me. The crazy broken widow living alone in the Territory. But you can skip it. I don't need your sympathy."

"I'm not doing this out of pity," Finn said. "I'm doing this because I want you. And I think you want me, too. We don't always get to decide the actual moment when we finally meet the right person. This isn't an ideal situation. I know that. But I also know there is a reason that you were the one to find me that night on the highway."

River was prepared to shut him down, but something stopped her. The truth of it, she guessed. Finn was right. You don't get to choose your moments. This was a chance for something, even if the future was uncertain. She felt it too, the connection between them. It had been a long time since she'd been with a man, even longer since she'd been excited at the prospect of being touched. Now, thanks to Finn, it was all she could think about.

"I think you may be on to something, Ivy League," River replied, feeling strangely giddy as she leaned in to kiss him. While the magic of adolescent romance had mostly eluded her, it didn't stop River from reveling in the shivers running up her spine, or the nervous anticipation she felt. Her state of mind was suddenly so hopeful that ordinarily it would have caused her to panic. She coached herself to stay calm, fervently hoping this one time she could relax and allow herself to enjoy the moment.

Their kisses grew from curious to passionate. Finn was gentle but ardent, his callused hands exploring her body. She trembled with delight at being touched, at being *seen*, recognized as something more than a relief stop for a troubled mind. She reached out to do the same, thinking momentarily of Marc, two hundred pounds of muscle honed by combat. Touching him was like trying to scale a wall; it was better to just let him come to you. Not so with Finn, whose sinewy body was all hard angles like the mountains he climbed. She didn't have to strain to embrace him, their bodies fit perfectly. His skin glowed pale in the faint light of the tent, her fingers detecting rough patches here and there, his skin like hers, weathered from working outside. Birds of a feather, she thought, improbably...somehow, the same, but so different.

Not long after, as he laid her body down, she closed her eyes and smiled. After tonight, regardless of what happened, at least she knew what it was like to be with the right person, to feel the knowing hum deep in her bones.

Later, Finn snoring next to her, she wanted to chastise herself for such romantic thoughts, for being so weak, but fell asleep before she could complete a proper browbeating.

The sun's rays woke River the next morning. She sat up part way, glancing at Finn, still nestled next to her, who began to stir under her gaze.

"Good morning," he said groggily.

"Who the hell are you?" River asked, a smile in her eyes.

Finn returned her mischievous look. "You're about to find out, sweetheart," he said, introducing River to yet another kind of peaceful intimacy she'd never known before. There was not a moment's hesitation in Finn's desire, his overtures confirming there were no regrets, no second thoughts in his decision. A long while later, she sat up again, this time searching for her clothing.

"We need to set up a firing range," she said, without preamble.

"How romantic," Finn said, laughing. "Do you make the same request of the all the men you make love to?"

River was hung up momentarily on the love part, but she let it pass. "Only the men I intend to keep alive," she said. "Last night was a wakeup call. We've been lucky. Sooner or later, we're either going to encounter a larger predator or security of some kind. I need to practice firing my weapon and the rifle if I'm going to keep us alive."

Finn frowned.

"You're not going to ask me to stop shooting a gun now that we've had sex, are you?" River said, scowling. "Because that's not going to happen."

"Don't insult me, River. I already said you're a better shot than me and I haven't forgotten you were a soldier," he said. "But you'll forgive me if I hate the thought of the woman I was just inside of a few minutes ago being injured or killed."

River paused a minute before she spoke, recognizing yet another new experience. She was being spoken to like a partner instead of an accessory. "I appreciate your concern," she said. "We'll have better odds of surviving if I practice. The more we anticipate, the better off we will be."

Finn stopped himself from protesting further. Mostly because she was right. They did need to prepare. It was also pragmatic if he wanted to keep her around. River had been on her own for a long while and trying to jump in and become her protector wasn't going to work. It was also incredibly sexist and plain dumb since she'd been fighting for her country while he'd been collecting algae in test tubes.

"I'm sold," he said. "We're going to hike into a valley today that should afford us a lot of privacy. As a reminder, I do know how to use a gun. You do not need to be the only person taking risks."

"Great," River said. "Why do you still look upset then?"

"I was just thinking," Finn said. "What if I'm wrong and my father isn't in Jackson Hole? What if I'm leading us into the wilderness for nothing?"

"What made you think he was there in the first place?" she asked. "You said you'd tell me why you thought this was the best route to take."

Finn reached for his backpack and pulled out his father's wool hat. "It's the hat," he said showing it off. "I think it's a map."

"OK, that is *not* what I was expecting to hear," River said.

"I know it's crazy, but do you see these pins?" Finn asked. "They're souvenirs from places he visited, sometimes with me, sometimes without. I didn't realize it until I was sitting in the back of the car with those guards. I thought I was about to die and wanted to remember something good about my life. I was looking at the hat...it's clear my father rearranged the pins. I thought it was all just nostalgia but the pins end with Jackson Hole, which was not our last trip together. It's not an accident. I think it's meant to be a map. A clue for how to find him."

"How long have you had the hat?" River asked.

"It was the last thing my father gave me before I left for Montana to go back to work."

"Then it could be a clue," she said. "Think of it this way. We're heading in the direction of Denver. If he's not there, we'll just keep going. We have to get to your mother one way or another."

Finn didn't say it aloud, but he hoped his father would be coming, too. It was long past time for his family to be reunited. The question was whether Richard Cunningham was waiting for them. Although he couldn't prove it, Finn believed he was.

TWENTY THREE

IT TOOK two days to reach the center of Yellowstone National Park and it would be another four and half days to traverse the valley before they reached the Tetons. They could see the ancient mountain range in the distance, its jagged peaks pressing against the heavens. They'd made remarkably good time, with very little snow to impede their journey. Finn's fugitive heart rejoiced at how easy the trek was, but his scientist mind registered the traumatic fact that it was too warm in the valley for this time of year. The ground should have been covered in a soft blanket of white. Instead, it was partially brown, the wheat-colored grasses of fall still blowing in the breeze. Even more jarring was the endless miles of debris. Rather than move their belongings during the evacuations, folks clearly decided to leave the majority of their worldly possessions to rot on the prairie. Without the helpful camouflage of several feet of snow, the land resembled a scrap yard waiting for its customers.

"I feel like I'm in a movie," River said, as they walked into a valley with a large lodge and a set of cottages perched in the distance. "One where a gigantic spaceship beams everyone in town straight up into the sky from where they were standing or sitting. What were people thinking?"

Finn suspected in those last hours and days it must have come down to priorities. Who needs a boat when you won't be living by a lake? Or maybe it was a vacation home, so it was easier to just leave everything behind. Whatever the logic, the result was a jumble of campers, snowmobiles, boats, and ATVs left parked outside homes and barns; a few had been driven into the middle of nowhere and left to rust. The boats were floating aimlessly in the lakes, unmoored from the dock.

"It's a bit spooky, but doesn't seem to bother the animals," Finn said. "The elk and moose are grazing right alongside this mess."

"Where are the bears?" River asked. "After your wild kingdom speech, I expected them to be out looking for food. We haven't seen any wolves either."

Finn was about to reply when he heard a high-pitched whining coming from somewhere off in the distance. Whatever was making the sound was far away, but easy to hear since there was no other noise except the crunch of their feet on the ground.

He glanced over at River, who'd already grabbed a pair of binoculars out of her pack. Thanks to her two tours of duty in the Middle East, she knew the sound meant trouble. The image through the viewfinder confirmed her suspicions.

"It's a drone," she said. "We need to get out of sight."

"Can we outrun it?" Finn asked.

"Probably, but whatever you do, don't turn around," River said. "It will be better if the cameras can't pick up our faces."

They took off running as fast as their packs would allow. The temptation to steal a glance as the buzz of the helicopter-like blades grew nearer was great, but Finn did as he was told. They ran hard, heading for the large building she'd noticed earlier.

River let out a stream of curses that would have made a sailor blush when she discovered the front door was locked, the drone gaining on them. Before Finn could say anything, she pulled her Glock from its holster and shot out the floor to ceiling stained-glass panel next to the door. She used her boot to kick the remaining pieces of glass out of the way, grabbed Finn's hand, and pulled them through the narrow opening. They skidded to a halt in the middle of a great hall with cathedral ceilings, stone walls, and dark wooden beams. River was about to sit down on one of the couches when she heard the whir of the motor and realized the other side of the room was a wall of floor-to-ceiling windows that framed the mountain range perfectly, but also left them totally exposed.

"Stay down!" River yelled, pulling Finn to the ground behind the couch. It was a large piece of frontier furniture, big enough to hide them if they lay horizontally. The drone was bumping against the exterior of picture windows, either because its operator was not all that skillful, or because it was overzealous in trying to track its prey. River hoped it was the former and they wouldn't have to overpower or outrun a security team like the one they'd faced in Williston. Adrenaline made it difficult to mark time, but eventually the buzzing subsided, and River gingerly raised her head above the red and black hand-woven upholstery to glance out the window.

"I don't see anything," she said. "I think we can get up."

They shrugged off their packs and sat on the couch, sinking into its deep cushions. Finn wasted no time asking the very question River had already been contemplating.

"Do you think they saw us?" he asked.

"I don't think so," she said. "Most of the drones I saw in the Territory had speakers. They would have issued some kind of command if they'd spotted us. I think this was just reconnaissance. It's still too close for comfort."

"Way too close," Finn said. "We shouldn't take any chances. Let's get out of this room and find someplace with fewer windows."

They settled on a suite on the upper floor of the lodge. The room came with a large sliding glass door that opened onto a patio, which they quickly covered with heavy drapes, blocking out the natural light. Jackson Lake Lodge had opened in 1955 and was considered a modern structure by National Park Service standards when the philanthropist John D. Rockefeller, Jr. commissioned it as a gift to the American people. Over the years it gained modern features, including solar batteries, which River was particularly grateful for because it meant she could take a hot shower.

As soon as the spray hit her body, she rejoiced, amazed at how such a small thing could feel so luxurious. They'd rummaged around the lodge and managed to find an abandoned housekeeping closet, stocked full of soap, shampoo, and towels. She ran a bar of soap over her body under the soothing water, trying to clean the dirt from her fingernails. She examined her hands, frowning at the large callouses on her palms. Two years of hauling hoses in and out of waste vats had taken a toll. She didn't have the hands of a woman. Glancing at the bruises and bumps on her legs, the lack of polish on her toes, she realized that nothing about her was feminine. Bit by bit, she'd shed those aspects of herself long ago. As she grabbed a towel to dry off, River wondered if it was possible to regain what had been lost to war and duty. Could she go back to being soft, girlish, and easygoing? Was she ever those things? Did having smooth skin make her more of a woman? Finn didn't seem to mind, in fact, he liked her just the way she was–at least until this emergency was over, the troublesome voice in her head cautioned. When this ended, the voice continued, maybe he would prefer someone more refined.

As she stepped out of the shower, she heard Finn calling. *"Oui je viens,"* she replied, letting him know she was on her way. After their first night together, at his urging, they'd begun speaking French to one another. It was their language, he told her. No one else would know what they were saying. Although it had been a while, the language she'd studied since childhood came tumbling back into her brain. It was another hopeful sign, and she tried not to snuff out the feeling of happiness that was blooming inside her. As she told Finn, in Syria, she mostly used Arabic. But in some places, French came in handy with more cultured locals. The other translators and the elite solders were also fluent in multiple tongues, but that was for work, not socializing. Among the rank and file, few had similar skills. Mostly they were broke, or from broken homes, all of them willing to put their lives on the line for a paycheck and a chance to go to college. Which meant there was no one around in the barracks to address with a jaunty *bonsoir.*

She found Finn sitting in a large leather chair in the main room of the suite, a glass of something amber-colored in his hands. He'd showered in one of the other bathrooms. His damp hair was draped across his shoulders, his skin pale and luminous. Everything about him was different and frankly beautiful, she thought with a quickening in her belly.

"How'd you do?" he asked, pleased at the way she looked at him. "I'd light a fire, but I'm concerned the smoke would attract attention."

"Are you kidding? There is hot water and soft towels," she replied. "Considering our afternoon, I'm grateful to be inside and cleaned up."

"Me, too," Finn said. "Shall we go down to the kitchen and see what was left behind? After our near miss I could use a good meal. I found a couple battery operated lanterns in the housekeeping closet. We can use them to find our way back."

The two ambled through the resort, admiring its treasures. Transporting the contents of a historic lodge built in the shadow of Grand Teton National Park clearly had not been a priority for the government. Finn hadn't given much thought to the aftermath of the evacuations, mostly because he'd been preoccupied with the damage to his own family. But after what he'd seen traveling through the valley the past few days, he wasn't surprised they'd just turned out the lights, closed the doors, and hoped for the best. Maybe they'd intended to send a historian to catalog the lodge's artifacts, or maybe they'd decided that in the scheme of things, losing a few hundred-year-old trinkets was a small price to pay for a fire hose of oil turned on twenty-four hours a day.

The refrigerators had been unplugged, but the pantries were filled with canned vegetables, dry beans, pastas, and various seasonings. It was more than enough to prepare a substantial dinner, one that they could eat at a proper table instead of on their laps inside a tent. The main dining room would have been perfect for a meal, but its panoramic views through an entire wall of glass made it too dangerous, so they settled for a small table in the kitchen, which could be lit by electric light since there were no windows.

"A penny for your thoughts?" River asked as they ate.

"A penny? We did away with that silly coin years ago," Finn teased. "Offer me a higher sum and I might tell you."

"Name your price," she said. "It's worth it to hear what's on your mind."

"I'm worried about that drone and what it means," he said. "I don't want to wake up to another hit squad. I'm thinking we may have to take turns staying awake tonight."

River nodded. "Good idea," she said. "I know I'm usually the one to worry, but from what I saw on the maps in the break room, it didn't look like they ever set up operations on this side of the state. All the extraction appears to take place on the eastern side. The main outpost is in Casper, which is miles from here."

"That eases my mind a little more," he said. "I just feel like things are way out of my control right now. I don't know what to expect next and it's driving me crazy."

"I understand," River said. "There were a lot of difficult things about my father dying suddenly, but one of the worst aspects was how abruptly my old life stopped. Everything after that felt like...."

"A roller coaster ride?" Finn asked.

"A little," she said. "We'll get through this. We have a plan, and we just need to stick to it. We're doing all the right things to keep a low profile. You said it yourself: they would never suspect we would walk right into another Territory. I think you're right and we're still one step ahead of them. Hey, have you thought about seeing your father? What might you say to him when we get there?"

"A bit, I'm just...." Finn said, pausing mid-sentence, a guilty look flashing across his face.

"It's OK," River said. "Of course, you'll be glad to see him. Don't feel guilty about that."

"Thank you," Finn said, reaching for her hand. "But we still have to find him and that assumes my hunch is right."

River nodded, returning to her dinner plate abruptly as if something fascinating had appeared.

Finn watched her for a moment before saying, "OK, now it's my turn. I'm offering a whole quarter to know what's got you brooding."

"Is it *weird*, your mother being President of the United States?" River asked.

"Yes, and no," Finn said. "For most of my life she's held some sort of elected or appointed office. I was used to that, but this...well, I'm not certain she wanted to be President. I don't think it occurred to her to refuse when the succession fell to her. This is no ordinary presidency, whatever that means. With my father leaving and all the blood-shed and upheaval, I think she's aged ten years since she took the job."

"So, you think she should have refused?" River asked.

"Yes," Finn said.

River thought about her life and the situations that had been foisted on her. "I think she did what needed to be done," she said. "Let's be glad there are people in this world who are still willing to do that."

Finn couldn't help but feel mildly reprimanded, but let it pass. "What about your mom?" Finn asked. "What does she do?"

"She's a librarian," River said. "At the Hailey Library. She doesn't make a lot of money, but it's a nice job. The town loves the library and she's been there for years."

"That must be where you got your love of books," Finn said. "I'm surprised you didn't pack any with you when you left."

"Believe me, I thought about it, but there was no time and no room," she said.

"We'll make sure they're replaced. At least some of them," he said. "I'm sure your mom will be glad to help."

River nodded. "My mother would *love* you," she said. "It's too bad you won't have a chance to meet."

"What do you mean?" Finn asked.

"You and me in real life? That would never happen."

"This *is* real life," Finn said cutting River off before she could finish.

"But...," River said, pausing.

"Is this because of my parents, or the fact that our family has money?" Finn asked.

River nodded.

"Let me put your mind at ease," he said. "My mother *will* love you. You're everything she admires: courageous, independent, and intelli-gent. She'll be proud of what you've accomplished. As for the rest, I'm not sure what you imagine our lives were like, but it wasn't glam-orous. My parents were all work and no play and had no patience for showing off. It's true we lived well, but we lived *quietly*. But that was my old life... for all intents and purposes my father *is* dead. He walked out on us and disappeared into thin air. We're out here chasing his ghost. Maybe he'll be where I think he is, or maybe he's vanished for good. Our family hasn't been together for two years. There are no dazzling parties, no closets full of clothing for fashion shoots. My mother was living submerged beneath the sea on a naval submarine for months at a time to avoid being murdered, and I've been hiding out in Montana, pretending my family didn't disintegrate."

"Wow, you're right," River said. "You are nothing special."

"I'm serious," Finn said. "You're the brave one. I've been...a coward."

"I'm not brave," River said. "I was broke and wanted a break from the house where Marc killed himself."

"There's nothing wrong with that," Finn said. "You did something to change your life, to try to make it better. You've got nothing to regret."

"Ava doesn't know what happened," River said. "She knows her father died, but not how."

"That's probably wise," Finn said. "It's hard enough for adults to make sense of things like that, let alone a small child. I'm looking forward to meeting Ava when all of this is finished."

The words hit River right in her sternum, or maybe it was her heart skipping a beat that caused the pain in her chest. Try as she might, she couldn't ignore the image of Finn and her daughter. Was it possible for someone like her to have a happily ever after, she wondered? For now, she would focus on helping Finn find his father. If they were successful and rid themselves of Universal's goons, then she would think about Finn and their relationship. There was no denying that it was a nice change of pace to contemplate something good waiting for her.

"I like your optimism, Ivy League," River said, squeezing Finn's hand. "We still need to find your mother and deal with Universal Industries before they try to kill us."

"True, but we have the advantage," Finn said.

"How's that?" River asked.

"They have no idea where we are or what we'll do next," Finn said. "It's easier to be optimistic when you have the element of surprise on your side."

TWENTY FOUR

THE SECURITY ALERT popped up on Cooper's tablet just as he was preparing to ride with Red to the airport. *Possible trespassers near Grand Teton* the message from his staff said, but the video was grainy and inconclusive. The operator wasn't sure if he saw two people or just animals moving across the valley. In the beginning there'd been a lot of trespassing, looters mostly, hoping to steal something or protest the conversion of the land. Eventually both stopped as the public lost interest and the Territories established a reputation for tight security. That was no accident. Red worked hard to create the impression. He knew most people were too passive to break the rules, which allowed him to focus more on serious threats versus the curious.

It seemed unlikely two random hikers decided to try their luck inside Wyoming in the winter. The timing tripped all of Cooper's wires. It was such a long shot, and yet it made a whole lot of sense. Why wouldn't a pair of fugitives go to the last place someone would look for them? It went a long way toward explaining why his team couldn't locate the couple. They were both tough enough to make the journey, but what was their final destination?

Cooper was itching to return to the office so he could activate another drone and get a closer look, maybe get a message to them. It was tricky to try to communicate–he would have to clear out the

command room if he wanted to say anything to them without his staff
knowing. He didn't doubt his staff's discretion, but Red would stop at
nothing if he suspected someone on his team was sabotaging him.

Carrying around this particular piece of news made Cooper's car ride
with Red to the airport even more uncomfortable. They were already
barely speaking. While the two men would never have been described as
close friends, they'd often passed their time together in amicable–even
animated–conversation. Cooper and Red's mutual respect had been
evident from the start to the entire senior executive team at Universal.
For his part, Cooper considered himself lucky to have transitioned out of
the military into such a fantastic job. It was not an easy set of responsibili-
ties. During the ten years he'd worked for Red, there had been moments
when they'd disagreed, but they had trusted each other.

That time was over.

Red sat rigid in his seat. His piercing gaze was fixed on Cooper. At
the Houston airport, the CEO would board his private plane to Pennsylvania for what they both knew was his last and final meeting with
the President.

"You're a hard man to find these days," Red said. "You're not in the
office regularly and when I call your cell phone, you don't pick up."

Cooper had anticipated this line of questioning. He'd been
rehearsing responses. "I've been reviewing our security," he said.
"Once you launch this plan of yours, they're going to come for us and I
want us to be ready. I took a few quick trips out to the Territories to
make sure everything is locked down tight."

"You didn't use our jet," Red said.

"I didn't want to tie up the plane in case you needed it," he said.
"You've been keeping pretty busy hours yourself."

Cooper watched Red simmer next to him. He knew his boss didn't
believe him, but he'd yet to do anything clumsy enough to justify Red
turning on him. Deniability was crucial if he was to survive long
enough to stop Red's plans.

"These are critical times," Red said. "I need to know I can trust you.
I need your absolute loyalty. I know you had something to do with the
President's son surviving. I can smell the scent of traitor on you a mile

away. No matter. But if I find out you are trying to derail my greater plans in any way, I will kill you. Is that understood?"

"Yes," Cooper said. "But you don't have to worry, Red. I know which side I'm fighting on."

Before Red could respond, his cell phone rang. The caller either didn't require a greeting, or was simply in a hurry to deliver a message because Red did not acknowledge the start of the conversation. After a few minutes he said "*Da*," yes in Russian, and hung up.

The call meant Red was going to get the support he needed to start a war. The Russians were particularly helpful when it came to purchasing illicit firearms. It seemed incomprehensible that there would be Russian soldiers on US soil. Surely the NSA satellites would pick up the movement of artillery before they reached Philadelphia, the city of brotherly love and the Liberty Bell.

"Do you want to review what you're going to say to the President?" Cooper asked, trying to sound unconcerned about the arms shipment.

"What for?" Red asked derisively. "Ever since her husband walked out, she's been bat-shit crazy. My meeting is a formality. A box to check off."

Cooper was well aware Red was setting a trap by insulting Elizabeth. If he appeared to come within spitting distance of defending her, Red would have more proof of his divided loyalties. So, he changed the subject.

"How is our team of go getters coming along?" Cooper asked.

"Very well," Red said. "Our staff has located a training facility and begun recruiting. There's an advance team in Pennsylvania as we speak, mapping evacuation routes. When others hear that I have the means to do this, they'll fall in line to help."

"Others?" Cooped asked.

"There are plenty of people in this country who are ready, willing, and able to stand up to a feeble, weakened government that would rather keep its head in the sand than prepare for a defense against its enemies," Red said.

"You're talking about the potential for armed conflict on US soil,"

Cooper said. "American against American. That's something that hasn't happened since the Civil War."

"Maybe it's time. Time for people to decide what kind of country they want to live in," Red said. "We're at that moment when the good of the many at the expense of the few is how we should be operating. What's a little inconvenience for *generations* of prosperity and freedom? And if none of that sways you, how about this: I expect the US troops to avoid firing on civilians, making my job easier."

"You mean you think they'll stand down because you won't?" Cooper asked.

"Precisely," Red said. "I expect them to use restraint, so I don't have to. It's good for you to know, too. I won't stop once this starts. I will make the government bend before I do, no matter the cost."

"Liberty or death?" Cooper asked.

"I think you're mocking me, but that is exactly what I mean," he said. "If this be treason, I intend to make the most of it."

Cooper had a vague awareness of nodding as Red finished his lecture, but after that, the rest of the trip was a blur. He conducted a security check of the jet and shook the captain's hand before leaving, but it was all autopilot. The Marine's mind was elsewhere. Things were accelerating. Red was preparing for battle. Cooper fervently hoped he had enough time to avert a catastrophe.

TWENTY FIVE

RIVER HAD NEVER PUT much stock in the concept of auras, but that was before she'd witnessed the halo of anxiety hanging around Finn as they made their way down a long, winding driveway. Sleep deprivation was fuel for the fire. They'd both been taking shifts to keep watch for security teams at night. Even when they should have been sleeping, they were awake, too restless and worried to get any peace.

"The house is just around the bend," Finn said.

"You ready for this, Ivy League?" River asked, hoping using the nickname would lighten the mood.

"As much as I can be," Finn said. "If he's not in there, we'll spend the night and then head straight for Denver in the morning."

River nodded. "Let's walk around the house and get a feel for things before we go in," she said.

Finn followed behind as she moved towards the back of the large wood and stone mansion, her gun drawn and ready. Finn's rifle was strapped to the back of his pack, but he knew he would be much slower on the draw in the event of a firefight.

"Keep close," River said, slowing her pace so he could catch up. They completed a full sweep of the rear of the house and were coming around towards the front when they heard a noise and looked up to see what appeared be a large black bird resembling a raven circling high up in the sky.

"Does that look like something you'd normally see out here?" River asked.

"Possibly," Finn said. "Except we haven't seen any birds since we started to hike. There used to be dozens of species out here including falcons, woodpeckers, owls, and of course eagles. Ravens, while not unusual, are not that common."

River didn't answer. She was too focused on whatever was moving in the sky to reply. It was coming closer, flying lower and lower in slow, concentric circles as if it were looking for something. Finn came to stand next to River as the thing landed, allowing them to both silently confirm it was a drone and not an actual bird, although its feather-like features had made identification difficult until the very last seconds. The device paused and turned its mechanical head, shuffling toward them. Before Finn could ask her what they should do, River aimed her gun at the device and blew it apart. The sound of the gun discharging echoed in the open valley, sending shivers up their spines as they realized she'd just fired off their own version of a flare gun.

"Sorry," River said. "I didn't think about the noise. I just wanted to stop the drone from transmitting back to its operator. Unfortunately, we have no idea how close by they are."

"Let's go inside and regroup," Finn said.

"We need to make sure it's not transmitting," she said. She used her foot to stomp on the broken pieces of the machine, especially the camera that was mounted inside the head of the device. "OK. Now we can go in."

Finn nodded and walked over to the front door, testing the handle. "It's unlocked," he said. They walked into the foyer, a large wooden chandelier above their heads.

"Do me a favor and don't shoot anyone until you hear from me," Finn said, their footsteps echoing in the empty house.

"You better speak quickly," she said, lowering her gun as she walked alongside him into the kitchen. It was a handsome room, with none of the horrible cowboy cookout décor so many rich people insisted on using in their homes. She'd seen it dozens of times in the expensive rentals she'd visited in Sun Valley as a teenage babysitter, the insistence on patriotic plaid upholstery and antler cabinet knobs. Instead, she observed a French Provençal kitchen, complete with distressed cabinets and a large farm table that seemed rather awkward in the middle of the room devoid of other furnishings. But even empty, it was refined and luxurious. The scenery jabbed at River, reminding her that Finn belonged to a world she had little connection to.

Finn, meanwhile, ran his hand along the countertops, stopping at the stove. For a moment he thought he smelled freshly baked cookies, but chalked it up to a childhood memory running amok–until he felt the oven door.

"This door is warm," Finn said, catching River's gaze.

"Interesting," River said, raising her Glock back up to eye level.

Finn moved from the stove to the adjacent cabinets, opening them to inspect the contents. There were a few wine glasses inside, certainly not the eclectic collection of Parisian flea market castoffs his parents had once displayed. He tried to recall if he'd been responsible for packing dishes when they'd evacuated, but couldn't remember. Next, he walked over to a set of drawers on the other side of the kitchen. He pulled one out, the deep kind that normally held hand blenders, measuring cups, and colanders, all balanced precariously and set to tumble with the first item removed. At least that was the state of things when he'd been a young man. Now as he peered in, he saw two dinner plates, two bowls and four drinking glasses.

"Somebody is using this kitchen," Finn said.

River walked over to the refrigerator and opened it. A wave of rank air almost felled them both as she slammed the stainless-steel door shut.

"If someone is living here, they're storing their food somewhere else," River said, waving at the air to move along the stench.

"So, we have a few dishes and a warm oven, but no food," Finn said. "What does it mean?"

"It could be anything," River replied. "Squatters, or maybe some soldiers or a defense team passing by on a tour of the area. Maybe the same people who own that drone. We need to search the rest of the house."

"That won't be necessary," a voice said, startling them both.

In a millisecond River had pivoted, her gun trained in the direction of the speaker. Finn was momentarily disoriented, trying to reconcile the image of his father, a man he hadn't seen in two years, being held at gunpoint by his lover.

"It's OK," Finn said. "This is my dad."

Richard Cunningham, his red hair dotted with grey and cut short against his head, stood stock-still, hands at his side. "You can put that away now," he said calmly. "You heard Finn."

River nodded but did not stand down. She recognized Richard from the gas station weeks ago, mostly because the vagrant's spooky warning had imprinted the whole episode on her brain. Nobody liked it when the crazy old coot turned out to be right. If she'd been in the field with her unit, they would have all pulled out their good luck charms and given them a squeeze just to clear the bad juju. It meant something, seeing him again. But what that something was eluded her. River couldn't tell if Finn's father recognized her. Nothing in his mannerisms gave anything away.

"I did," River said. "But first I'd like to ask you a few questions, if you don't mind."

Finn watched his father nod in agreement, wondering what the slight gleam in his eyes meant.

"By all means," Richard said. "Fire away."

"Are you alone?" River asked.

"Yes," he said.

"Are there any security teams in the vicinity?" she asked.

"None," Richard said. "They didn't stay on this side of the state after the evacuation. It's too far from the oil and difficult to patrol except by drone, which I gather you just figured out."

"Does this seem funny to you?" River asked. "We just blew a drone to pieces. They could have a group here within an hour to kill us."

"Nothing like that has happened since I've been here," he said. "It's amazing, the fabulous illusion they've created. The public is certain this place is off limits, crawling with troops, and yet here I am cooking in my own oven."

"How did you know it was safe to come in here and approach us?" River asked.

"I didn't, not until I peered through the peephole I drilled in the door that leads to the basement. I have a rifle sitting just outside the door. I heard voices, but if I'd looked in and seen anyone else…well, let's say I would have reacted differently."

"It's OK," Finn repeated, catching River's eye. "You can relax."

River and his father exchanged nods, but she did not lower her weapon immediately. Although she knew it was Finn's father, the resemblance was irrefutable, it was obvious he was loaded with secrets. What had he been doing that day when she saw him, she wondered? She hoped that his past behavior wouldn't cause more pain for Finn.

"I guess there's no mistaking the red hair," she said, finally lowering her gun. "And you have the same eyes…."

"He has his mother's eyes, actually," Richard said. "Something I expect you'll see for yourself soon enough."

TWENTY SIX

RIVER AND FINN followed Richard out of the kitchen, into a hallway, and down a musty staircase that led under the house. Finn looked genuinely perplexed as Richard took out a set of keys and opened several locks on a door that led to an apartment.

The furnishings were nothing like the main house above. It was sparse, a cliché–the divorcee's apartment. Short on furniture, long on stuff. There were teeming shelves and ancillary piles of books stacked nearby. It was a tremendous distraction from the immediate situation. River tried to keep her focus on Richard.

"You're wondering if I'm a coward or a patriot?" Richard asked as he took a seat on a couch in the living room. "I've posed this question to myself many times."

"I vote for coward," River said.

"I don't think you know me well enough yet to be that critical," Richard said.

"Oh, I feel like I do," River said, arching a brow.

She detected a message implicit in his inscrutable countenance. He did not want her to mention their encounter at the gas station.

"Why did you disappear?" Finn asked, redirecting the conversation. "When you told me you weren't going back to Washington, I thought you would stay away for a few weeks."

"I was foolish," Richard said. "I was angry. I thought the Territories were a terrible mistake. I regretted it almost immediately, but as time passed, I couldn't find the words to approach your mother and apologize."

"We've all done things that make it difficult to face the people we love," Finn said. "But two years? Where have you been?"

"I think we should all have a drink before the interrogation begins," Richard said.

"I could use a shot of something, actually," Finn said, glancing over at River.

"Fine," she said.

Richard walked over to a small table in the corner that was set up as a bar. There was a silver tray with three lowball glasses, a small glass pitcher that probably was used for water, and a collection of various hard alcohols including gin, whisky, and rum. Richard opened the bottle of Jack Daniel's and poured the dark brown liquid into the glasses, handing one to River and one to Finn before sitting back down on the couch.

"To answer your question, I traveled everywhere and yet nowhere particularly far away. I crisscrossed the country, sometimes staying with friends or colleagues, other times I camped in National Parks," he said. "I don't have a passport with a Western Alliance/NATO security chip so I can't travel abroad. I always planned to return to Wyoming. My initial idea was to enter the Territory to protest Universal's occupation, but it turned out to be unnecessary. Imagine my surprise when I realized there was no real security guarding the perimeters. At least not the west side of the state that borders Utah and Idaho."

"Where are we?" River asked. "Is this some kind of bomb shelter?"

Richard nodded. "The shelter came with the house; the original owners were big believers in the nuclear *deterrent* and built this two-bedroom space complete with a bathroom. It's several feet below ground and has its own heating and cooling system. I added a solar battery when I moved down here to run some basic appliances, including a small refrigerator. We decided not to use the space when we lived here as a family. Finn, I don't think we even showed it to you when you were growing up. After I came back, I thought it prudent to keep a low profile just in case troops decided to return to the area. Occasionally a drone flies over, but they don't waste much time over here."

"You've been living here in this apartment the whole time?" River asked.

"Mostly," Richard said.

"I can't believe you didn't try to call Mom," Finn said. "Or me. She's been alone all this time."

"I gave up my mobile phone so the secret service wouldn't be able to trace me," Richard said. "And I don't use email regularly for obvious reasons. But I did give you the hat. I hoped it would lead you to me eventually."

"You gave him the hat as a road map back to what?" River asked. "You had no way of knowing what you would find when you returned, but you were willing to send him *here*? So he could find you and then be arrested and detained for treason? If you wanted to be a patriot, why not go back to the White House and raise hell instead of living as a recluse? What makes you so special that you get to disappear?"

"That's my right as a person," Richard said. "What change was I going to make in Washington? Those fascists were determined to undermine our country's law. What makes you so certain I could have done something?"

"I'm not certain, but your wife is the President," River said. "And, for the record, I didn't spend months slogging my way through Syria so you could just *opt out*. The Territories were created so that people like me could come home. Who are you to complain? What inconvenience have you had to endure lately?"

Finn watched his father closely. Normally this was where Richard would have unleashed his sharp tongue, but to Finn's surprise, he didn't.

"There was a period in my life when I would've argued with you until we were both exhausted," Richard said. "But I've been alone with my own voice for a long time and come to understand its shrillness. Maybe we did establish the Territories to protect our people, but the consequences are so much greater than just that one idea. We altered our landscape and the country's history with one swipe of the pen. I'm not sure it was worth it."

"I think I'm going to stick with *coward*," River said, abruptly popping up from her seat. "I'm going to lie down."

"Take the second door," Richard said. "That's the guest room."

Finn watched her leave, admiring her courage. He loved his father, but he did think him a coward, too, although he would be hard pressed to say so aloud. How did you tell the man who helped you catch your first fish and pitch a tent that you were disappointed in him? That had been Finn's curse all along, not being able to express himself. And look where it had gotten him, he reflected. He was going to have to change.

"I wasn't sure if I would find you here," Finn said. "Your big clue wasn't all that obvious until I got into a spot of trouble. If things had been different, I might still be wondering."

"Trouble?" Richard asked.

Finn recounted his saga inside the Territory for his father, including their trek through Wyoming, emphasizing how River had risked her own life to save his.

"Is she your girlfriend?" Richard asked.

"After everything I just said, that's what you kick off with?" Finn asked.

"I don't know. A lot of what you told me is pretty self-explanatory," Richard said. "But she's the mystery, right? By the way, I don't think she likes me very much."

Finn, who had remained standing, came over to the couch and sat beside his father. The moment their bodies touched he felt the connection of blood and bone, sinking into the cushions to rest against him. Richard lifted his arm and brought it around Finn and the two sat there, wordlessly, allowing some of the hurt and sadness to dissipate. It was yet another new gesture from a man who'd never been all that effusive in the past.

"I think the girlfriend thing is sort of up in the air," Finn said. "She'll probably leave me the second this is all over."

"Why do you think that?" Richard asked.

"She has a daughter back in Idaho," he said. "I've managed to keep her away from her family, tied up in my mess."

"I don't know. After everything I've heard, I'd say she's perfectly capable of making her own choices. If she didn't want to be a part of 'your mess' as you put it, I think she would have left you for dead," Richard said.

"Maybe," Finn said. "I've been talking to Mom, trying to keep her informed."

"She must be chagrined that her business partners tried to kill you," he said.

"What are you talking about?" Finn asked.

"Universal, the people who shot at you," Richard said.

"That's not fair," Finn said.

"Your mother went into business with them," Richard said.

"No," Finn said. "That's not really true. I've had a lot of time to think about this. The United States created the Territories, not Elizabeth, the woman who made us cookies in the oven upstairs. She didn't have a moment to think about what she wanted. She was sworn in and forced to deal with this as the President of the United States of America, and neither of us stood by her. I'm embarrassed to say I haven't seen her for almost as long as you."

Richard adjusted his arm and pivoted so he could face his son. "I wish it was as black and white as that. I regret leaving your mother, but I'm also furious with her for agreeing to the Territories. One of the things I love about being married to her is that she never asked me to change, never asked me to subvert my values."

Finn winced at his father's selfishness. River was right. He was a coward, running away from things he found unpleasant. They both were. "No, she never asked you to change," he said. "But Mom didn't have a choice about what happened to her. She needed us and we both walked away. We have to do better."

Richard felt the blunt end of the truth stab him in the heart. He hung his head. "I'll think about what you've said. To be honest, I don't care who's right anymore. I miss my family. I don't know if it's possible, but I want an opportunity to repair the damage I've caused."

Finn looked at the man sitting in front of him and tried to reconcile all that had happened. How does forgiveness work, he wondered? It starts with belief. Did he believe his father was truly sorry? How do we know if the people who wrong us are telling the truth? In the end, Finn didn't believe he had a choice. He wanted his father back. For his own selfish reasons, he would forgive him and hope that his trust was not misplaced. He needed to forgive him to survive, to find his mother and to hold on to the woman he was falling in love with.

"We have to get out of here and get to Mom. She's the only person who can protect us," Finn said. "She's going to be in Denver in a few days to give a speech to announce the resumption of national elections. Come with us."

"My God, elections already?" Richard asked.

"Already?" Finn said. "It's been two years."

"Denver," Richard repeated, suddenly feeling like time had collapsed on him. "Are you certain I should come with you?"

Finn looked at him like he had three eyes. "Didn't you just tell me you wanted to try to make things right between you and Mom? What are you waiting for? I was almost killed in North Dakota. What if I had been? Would you have known your only son was gone? You're running out of time to put your family back together again."

Richard nodded. "You're right," he said. "We'll all go together, and I'll, umm, face your mother. Why don't you go and get some rest? We'll leave first thing tomorrow. My car is already packed with supplies."

Finn and his father made arrangements to each take a shift to watch for intruders. After saying good night, Finn crawled onto the air mattress next to River and felt her body relax as he enveloped her.

"I was worried you'd be angry with me for criticizing him," she whispered.

"You're entitled to your opinions," Finn said. "For me, it's a bit more complicated."

"I did it so you wouldn't have to," she said.

"You don't have to stick up for me," Finn said. "I can take care of myself."

"We'll see about that," she mumbled, burrowing closer to him.

Finn smiled as he drifted off. It was nice to have someone on his side, someone to defend him. He also liked the feel of River in his bed. Just for a moment, sleeping in his home, his father next door, life felt almost normal.

TWENTY SEVEN

ELIZABETH SAID goodbye to the local party officials and watched through a window as two secret service agents escorted them down a small set of portable stairs, away from the train car, and into waiting sedans with actual drivers. They were parked on the outskirts of Philadelphia's train station. Autonomous vehicles were prohibited near presidential compounds, vehicles, or convoys, a necessary precaution after several serious hacking incidents.

So far, the first stop on the tour was going well. Her initial meetings had been productive; it was perhaps the first time in a long while the two main political parties had agreed on something. They would both initiate voter registration programs and other election-related activities. The new, smaller political coalitions made up of the relocated and digital privacy advocates did not have quite the same machinery in place, but they would also be contacting voters. Normally, her duties would fall to party leaders, former members of the House and Senate charged with raising money and marshaling the forces, but this was no ordinary election year. Sending surrogates wouldn't do.

As she returned to her desk inside the coach, a shudder racked her body, a reminder from her nervous system that it had been two days since she'd slept more than a few hours. She was worried about Finn, of course, but the nightmare had also returned with a vengeance. For months she'd been plagued in her dreams with the sensation of being surrounded by fire. Flames steal the air from the room. The hair on her arms begins to singe, the searing heat creeping over her skin. The whine of steel collapsing is always the last sound before she wakes, her breath coming in gasps. Such horrible images, but it wasn't a memory of something she'd seen, of that she was certain. She knew Red's visit was likely the trigger for their reoccurrence. She'd been at the cusp of too many tragedies not to sense the change in the air. Trouble was coming, and Red was the delivery boy.

A knock on the door pulled her out of her thoughts and sent her skyward out of her seat.

"Sorry to disturb you, Madam President," a secret service agent said. "FBI Director Robert Gray is here to see you along with Cooper Smith."

"Send them in," she said.

The two men walked in. "Good afternoon," Gray said. "We've completed our final security checks."

Elizabeth mustered a weak smile. "Thank you," she said. "And Red? Where is he now?"

"On his way," Cooper replied.

"Listen, I know you will think I'm crazy, but I want you to leave me alone with Red when he arrives."

Cooper let out a piercing whistle. "It's a big risk," he said. "Why would you knowingly put yourself in danger?"

Haven't I been in danger from the start? Elizabeth thought to herself. From the moment I walked off the plane? But there was nothing to be done. A man like Red would run circles around the authorities unless someone put themself in his way. She didn't have a death wish, far from it, but deep in her heart she knew she was their only chance to try to catch him.

"He won't say or do anything with a room full of security," Elizabeth said. "He's too smart for that. This room is wired, isn't it? I want him to confess, maybe boast a bit, do something that will allow the Attorney General to charge him with treason. Bring me a bulletproof vest to put under my clothing, just in case. I won't do anything crazy, I promise."

"Lord above," Gray said. "I don't like it, but it does make sense. Try to get him talking, Elizabeth, and *quickly*, I don't want to put you in danger for any longer than is necessary. I'll post sharp shooters and undercover agents around your train car and in the yard."

"Oh, it won't be difficult to get him talking," Elizabeth said bitterly. "He and silence have never been introduced. Cooper? Where will you be?"

"In an adjacent train car," he said. "Red doesn't know I'm here and it would be better if it stayed that way so I can continue to monitor his activities. If I have to come out of hiding, though, I will."

"I'm sure that won't be necessary," the President said. "Your agents will come immediately if he threatens me?"

"Of course," Director Gray said, as he and Cooper headed for the door. "We're almost there, Madam President. Try to hang on."

Elizabeth nodded. They were certainly on the verge of being some-place, but whether it was hospitable Territory remained open for debate. Another twenty minutes elapsed before Red arrived at the rail yard and agents escorted him inside. Upon entering, he took a seat in one of the brown leather chairs set up next to a small coffee table.

"Thank you for seeing me," he said in a tone that lacked sincerity.

"Your people said it was urgent," Elizabeth said, choosing to remain standing near one of the windows. "What's so critical that I need to take time away from my trip?"

Red didn't reply. Instead, he rose from the chair and joined her at the window. "Are you looking for something?" he asked.

"No," she said. "Just trying to avoid sitting down for hours at a time."

"As accommodations go, this isn't too terrible," he said. "It's small, but then after a submarine you're probably used to tight quarters."

"I've learned to live with a great many hardships in the last two years, Red," she said. "Now, are you going to tell me why you're here? You may have noticed I have a rather packed schedule trying to restart national elections."

"To what end?" Red asked, wrinkling his nose. "Haven't you preferred making decisions without having to wait for an ill-informed public to issue their opinion? Before the attacks, Congress was frozen, paralyzed by partisan disputes. Such a tiny percentage of the country voted and they sent *idiots* to govern. Your beloved State Department rarely had its budget renewed on time—why would you want to return to that?"

"You have a very low opinion of your fellow man," she said, grimacing. "I'm surprised a self-professed patriot like yourself would be so quick to abandon the founding principles of this country: one citizen, one vote. We're a secular democracy, Red; we elect our representatives—for better or for worse—and let them govern. The National Pause was implemented to prevent politicians from capitalizing on a national tragedy, not to rob people of their birthright. We have an obligation to restore things to their rightful order."

"What if that *order* is no longer relevant, practical, or suitable?" Red asked. "What if we've learned that certain decisions should remain in the hands of an informed few?"

"That's the same excuse used throughout the ages to justify all kinds of horrors," Elizabeth said. "Who are we to rewrite the rules in our favor?"

"After everything that has happened, why can't you just admit that the American people are clamoring for certainty?" Red said. "Giving them so many choices again will only scare them. They're desperate for a leader with the courage to tear down old systems and bring order to the chaos of our times."

"The country may be desperate, but I don't think it's for what you're suggesting," Elizabeth said. "Some may want more control over their lives, but quite a few are worried their country is becoming unrecognizable."

"Why? Because we don't allow anarchists and women with headscarves to roam our streets?" Red asked.

"That's a bit of an over-simplification, don't you think?" Elizabeth said.

"Hardly," he said. "We were complacent before the attacks, in love with the idea of our country as a melting pot and thought the world was, too. Of course, they weren't—a lesson we learned the hard way."

"What does that have to do with the millions of people living in the

United States?" Elizabeth asked. "How many of them participated in the terrorist attacks?"

"That's not the point," Red said.

"Oh, but it is," Elizabeth said. "You want to keep the US in a state of emergency so you can justify bullying me into making Pennsylvania another energy Territory. But I'm not convinced that what you're proposing is necessary."

"It's not necessary to have an unlimited supply of crude at our disposal? It's not necessary to export oil and dominate the world markets? It's not prudent to offer Russia's satellite countries fuel at a better price and draw them into our sphere? You're a former Secretary of State. I would've thought these benefits would be obvious to you."

"In a vacuum, what you suggest would be ideal, but as President, I don't have the luxury of such one-dimensional thinking. I have to think about the cost of those decisions, the displacement, the upheaval of lives. The first two energy Territories have more than met the goals we outlined. But..."

"But what?" Red asked.

"You knew that I wouldn't agree to a third Territory, at least not in Pennsylvania. And by now you must also suspect that I know you tried to kill my son. So, I'll ask again, why did you come here today?"

"Justifiable cause," Red said.

"Cause for what?" Elizabeth asked.

"Removing you as an obstacle," Red said. "The world must operate on a simple maxim: the good of the many at the expense of the few. Your timidity is going to cause a national tragedy."

"Hardly," Elizabeth said. "The world cannot be governed by your silly affirmations. Life is not a poster in a golf shop, Red. You should really seek some help. You're obviously coming unhinged."

"Me?" Red replied. "I have never been more certain about things in my life. It's you who excels at making excuses to avoid doing difficult things. Honestly, it's sad."

"You know, I'm really going to enjoy ending this conversation," Elizabeth said, just as the door to the train car opened. "The Secret Service and FBI are here to arrest you for treason and after an investigation, I'm sure a host of other crimes."

Red stood stock-still as a group of agents entered, followed by Director Gray.

"Redmond Pierce, please raise your hands above your head and keep them where I can see them," an agent said as she approached. "I am placing you under arrest."

Just as Red raised his hands, shots rang out. A bullet hit the Director in the head. He collapsed to the floor. The agents grabbed the President and Red, taking each in opposite directions. Elizabeth was ushered into an adjacent safe room, while Red was dragged outside.

Cooper, who had been monitoring the conversation, heard the gunshots and picked up one of the radios the secret service agents used to communicate.

"This is Cooper Smith," he said. "What's the situation?"

There was no reply as more shots rang out, including a bullet Cooper would later learn felled one of the agents guarding Red.

"We've got another agent down," someone screamed. "We need back up!"

"Looks like you've been compromised," Cooper yelled into the radio. "Let the CEO go, I repeat, cut him loose. Your primary objective is the safety of the President."

Cooper listened as more chaos unfolded, trying to bide his time while Red escaped. He wanted to help, but knew many more lives would be spared if his involvement could remain a secret. Forty minutes later, the wounded had been taken away by ambulance and the compound secured. Cooper walked into the Presidential train car to find Elizabeth sitting on the floor, her blouse covered in blood. She looked up, her face a grim mask. "Somehow he knew and brought his soldiers," she said.

"Looks that way," Cooper replied. "I'm sorry. I asked you to trust me, but I let you down. Red is farther along in this thing than he's let me see. Your agents did manage to shoot and capture one of his sharp-shooters: he's Russian, heavily armed. Although for the record, the shooter was just lucky: this train is outfitted with bulletproof glass. Whoever killed the director maneuvered their shot through the open train window. Red's troops neutralized most of your perimeter security, which made such easy shooting possible."

"The Russians are willing to help overthrow the US government?" Elizabeth said, rising from the floor. "They killed our men? That seems extreme, even for them."

"I don't think the Russians expect Red to be successful," he said. "But they will enjoy the bloody mess it creates along the way, and make some money in the process."

"I'll call the ambassador directly in a few minutes," the President said.

"If I might make a suggestion," Cooper said. "Calling the Russians will only reward Red's megalomania. I would stay silent and let them, *let him,* wonder what you're going to do next."

"You don't think his insanity has already reached peak proportions?" the President asked. "He just killed my FBI director."

"Maybe you should cancel the trip," Cooper suggested.

"No," she said. "We need to get this train moving and be in Denver in time for my speech. The American people are depending on me."

"There's one more thing I need to tell you," Cooper said. "It's about your son."

"If you tell me he is dead," Elizabeth said. "I will wish that Red had succeeded in putting me out of my misery."

"No," he said. "He's very much alive and traveling with a woman named Jennifer Peterson. She goes by the name River. I think I know where they are...it involves Wyoming."

"Wyoming?" Elizabeth asked, butterflies forming in her stomach.

"How long has your husband been living there?" Cooper asked.

Elizabeth waited a second to speak, amazed that the issue hadn't come up sooner. "About a year, maybe more," she said.

Cooper lost his ability to maintain a poker face and just stared at her for a second.

"Ever been married?" she asked.

"No ma'am," Cooper said.

"One day you might be," she said. "And God forbid a tragedy strikes. In the terrible moments afterwards, you'll come to understand that the truth is more malleable than you suspect. You'll come to see that it's sometimes helpful to give your spouse some space rather than force them to make a choice. How did you figure it out?"

"I did a few focused drone sweeps of the Territory and picked up on some human bio stats—just a faint heart rate," Cooper said. "We don't usually use such sophisticated equipment in that region. No one would have detected him. Had I not been looking for something specific, I wouldn't have noticed. A few hours ago, I managed to get a visual on Finn and River in front of a home, which I assume was yours. Before I could get a message to them about a possible rescue, River shot the drone to pieces."

"She shot it?"

"Yes, ma'am. River is a former soldier who did two tours in the Middle East," he said. "She's been working inside the Territory as a truck driver. I don't yet have all the details about how they met, but I can tell you that she saved his life, injuring two of my best men in the process. She is formidable."

"Somehow that doesn't surprise me if she's with Finn," she said. "He must have figured out his father was living there."

"Yes, and they are no doubt heading straight toward you," Cooper said. "I want to reiterate, it might be a good idea to cancel the speech, for the safety of everyone."

"They're coming to Denver," Elizabeth said. "Finn called me after they'd escaped from the Territory. He also told me he was going to look for his father, but he didn't mention going home. If he had, I would have warned him against entering another Territory."

"I don't like it, but it makes sense," he said. "They need to get to you to be truly protected."

"Then why are you reacting as if it were a bad idea?" Elizabeth asked.

"Because it puts all of his enemies in one place," Cooper said. "It's never a good idea to make things easy for Red."

TWENTY EIGHT

"So, you drive a Range Rover?" River asked, letting the question hang in the air. Although she sensed Finn's father was against it, she'd been debating whether to tell Finn she'd seen Richard at the gas station that day. The old River would have just let the truth out, both barrels blazing, but that was before. She felt the need to be more careful with Finn's feelings, especially since she knew how upsetting it was that Richard had cut off contact with his family. Who was she to spill their secrets? On the other hand, Finn had a right to know the truth.

"A little conspicuous don't you think?" she continued.

"I suppose in some circles," Richard replied, catching River's gaze in his rearview mirror. "But as you know, gas is plentiful and I need room to haul things."

"Like what?" River asked. "What have you been doing?"

Richard caught the meaning in River's gaze. Seeing as he was overdue for a recounting of his whereabouts, there was no harm in being honest. "I've been visiting the refugee cities," Richard said. "Delivering supplies to some of the families there."

"Why?" Finn asked.

"I wanted to see for myself," Richard said. "I wanted to bear witness to what had happened."

"What are they like?" Finn asked.

"Miserable and sad," River said. "I thought the Territories were the worst place on earth until I visited."

"What are the Territories like?" Richard asked.

"We're talking about you," River said.

"Come on," Richard said. "Few people have ever stepped inside; you were there for almost two years."

"Desolate," River said. "The land is bare; all the plants are gone. It's dirty, dangerous, and most of the workers are crazy. It's like landing on the dark side of the moon only here on earth...*like a hell broth, boil and bubble.* I went because I had no choice."

"She quotes Shakespeare," Richard said.

"And now...*you!*" River said. "Let's hear about your time on the road."

Although he felt put on the spot, he was impressed. The woman in the back seat had moxie. She was someone who was worthy of his son. Would he ever be worthy of his family again? The question hung at the back of his mind as he drove towards what he knew was his moment of reckoning.

"At the risk of sounding melodramatic, it's a national tragedy," he said. "Finn, I know your mother must be heartsick. The folks there are trapped. They want to get out, but don't know how. There wasn't much I could do but try to help make life bearable for the people I encountered. I've been delivering supplies, mostly food and medicine, sometimes alone, and sometimes with volunteers."

"Volunteers?" River asked. "Are you a member of some kind of group?"

"It's not as organized as you make it sound. It's just a group of like-minded people who care about those affected," Richard said. He toyed with the idea of telling Finn that he suspected Elizabeth had known about his movements from almost the very beginning, but decided against it. It was a secret between him and Elizabeth; it was a part of their marriage and not to be shared with the rest of the world. It was a selfish position in some ways. Selfish because he knew that if others were aware of the circumstances, they would chide Elizabeth for being so accommodating. It also limited his exposure, narrowing the audience he was required to be accountable to. The fewer people who knew, the smaller the circle, the more likely he might be forgiven.

"Sounds like a *resistance* group," River said, interrupting Richard's thoughts.

"I disagree. There is a big difference between rejecting an idea and rejecting your government," Richard said. "Besides, all we did was bring comfort to very impoverished individuals."

"Can we call a truce?" Finn asked. "We have at least seven hours together in this car."

"We're not fighting," River said. "I'm just asking questions."

"She's questioning my integrity," Richard said. "Understandable, given how we met, but I assure you I love this country as much as you do."

"If you wanted to make a difference, why didn't you go back to teaching?" River asked. "Colleges and universities eventually re-opened after the attacks."

Richard thought briefly of the note he'd sent to the president of Yale, requesting a leave of absence. In it, he'd relayed his deep love of teaching: his appreciation for the complexity of breaking down infor-mation so it could be taught to others, his thrill at searching out new texts and conducting research to make the best possible experience for his students. Learning was supposed to be a wondrous thing, he'd written, difficult perhaps, worthy of sacrifice and concentration, but still joyous. How then could he participate in something so life-affirming when he'd made such a mess of his life? When the country he loved was so deeply wounded? He couldn't. That was the short answer, and so he'd asked for a leave of absence.

"It hardly seemed right to go back to the life I'd known, a life as comfortable as the shoes I'm wearing, after what happened," Richard said.

"Now is your chance to turn things around, professor," River said. "After this, you could go back to Yale and teach."

"Maybe, River," Richard said, smiling at her in the rear-view mirror. "We're all entitled to a second chance, right?"

Finn watched the growing thaw between River and his father with relief. He couldn't explain what was happening to him. For a man that had been happy to hang in a hammock in the wilderness with nothing but bears for company, he now suddenly wanted his parents to like his girlfriend. And he wanted his girlfriend's mother and child to like him. Life felt urgent all of a sudden, like it had a purpose, and that was for them to be together. It was ridiculous to be making plans for the future; they could all be dead in a few days' time. The worst that could happen, other than ceasing to exist, would be that nothing would come of his daydreams. But it was also possible that things would go the other way and they would live. For Finn, the idea of being alone no longer held any allure.

"When we get to Denver, I think you should contact your mom," Finn said to River. "How many days has it been since you spoke to Ava?"

"I think we may want to wait until we know what's happening," she said. "I don't want to put them in harm's way by talking to me."

"Once we get to Denver, we'll be fine," Finn said. "The FBI will sort this out."

"Let's hope so, but don't underestimate Universal Industries, or its CEO," Richard said. "That man has visions of grandeur that rival the kings of the ages."

"Do you know him?" River asked. "Redmond Pierce? His picture is posted all over the buildings in the Territory."

"I'm not surprised," Richard said. "He wants everyone who works for him to know he's responsible for their existence. I met him in the days after the attacks when he, along with other business and political leaders, was summoned to a series of meetings with my wife. The country was reeling from what had happened and Elizabeth was searching for the best ideas about how to move forward. Mr. Pierce was not a wallflower and expressed his opinions freely."

"The Territories were his idea then?" River asked.

"I wasn't privy to the conversations," Richard said. "The security clearance required to be in the room didn't exist prior to that day. There was a closing of the ranks in government. People were terrified."

"I don't envy the President," River said. "I served two tours of duty and saw firsthand what the Republic was prepared to do to our soldiers and to their own people. I couldn't wait to come home. There were soldiers who wanted to stay behind after the attack at the mall, but they were recalled, forced to abandon their posts. It was very confusing."

"War is like that, regardless of the era," Richard said. "My father was an officer in the Vietnam War, which seems like something fought during the stone ages, and yet it wreaked its own havoc on a generation of people."

"Women weren't allowed in combat then, right?" River asked.

"Correct," Richard said. "Those years were the beginning of many changes for women that eventually allowed them to have greater equality, including holding a combat position in the military, if you consider being able to die in battle a right."

"I think being able to serve your country to the best of your ability, regardless of your gender, is a good idea," River said. "I knew a number of women who saw combat and they were good at their jobs. Better on some days then the men."

"I believe it," Finn said. "Watching you take care of yourself out there in the Territory, I believe it."

"I did what I had to do, Finn," River said. "And so did you. Given the circumstances, we're all capable of rising to a challenge."

Richard caught River's eye again. "But that isn't want you wanted to excel at, is it?"

"What do you mean?" River asked.

"I mean, what did you want to do, before everything was interrupted?" Richard said.

River hesitated, but decided she'd had enough of censuring her emotions. "I wanted to study abroad and use my language skills," she said. "I was interested in diplomacy, maybe working as a translator. I'm a small-town girl from Idaho. I wanted to see the world."

"And now?" Richard asked, keeping his eyes on the road.

"You sound like my mother," River said. "She wants me to go back to school."

"Once this business with Universal is cleared up, you are free to do what you wish," Richard said. "Yale has all kinds of programs for veterans, and it won't be long before Ava can attend kindergarten."

"He's right," Finn said. "You could pick up where you left off."

The picture of endless possibility they were painting made River horribly nervous. Finn and his father were confirming what she knew in her bones, but didn't want to admit: there were no more excuses left, no further obstacles to her getting her life back on track. The thought left a ball of dread in her belly, because it would all be on her now. No more bad breaks to lament.

"Change is daunting," Richard said. "But here we are heading to Denver together. Maybe, just maybe, we're all going to have a shot at a new beginning."

TWENTY NINE

COOPER WATCHED the directional signs for the William P. Hobby Airport in Houston whir past, his driver hitting speeds not even contemplated in the Texas vehicle code. No matter. One of the many benefits of living and driving in a company town was that the highway patrol ignored you. It would be his last perk, though. Cooper was on his way out.

After the shootout at the train depot, Red did not return to the company's headquarters. His absence was an open secret, something everyone noticed but did not discuss. Like Noah and his Ark, Red had already deployed staff he deemed worthy of his new world order. Anyone left behind would likely not be invited to the revolution.

For his part, Cooper returned to work as if nothing had happened. Keeping up appearances was certainly a necessity, but behaving as if everything was normal after Red's mercenaries murdered a member of the government was tough, even for a seasoned soldier.

Cooper felt partially responsible for the death of the FBI director. He'd underestimated Red's frame of mind. Underestimated his willingness to ignore all of the established norms and agreed upon rules of engagement. It was all disruption with Red, his hubris driving the train. If he was going to be successful, Cooper was going to have to relearn the rules, specifically *that there were no rules*. It was every man for himself, sink or swim by your own blood and tears; that was Red's version of America. His former boss was too blinded by his voracious ambitions to see the ruin that lay ahead, to see that he was the prover- bial Kurtz, already down the river too far to come back, the *rat, tat, tat* of the machine gun the background music of his life ahead.

Cooper also regretted that he'd been unable to communicate with River before she'd destroyed the drone. He could still see the look on her face as her boot came down upon its camera. He'd seen it in the eyes of hundreds of soldiers in the field: determination. The act of having a purpose, in this case to survive. If it had been him, he would have blown the thing sky high, too. There was no way for her to know his intentions, and he'd been too slow on the draw to use the speakers to communicate. Although he was aware River was an accomplished marksman, it did not prepare him for the experience of watching himself get shot *virtually* between the eyes. It was quite a series of blows coming days apart. Things had spun out of control quickly and the ties to the world he knew were coming undone. Cooper wasn't used to feeling such upheaval and uncertainty after a life of prepara- tion and order, and he knew there was more to come.

As the outline of the airport came into view, Cooper consoled himself with the thought that whatever violence and betrayal were about to happen, the fault for all of it lay with Red. The question he couldn't answer was why. Why risk it all now? It was a full-time job just to pull the oil they had out of the ground day after day inside the Territories. Cooper was astonished at the mathematical and chemical symphony required to dive into the geological burial grounds, locate the fossil fuels trapped between the earth's layers, and extract them from their deep, dark pools. But Red knew. He was the master at understanding how to get the earth to give up its quarry.

But what did Red know about running a government? Education, national parks, veterans...the country was a vast hive of needs and wants. Cooper could count on both hands the number of business leaders over the years who'd boasted that they could run the country better, if only given a chance. As if someone who made computers or sold real estate could magically straighten out the messy business of tending to four hundred million people. But Red wasn't interested in better government; he had something more elemental in mind. Red wanted to build an empire, a kingdom of crude to rule the world and in the process bind everyone to his will.

It wasn't a worthy enough goal for Cooper to stick his neck out. He knew what it was like to fight for liberty and freedom, whatever those concepts meant to people nowadays. So, he'd switched sides, abandoned his post. Given the circumstances, he would have done it regardless, but having the President ask for his help soothed his sense of honor. He only hoped the Russian mercenaries Red had hired to help fight in his revolution didn't try to kill Red in a double cross before the fighting actually got started. Cooper wanted the task for himself.

THIRTY

As RED'S car sped along the highway towards his new compound in Virginia, he reflected on how easily he'd managed to escape from the rail yard in Pennsylvania. Marveled at how, despite all of the bloodshed, he'd walked away without a scratch. It was truly a mark of his genius, a sign that the gods were on his side. He was *incontrovertibly* invincible and fully expected the spoils of war to flow to him in the end.

A small part of him did regret the death of the FBI director, but it was an accident—Russian mercenaries could only be managed so much, given the language barrier. In the end, though, he was not the catalyst for these events. It was the President's fault a man was dead. If she had been a stronger leader, the entire tragedy could have been avoided. Weakness. It was a plague upon the nation. And none exhibited weakness more than his chief of security. It was damn sad to see a Marine go soft. Cooper had clearly gone over to Elizabeth Cunningham's side. Red had made peace with the fact that his second in command had proven to be a coward; it was better to know of it sooner rather than later. Better to know now, before they were in the middle of a war.

Finding loyalty, true loyalty, in people was tough these days. In another time he would have found folks who'd have laid down their life for him without a second thought. Now everyone had their own angle to manage. The only reason Red didn't have Cooper killed immediately was because he knew he'd have another opportunity in Denver, and it would be better there, more dramatic or poetic, depending on how you looked at it. Cooper, the decorated Marine, dying alongside the C Team–all of them expelling their last breaths to protect a failing way of life. God, it was tiring to be the best and smartest all the time. When, Red wondered, was someone going to finally surprise him by being one step ahead?

Red's car arrived at the new training facilities, which, given more time, would have been a gleaming campus of warfare with the latest in technology. But this was a rush situation, so they'd merely rehabbed an abandoned manufacturing complex, pulling out machinery on the factory floors to make room for storage and training. Two warehouses had been converted into dormitories for the all-male force. The idea of women in combat always bothered Red, and after the incident with the truck driver in the Territory, he'd decided to exclude females from his units. Females were untrustworthy and unstable. It was best to leave them to what they were created for: to carry children and serve their husbands. Obedience was a woman's greatest gift to a man, in his humble opinion. In any case, it wasn't a grand compound in the way he would've wished it to be, but it was functional. They were almost ready to commence their objectives. He'd written a note to his wife saying goodbye. He doubted he would ever see the poor thing again.

Red exited the vehicle and walked briskly towards Building A, where the bulk of his troops were waiting for him, along with the Russian *specialists* he'd acquired. His shoes made a slight squeak on the cement floor as he entered the cavernous space, thousands of faces staring back at him. The men had been waiting more than an hour to hear him speak. He stepped up to the podium, adjusted the microphone, and took his remarks out of the inner pocket of his suit coat. He unfolded the papers, smoothing them out as he prepared for what he knew would be one of the most important speeches of his life. He looked out at the sea of faces before him, young and fresh, soaking in their adoration.

"My fellow patriots," Red said. A thunderous wave of applause and catcalls erupted as he began to speak. "Turn and look at what you have built in just a few weeks' time. Is it not an impressive undertaking? Are we not a force to be reckoned with? You are the chosen, an elite group of soldiers selected to carry this great nation into its next chapter, and in doing so, protect its future from all manner of savages and terrorists who would seek to end our way of life. It is a sad day to say that our government has failed us. It is a serious thing to challenge its authority, its very existence and the rule of law. At the moment I'm nothing but a fugitive, a man wanted for treason. But I'm at peace with this, just as our forefathers were in the face of an unjust system. It's times like these that I look to men like Patrick Henry for solace, a man who once uttered this call to action: 'Is life so dear or peace so sweet, as to be purchased at the price of chains and slavery? Forbid it, Almighty God! I know not what course others may take, but as for me, give me liberty or give me death!'"

The audience exploded into a frenzy of whistles and hooting. Red paused to let them settle down.

"I tell you now...I tell you now that we face the same stark choice. That we must tear ourselves from the comfort of our lives and fight for what is right. I'm honored that you have signed on to take this journey with me. Together we will restore the United States to its former glory, allow it to be the force in the world it deserves to be. Now is the time to draw a line in the sand, to stop the impending carnage of our people and their false sense of security and peace. Without sacrifice there can be no victory. And victory will be ours!"

More applause followed as Red stepped away from the podium. He raised his hand in salute to his troops, and in response the men began to stomp their boots in unison, filling the space with the steady drumbeat of war. Red smiled as he moved towards the exit; he had his well-run militia, and would see his destiny fulfilled.

THIRTY ONE

ELIZABETH STOOD next to the technician, waiting for her speech to load onto the teleprompter, her anxiety growing. While no one on her staff had said it aloud to her, she knew the speech in Denver would be the most important of her life. Although it was not the annual State of the Union, in thirty-five minutes, she had to succinctly convey the condition of the nation. She would not be addressing Congress in the grand hall of the Capitol Building. There would be no pomp and circumstance, and that was, in many ways, the crux of the problem. Becoming president through succession, she'd had the enviable political luxury of upending the American public's comfort level without immediate repercussions or oversight. When she walked on stage in a day's time, she would finally face her employers and learn whether the job she'd done had been sufficient to the cause.

Nevertheless, looking for inspiration, she'd reviewed previous State of the Union speeches. What tone to take? Whose voice to borrow? Should it be Roosevelt, who had earnestly told the American Public that *"Everything we are and have is at stake. Everything we are and have will be given."* No, she decided, it would be Lincoln whose words she would carry with her. She chose him because he was a president who knew the pain of a deeply wounded nation, forced to reconcile its traumas and injustices.

Elizabeth had no Civil War to contend with, but her country was divided nevertheless. Combing through the White House's vast library, she'd found one of Lincoln's inaugural speeches, given, ironically, as he traveled by train after his election. Having retraced his steps to Philadelphia, she took an interest in his telling the audience, *"You have kindly suggested to me that in my hands is the task of restoring peace to the present distracted condition of the country."*

Later, she combed through a copy of the Gettysburg Address, drawn in as Lincoln contemplated the task of *"testing whether... a nation so conceived and so dedicated can long endure."* Despite the hours of work she'd put into her remarks, Elizabeth's greatest worry was that she would not sufficiently answer the question she knew was on the minds of everyone that would enter the arena to hear her speak: *who are we as a nation?* Like a lover who delivers assurances in whispered tones, it was her job to proclaim the country safe and stable. Every fiber of her being ached with the hope that she would be able to fulfill her responsibility as others had before her.

A stagehand, who looked to be in his mid-twenties, stood with his back to her, tapping a handheld microphone *"Check, check, check...Hey man, I don't think this thing is on,"* he yelled to a distant figure sitting at a mixing board. Elizabeth would have remained on stage indefinitely — ignored by the cadre of indifferent roadies and technicians—as she second-guessed her remarks, had her phone not begun to ring. She fished it out of her jacket, excited to see Finn's number appear.

"Is that you?" she asked.

"That depends," replied a familiar voice. "Who were you expecting?"

"Richard?"

"Yes, it's me," he said. "I...umm. Look, we're together, Elizabeth, *all of us*. We're just outside Denver. Where are you?"

"I'm at the Convention Center with my advance team," she said, her words coming out in an excited jumble. "Come to the rear doors of the main auditorium near the loading docks. My security detail will let you in."

"We'll be there in twenty minutes," he said and hung up.

Elizabeth slipped her phone back in her pocket. She could barely concentrate as she ran towards the exit, the sound tech finally calling her name as she sped away from the teleprompter. She raced towards a set of double doors where the Secret Service was stationed, whispering the news to a senior member of her detail. Even as she said the words, she was in a state of disbelief. Somehow, the impossible had happened. After two years of silence, Richard was on his way to her with Finn. Their family would be reunited. It qualified as a miracle, but it also opened a whole other set of issues. How had Richard changed while he way away? Should she forgive him? Would he apologize?

Time slowed to a crawl as Elizabeth waited with her tangle of thoughts. She used the minutes to prepare for seeing Richard. She was undecided about whether to reveal that she knew of his whereabouts during his absence. On the one hand it seemed important to clear the air and confess all that had happened. On the other, it seemed petty and somewhat cruel: an easy way to destroy any illusion of independence he might have felt he had. Try as she might, she couldn't summon any rage or fury. What she felt was an overwhelming sense of sadness. Regardless of how it started, for two years they suffered, alone. As far as she was concerned, it was time for a fresh start, even if they had to work towards reconciliation.

Finally, after what felt like an eternity, smart phones began to vibrate, and her secret service agents smiled. The double doors opened, and Richard walked through, immediately catching her gaze as he stood stock still while the Secret Service patted him down. Finn followed, holding hands with a young woman she assumed was River. Her green eyes were fixed on the guards as they searched her, her wary gaze seemingly recording every detail as she waited for them to finish. After they'd completed their inspections, Richard stayed back, standing some distance from Elizabeth. Finn needed no encouragement and ran straight into her arms.

"I've missed you so much," he said. "Let me take a look at you."

Finn took a step back to scrutinize his mother, the way grown children do, to look for assurances of their parent's dependability.

"You look worn out," he said, frowning.

"It's been a long few days," she said. "There's a lot to tell you."

Finn nodded, knowing from her expression that something terrible had happened. "Let me introduce you to River," he said.

*And I love her...*Elizabeth thought to herself, watching the way her son gazed at the young woman standing off to the side. Poor River. Meeting your boyfriend's mother ranked up there as a challenging experience regardless of the person. When said mother was also the President of the United States–and you'd been on the run because your life was in danger–that certainly raised the level of awkwardness into the stratosphere. Elizabeth walked over to River, determined to defuse the situation.

"I know this is all probably too much to process," Elizabeth whispered in River's ear while wrapping her in a warm embrace. "For now, please try to think of me as a mother who is very grateful you helped bring her son home safe."

"I'll try," River said, feeling slightly disoriented at being hugged by the President of the United States.

The only person left to greet was Richard, who continued to keep his distance. Elizabeth, remembering her thoughts earlier, took the initiative and quickly closed the gap, enveloping him as she would have in their better days.

"Hello, stranger," she said. "I know we have a lot to discuss, but God, I've missed you, It's good to see your face."

River thought she caught a hint of moisture in Richard's eyes as he met Elizabeth's gaze. "I've been a damn fool," he said.

"Yes, you have," Elizabeth replied. "But today is a new day, Richard. Let's see if we can't find a way forward."

A sense of relief enveloped Finn as he watched his father nod somberly and then lean in to say something for Elizabeth's ears only. Whatever it was, it caused her to reach out and squeeze his hand. Although he was a grown man living on his own, his parents' separation had been painful. In the blink of an eye their family had been pulled apart and it had, he realized, left a gaping hole in his heart that he'd tried desperately to ignore by hiding out in the wilderness. But solitude can't always heal an emotional wound, no matter how beautiful the setting.

River watched Finn's expression as his parents embraced. She gave his hand a squeeze in support and to catch his attention. She was doing her best to act normal, whatever that meant, but now that they were back in civilization, she was anxious for some answers and a proper explanation for their predicament.

"We should find a place to talk," she said, catching Elizabeth's eye.

"Absolutely. I have a set of private rooms we can use," Elizabeth said. An agent led them a short distance down a hallway. They came to a door and the rest paused as the agent conducted a sweep.

"All clear," he said.

The four walked in and sat down on a couch. A tray of water and four glasses sat on a small coffee table in front of them. They stared at one another in polite silence; perhaps unsure who should go first. River, never very good at waiting, was about to seize the initiative and fire off a barrage of questions, when there was a knock at the door.

The acting FBI director entered the room with a contingent of his agents, looking even grimmer than he had the day his boss had been assassinated. He was under six feet tall and blessed with a youthful appearance. When combined with his penchant for wearing suits that were a tad too big, he looked like a teenager playing dress-up. He was coming into his job years earlier than he would have otherwise. His boss had not been expected to retire for some time. Like Elizabeth, he now found himself thrust into a volatile situation with little warning.

"Madam President, I wish there was more time for you to exchange pleasantries with your guests," he said. "But we have a major security situation on our hands and need to brief you as quickly as possible."

"Understood. But I want them to stay," Elizabeth said. "They are a part of this and should know what's happening."

The director agreed and explained that he actually wanted to question Finn and River before delivering his report.

"Bear with me," he said. "It will all make sense when we're through."

At the assistant director's request, Finn recounted the night he was shot and their backpacking trek into Wyoming.

"It sounds crazy when I describe it," Finn said. "This all started because of the data I was collecting...there is no question the streams and river segments in the northern part of the state are getting warmer."

"Can you explain it?" the acting director asked.

"I can't," Finn said. "Not yet. The problem is that was only *one* of the anomalies. The other is that in some places the water simply does not freeze, even in the most extreme temperatures."

"That's impossible," the acting director said.

Finn smiled. "Yes, you're not the first to tell me that, but I assure you, it's happening. I was documenting the situation for a field report, believing I had safe passage to visit the Territory…"

"I've spoken with Cooper Smith," the acting director said. "He told me Red ordered him to kill you as soon he learned you'd requested permission to visit. Cooper established an elaborate ruse with his men to make it look like they'd tried and failed. He was about to help you escape from the Territory when River stepped in."

"It sure didn't feel like a ruse when I was floating down the river bleeding from a gunshot wound," Finn said. "Or when the security team pulled me out of River's apartment with an assault rifle aimed at my head. We both thought we were going to die."

River fought to maintain her composure upon learning about Cooper's subterfuge. It didn't feel like a hoax when the guards came banging on her door. These were the machinations of people whose lives were far more complicated than her own. How was she ever going to survive being with someone caught up in this kind of dangerous intrigue? A swirl of regret started to form in her belly. Maybe her first instinct with Finn had been right, maybe she should have just run in the opposite direction and gone home to her family when her contract ended.

"River," the assistant director said, pulling her out of her thoughts. "You were a hauler inside the Territory? That's how you came to meet Finn?"

"I *came to meet* Finn when he stumbled onto the road, bleeding, at the end of my shift," River said. "He asked me to help him."

"And you did?"

"She did," Finn said. "She brought me back to her room and patched up my wound. She was amazingly brave."

Elizabeth grabbed Richard's hand. "I created a monster," she said. "I would never have forgiven myself if Finn died inside the Territory."

"You didn't create this mess," River said. "That man did."

"And before the Territory," the director said, bringing the conversation back to his investigation. "You served in the Army as a field interpreter?"

"You know all of this," River said, her exasperation coming through. "Why ask again?"

"Be patient, I'm getting there," the director said. "While you were in the Territory, did you ever see any troops bearing unusual or foreign insignia, or witness any movement of military equipment?"

Now he had River's attention. "No sir," she said. "The Territory is full of ex-military acting as security. They have cameras and surveillance, and use military grade weapons, but the rest of the operation is strictly industrial."

"And the guards that confronted you, Finn, did they speak English?"

"Yes," Finn replied. "They were American without a doubt."

"What does this have to do with us?" River asked.

The director looked at Elizabeth, checking one more time for permission to speak frankly, and received it.

"You are no longer the target of Red's anger," the director said. "While you two were incommunicado, his behavior rapidly escalated in another direction."

"Please tell me what could make the attempted murder of two people seem unimportant now?" River asked. "Do you have any idea how absurd this all seems? This wasn't a game to me. I thought I might not see my daughter again."

"I understand your anger, but it's worse than you think," Elizabeth replied. "The CEO of Universal is planning to overthrow the government. I know of his plans firsthand. A few days ago, he killed the FBI director as we tried to arrest him for treason. He's building an army of his own using his existing security forces, sympathetic veterans, and Russian mercenaries."

"He's preparing to go to war against his own country," the assistant director said. "Our sources tell us he's prepared to kill civilians to make his point."

"The good of the many at the expense of a few," Richard said. "It's his *modus operandi*."

"What about us?" River asked. "How can you be certain we're no longer in danger? I haven't contacted my mother or daughter for days out of fear that it might put them at risk."

"You were wise to take precautions," the director said. "We don't have a profile model for this kind of behavior. This man is unstable and prefers to keep his perceived enemies guessing. He only cares about himself and his authority. We'll never know, but you might very well have saved your daughter's life before Red became distracted by his greater plans."

"I don't know whether to be relieved or appalled," River said. "After everything he put us through. How can one man have so much power?"

"Elizabeth, you've got to cancel your speech tomorrow night," Richard said. "Red is too unpredictable. You'll be a sitting duck out there on that stage."

"Impossible," Elizabeth said. "Too much work has been done by too many people to restart national elections. If I don't appear on television, it will send the country into a tailspin. I have to be on that stage tomorrow night."

Finn watched his father out of the corner of his eye. The old Richard would have protested and cajoled until he'd whittled away all opposition.

"I don't like it, but I understand," Richard said, knowing full well he was a pheasant under glass. "You're the President of the United States and people will be looking to you for leadership. But that doesn't make it any easier, knowing you'll be in danger."

Elizabeth caught Finn's eye, surprised at her husband's less strident tone. Perhaps his time from away from her had done him some good. "We'll speak with the Secret Service," she said. "They've got a plan in place to secure the convention center."

"Don't forget the FBI," the acting director added. "We'll make sure things are locked down tight."

"I have a weapon," River said. "I left it in the car to avoid any trouble with the Secret Service, but if they'll allow it, I can help protect you, too."

"Let's hope that won't be necessary, but thank you," Elizabeth said. "It's very humbling to have someone make that kind of offer. I'm grateful."

River blushed, realizing that much of what she'd assumed about the most powerful woman in the country was wrong. In her mind she'd conjured up an image of the President as a formal person, a stern woman with little warmth or charm because of her job. Up close, Elizabeth Cunningham was kind and patient with her staff. Her clothing was expensive but understated, and she wore no makeup, or at least very little, making it easy to see she hadn't slept well in months. But it was her strength that caught River's attention. It radiated from her, like you could knock her down and she'd get back up. As corny as it seemed, River felt they might be kindred spirits. River knew what it was like to face one calamity after another and have no choice but to go on, and she understood the pain of being separated from the people you loved because there was no other choice.

"I think we should go back to the train where we can all get some rest," the President said. "The car adjacent to mine has been made up as guest quarters for visitors. Finn, you and River can stay there."

"If you don't mind me saying so, you look like you could use some sleep, Elizabeth," Richard said. "*Uneasy lies the head that wears the crown?*"

Elizabeth nodded, giving her husband a knowing glance. There was so much to say, but at the moment, just the thought of lying beside him was enough. "*To sleep: perchance to dream: ay, there's the rub,*" she replied. "But I have a feeling tonight will be different."

THIRTY TWO

LATER THAT EVENING, River tried to decide what was more surreal: bedding down for the night in an official presidential residence, or sharing a bed with the President's son. Both were beyond the realm of what her imagination was capable of conjuring up. For some reason, her thoughts drifted back to middle school study hall, when, like most adolescents, she spent her time answering impossibly intrusive questions passed from student to student in notebooks like *who would you marry* and *how many kids would you have?* Who had she chosen? Some popular boy whose name she couldn't even remember now. She could almost picture him; after graduation, he'd married a local girl and moved one hundred miles south of Hailey to Burly to manage her grandfather's farm.

"I can hear your wheels turning," Finn said, rolling over to face her. "*Qu'est-ce que c'est?* What is it? What's the matter?"

"I can't believe I was sitting at a table tonight eating dinner with the President of the United States," she said.

"She has to eat like the rest of us," Finn said. "Frankly, I think this may have been the first meal in a long while she actually enjoyed. It's obvious she hasn't been taking care of herself. I feel partially responsible. I should have come to see her sooner."

"No offense, but I think it's your father that really made the difference," River said. "I'm surprised she forgave him so easily. I don't think I could do that."

"I don't think she's forgiven him yet," Finn said quietly. "But they've been together a long time and…"

"And what?" River asked.

Finn was trying to figure out what to say. He didn't want to scare River off with a bunch of lovesick nonsense. But he also knew in his heart that his parents, despite their conflict, remained deeply in love. Finn wanted that for himself. He wanted the life that kind of commitment brought. "I guess I was going to say that after so many years they understand one another. They know they let this go too far, and go on too long," Finn said. "When you love someone, you have to be able to forgive them."

"I don't know if I could do that," River said.

Finn smiled, thinking about all the skittish animals he'd met in the wild; the ones who'd never seen a human before. "You might," he said softly. "You might if it was important enough."

River let it pass, but she had a feeling their conversation was some kind of test, one she might fail. It wasn't that she didn't want a good life. She did. It wasn't that she didn't want to be in love, she did. She craved the kind of love that knew the sound of your voice in a crowd, the feel of your skin in the dark. The kind of love that could tell when you were having a nightmare by the cadence of your breath in your sleep. The kind of love that took the baby so you could sleep and brought cold cloths for headaches and aspirin for hangovers and never said, *"I told you so."* But she was also afraid that she wouldn't be able to reciprocate that kind of devotion and therefore would *never* be the recipient of such a rare and valuable thing.

"Have they always been like that?" she asked. "So intense with one another?"

"Always. They've been known to finish each other's sentences," Finn said. "Don't worry, you'll get used to it. Try to get some sleep."

River lay there, feeling the heat of Finn's body, a lump forming in her throat. There it was again. Certainty. *"You'll get used to it."* As if the next chapter was written.

Here was another place she didn't share his confidence. River wasn't certain they'd survive, his mother included. The briefing from the FBI certainly spelled out the basics. There was a mad man on the loose trying to create his own reality. That alone was dangerous enough, but there was something else. River knew more about Universal Industries than most people. She understood their devotion to the bottom line, their ruthlessness to achieve results. Now their CEO had applied his principles to something far more dangerous than oil extraction. As she listened to Finn drift off to sleep, her soldier's brain turned on, wondering what was coming next.

———

IN THE TRAIN car next door, Richard and Elizabeth sat across from one another feeling like two strangers on a first date. A half-drunk bottle of red wine sat between them, a useful lubricant for rusty conversationalists.

"Do you remember when you first told me you wanted to run for Congress?" Richard asked.

"Vaguely," Elizabeth said. "It was such a long time ago."

"It seems like yesterday to me," Richard said, swirling the cherry-colored liquid around in his glass. "You came running into the kitchen one afternoon and said 'old Pat Barnes has lost his marbles and needs to be replaced by someone who can look after the district.'"

"Oh my." Elizabeth giggled. "I do remember. As I recall, you didn't want me to do it. You said it would be tough to beat someone so respected in the community."

"Yes, I did, but you didn't care," Richard said. "You straightened up your spine and looked at me and said 'I'll just have to go out and talk to people and make them understand.'"

Elizabeth smiled at the memory. "I did and I won the race."

"You won the next several elections," Richard said. "And then you became the beloved incumbent until…"

"Until I was appointed Secretary of State," Elizabeth finished his sentence. "You asked me not to accept that job, too."

"I did," Richard said. "I was worried we would see even less of each other than we already did with my teaching at Yale and you being in Washington. But it was more than that."

"What?" Elizabeth said. "You never mentioned anything."

"I know," Richard said. "I was intimidated. You were about to become one of the most powerful people in the world. I was worried you wouldn't need me anymore."

"How absurd," Elizabeth said. "I think I needed you more at that moment than I ever had in my life. Just as I need you now."

"Why on earth do you feel that way?" Richard asked. "You've gone toe to toe with the most dynamic leaders on earth, faced down great evil, and run our country in a time of chaos and peril. What do you need me for? An aging professor steeped in history, something no one cares about anymore. My mind is full of useless details that have no relevance."

"That's just melancholy nonsense," Elizabeth said. "It reminds me of the day you walked out. I need you to resist such impulses in the future. I've come to understand that things are not so black and white. Your relevance *or irrelevance* to this world is not written. You will decide your fate by what you do next. When you left, you took away something precious to me. Do you know what it is?"

Richard felt his throat constrict. "I think I know, but why don't you tell me?" he said.

"You may have thought you were making a statement to the President of the United States when you walked away, but you didn't abandon the leader of the free world. You ghosted your wife," Elizabeth said. "I lost my best friend the day you disappeared. I had no one to turn to for solace or laughter. There was no one to express my gravest doubts to. I have been without my greatest confidant for two years."

"I felt I had no choice," he said. "I hate the Territories and all that they stand for. I wanted to be true to my principals. I still do, but..."

"To hell with your principals, Richard. Did they keep you warm at night? Did they bring you closer to your son? It's the coward's way to walk out in the middle of a fight," Elizabeth said. "You could have stayed and lent your voice to the discussion. You could have been the nation's conscience; played the Devil's Advcate. No one was keeping you from expressing yourself, except you."

Richard grimaced. Could it have been that easy and instead he ran away in a selfish snit?

"I see a light bulb is going off for you," Elizabeth said. "I may be the president, but I am also a human being, capable of listening. You do not need to censure yourself or walk away just because we don't agree. I've been furious at you for so long. I'm willing to put aside my hurt because I love you, but I want to know you've grown from this and don't plan on leaving again if things become uncomfortable."

"I promise. The truth is that not long after I left, I knew I'd made a terrible mistake, but I was too ashamed to return," he said. "I am sorry, Elizabeth. I will spend the rest of my days trying to make it up to you."

"No," she said. "I don't need a martyr for a husband. I need a partner. If you really want to apologize, I suggest you get up and come with me now so we can finish this discussion properly and put an end to this sorry chapter in our lives."

Later, as Richard lay awake listening to Elizabeth sleep the sleep of the exhausted, he reflected on how he'd been given the precious opportunity to understand the value of what he'd left behind. He did not intend to squander his good fortune.

Although clearly worn down, his wife was more beautiful than ever. When he first set eyes on her inside the convention center, he'd been reminded of the day he'd spotted her at college, the confident young woman who'd refused to join a sorority. Captain of the debate team and a volunteer at the battered woman's shelter near campus, she'd declined his first two offers of dinner. *Too handsome,* she'd said, as if it were a flaw in his character.

Finally, she'd agreed to go out, but not for dinner, only coffee. From there she'd allowed him to escort her to a photography exhibit and then later a play and dinner afterwards. It had taken him an entire month to be able to spend more than a few hours with her at one time. She was careful with her affections.

When he was finally allowed to visit, he discovered her dorm room was covered with old issues of *The Economist* and the *Paris Review,* and with books, some new, some used, all of them scribbled with pen or pencil, maybe a torn piece of paper marking a critical thought. Many of his friends found her too brainy, but he loved it. He wasn't afraid of her ideas or her energy. She ignored her own beauty, but often complimented others, and it made her lovelier. She was athletic, riding a bicycle between classes and playing tennis on the weekends.

He knew that he loved her early on in their courtship, but was careful not to rush things. Both their families were old money, concerned with expectations for marriage and status, but Elizabeth didn't seem to care. She wanted to have her own life and be free of the trappings her birthright brought her. And yet she failed to escape the outlines of her destiny, for here she was, President of the United States, preparing to address the nation. He had not handled her ascension to the position as gracefully as he should have. As he lay there, he thought back to how she had carefully allowed him into her life all those years ago. Once she did, she loved him with all her heart, no exceptions. He had not done the same thing for her, and he regretted it.

Richard thought about how far he'd drifted from his family, his career, and his life. If there was such a thing as miracles, then he'd witnessed one, certain he would never know why such grace had been bestowed upon him. As he drifted off to sleep, he thanked whatever forces were at play for reuniting him with Elizabeth, for allowing his impulsiveness to be repaired, and for giving him a second chance.

THIRTY THREE

RIVER GAZED across the table as the White House traveling staff served pastries and coffee to Finn and his family. Despite all that had happened, it was obvious that if given the option, they were a family that preferred to stick together. They'd been put through the ringer, and were more than entitled to wallow in recriminations, but instead chose to savor their proximity much like a good meal.

She was astonished how beguiling it all seemed to her as an outsider. No one in her household ate together. She'd gotten up with Ava at the crack of dawn; her mother was usually out the door to open the library up for the morning. Marc never rose before noon. Despite the noise and chaos of three adults and a baby, her home was steeped in silence, a place of concealment and secrecy, with a good deal left unspoken by tacit agreement. This morning though, River realized she was enjoying the silence. She savored her croissant, reading a printed copy of a national newspaper until a frantic knock at the door interrupted their peace. A member of the President's security team opened the door, allowing the acting FBI director to burst into the room.

"Good morning, Madam President," he said.

"Good morning, Michael," she said. "We were not expecting you until later. What is it?"

"It may be nothing," he said. "During one of our perimeter

searches this morning, we came across a piece of paper containing something unusual. We're wondering if River could review it for us."

"Why me?" River asked.

"If you take a look, you'll understand," he said.

River took the scrap of paper and looked at it for several seconds, her brow furrowed.

"It doesn't make any sense," she said, handing the scrap back.

"Do you agree it appears to be a photocopy from a book?" Michael said.

"Yes," River replied. "But not one that would have been allowed in the United States in the last two years, at least not without supervision."

"Could you loop the rest of us into this conversation please?" Elizabeth said.

"Right. Sorry. The scrap of paper is from a poem in Arabic," River said.

"What does it say?" Finn asked.

"It's about pledging total devotion to God," River said.

"Can you tell how old it is?" Michael asked.

"The printing and paper look contemporary," River said. "Is there a trash dump nearby, or storage facility? Maybe someone was clearing out an old space?"

"Not that we know of," he said.

"I don't want to sound overly dramatic, but this is the kind of thing a martyr would carry," River said. "A devotional text to bolster their resolve."

"That was our conclusion as well," Michael said. "Our agents are investigating."

"Maybe it's a trick," Richard said. "A red herring from Red to throw us off his trail and make us think there's another threat. He loves to blame Muslims for our troubles."

"Plausible," Michael replied. "It's another angle to investigate. Meanwhile, our satellite images show the bulk of Red's troops and equipment still parked on his compound in Virginia. He hasn't made any significant shifts in the last forty-eight hours."

"What do you make of it?" the President asked.

"We're not sure, to be honest," he said. "Cooper Smith arrived last night and is trying to anticipate Red's next move. He thinks Red may be waiting until after your address, hoping he can use your speech to justify launching his attack."

"That sounds like him," Richard said. "He'll no doubt employ his *selective* use of American history to try to stir people into a frenzy."

"The problem is deterrence," Michael said. "Given the civilians in the area, our military advisors tell us it's unlikely we can use airstrikes to destroy his base, but our surveillance is incomplete. We have one more pass to make and then our photography can be compared with maps and satellite imagery."

"Airstrikes on American soil?" the President asked. "That's not something I'm ready to sign off on. My God, that would scare our people half to death. I need to speak with the Secretary of Defense, and we'll have to assemble the cabinet."

"This is not your typical homegrown rebellion, Madam President. We're not talking about a bunch of frustrated ranchers trespassing on public land. Red is amassing real firepower. Extraordinary measures may be required...."

"For extraordinary circumstances," the President interjected. "You're the not the first person to present me with that argument. I will tell you the same thing I told *him*, the United States doesn't abandon its principles in an emergency, that is the time when they're needed most. We will not use our troops on US soil, at least not yet."

"Understood," Michael said. "But it may be our only option to thwart him before he enters more populated areas like Philadelphia."

Elizabeth looked over at Richard, wondering what he made of this matter-of-fact conversation about an action that could tear the country into pieces. Not since the Civil War had the country pitted its own soldiers against one another. As Commander in Chief, she would not give such an order. She'd rather see the Russians march down the street in front of the Liberty Bell than ask neighbors to draw arms against one another. The sight of foreign invaders would be an insult, but it would not be a lethal blow to the soul of the country. She wouldn't be the one to inflict such a mortal wound, accomplishing what years of terrorism could not: turning neighbor against neighbor.

"Richard," Elizabeth said, looking to her husband for his thoughts.

"We must not be enemies," he said. "We must be the better angels."

"Yes," she said. "Quite right. Michael, I understand your position, but we will not pit our armed forces against their countrymen. I will not drop bombs on innocent people. Instead, you will send our best people to infiltrate the compound and deal with this directly. You...*they* have full authority to stop Red from leaving the compound."

"Understood, Madam President," Michael said. "As a reminder, you are expected at the Convention Center in a few hours. We'll be sealing the facility and doing a security sweep before we let folks inside. You and your group need to be there at least two hours before the speech."

"We'll be ready to go," Elizabeth said.

But in her heart, she wondered. She suspected the rest of the room felt the same way.

THIRTY FOUR

THAT AFTERNOON, Elizabeth sat uneasily in her car as it sped towards the Convention Center, a shiver of dread creeping up her spine. The Secret Service insisted she travel alone in an unmarked car for security purposes. Despite a late afternoon briefing confirming Red was still in Virginia, she was worried about being ambushed. Elizabeth knew from her time as Secretary of State that the Russians excelled at executing officials in public. She had no desire to die on the open road like some enemy of the Kremlin when she had just repaired her marriage and reunited with her family.

After what seemed like an eternity, her motorcade arrived at the Convention Center, and she expelled the breath she'd been holding. A secret service agent opened the door within seconds of her vehicle pulling up to the curb. Two more agents shadowed her as she entered the massive facility, using the rear loading dock. Even more agents surrounded her as she walked through the rear doors. She was relieved when she stepped inside and found her entourage waiting for her in the hallway.

"There is the star of the show," Richard said, coming forward to greet her. "Tonight is your night, Elizabeth. Try to look ahead at what you are about to do, the legacy you leave behind. I promise Red's deeds will pale in comparison when all is said and done."

"If you weren't an expert in American history, I might think you were just trying to butter me up," she said.

"You're long overdue for a compliment," he said. "Especially one from your husband."

Elizabeth smiled and took Richard's hand, leading them back to her suite of private rooms, to pass the time until her speech. Elizabeth reviewed documents that required her attention. Richard had unearthed an old picture puzzle of the Unites States from the train's library, complete with notable landmarks such as Mt. Rushmore and the Statue of Liberty. It was 1,000 pieces, plus or minus, and carried the familiar scent of dusty cardboard. He'd set it up on a table in the corner of the room. River was carrying a few things Richard lent her from his library in Wyoming. She'd been curious about an old dog-eared biography of a woman named Kay Graham, who'd been the publisher of the *Washington Post*, a newspaper she thought had been founded by the CEO of Amazon. There had also been a copy of poems by E.E. Cummings, a poet River had been obsessed with since high school. None of those diversions worked on Finn, though. He could barely sit still, the apprehension causing his legs to vibrate. The tap, tap, tap of his hiking boot finally pulled River's nose out of her book.

"He's been like that since he was born," Elizabeth said, noticing her son fidget. "When he was little, I solved the problem by just opening the back door and letting him run outside."

Finn smiled. "She's right," he said. "I need to roam."

"It is beginning to feel a little confining," Richard said. "Soon we'll all be out of this place. It's too bad you didn't bring some flies to tie."

Finn smiled. "Man, what I wouldn't give to be fishing right now," he said. "Outside in the sun, knee deep in a river."

"That even sounds good to me," Elizabeth said. "And I am the least enthusiastic of us three."

"Patience, everyone," Richard said. "That day will come."

Eventually the knock on the door they'd been waiting for arrived and an agent popped his head inside the room. "It's time, Madam President," he said. "The audience is taking its seats."

Elizabeth set her laptop aside and rose from her chair, focusing her gaze on Richard. "Are you coming with me?" she asked.

"Of course," he said. "Finn, you and River stay here. It'll be easier if there are fewer of us to manage. You can watch the speech on the flat screen here in the room."

"Of course," River said. "We'll hold down the fort."

Elizabeth smiled. She liked River and admired her strength. She fervently hoped Finn had finally found someone he could walk into the wilderness with. She also hoped she would live through the night, live long enough to see her son happy.

"I'm ready," Elizabeth said to the group. "Let's get this show on the road."

Finn suppressed a shudder as his parents left the room, the frantic pulse of his blood whooshing in his ears. He leaned back against the wall, trying to get his bearings. This was why he lived like a hermit in Montana. He possessed physical grit and endurance in spades, but it did not extend to emotional fortitude. His belly churned with worry at the possibility that somewhere in the audience lurked an individual with the power to end life as he knew it. He did not want to witness his mother's murder.

"Hey, it's going to be ok," River said, noticing his discomfort. "Your mother is not a fool. She'll follow directions. Security is posted everywhere. They'll be safe."

"And what happens after?" Finn asked. "I thought when we got here that everything would resolve itself. That life would go back to normal. But this is just the beginning of our troubles; it could be weeks or months before he's caught. My mother will not be safe until he's dead. We might not be safe."

River shared Finn's worries and then some, but the soldier inside her told her not to get too bogged down in the what ifs of an unknown future.

"I'm as anxious as you are to put this mess behind us, but we have to try to stay calm and take one moment at a time," she said, pulling out her gun. "I don't want to frighten you, but I need to check my weapon. I want to make sure everything is ready…just in case. OK?"

"It's fine," Finn said, and then a moment later asked, "Do you really think the poem the director showed you belongs to a terrorist?"

River paused in her work, setting the clip of bullets down on the table. "I don't know," she said. "It's not the kind of thing you usually see lying around."

"The director thought it was possible," Finn said. "But my father didn't. You were a soldier. What does your intuition tell you?"

"You don't need intuition to know something bad is going to happen regardless of where the paper came from," she said. "I'm worried, too. I just don't know what we're looking for."

"That makes three of us," a voice from the doorway said.

Finn turned to see a hulking figure standing in the entryway. He was purposefully bald, a pair of aviator glasses tucked in the opening of his black fleece.

"I'm Cooper Smith," he said. "It's nice to finally meet you. Honestly, I've never had so much trouble trying to keep two people alive. Finn, you surprised the hell out of me, finding River like that. The way you two disappeared into thin air, well, you have my respect."

Finn extended his hand. "You helped save our lives regardless," he said. "Thank you."

"It was a team effort," Cooper replied, fixing his cobalt eyes on River. "I'd say your girlfriend had a lot to do with it."

"You'll get no argument from me," Finn said. "I owe her my life."

Cooper nodded, watching River. He walked right up to where she was seated, but she remained focused on her weapon. He knew she wouldn't acknowledge him until she'd finished. He heard the safety snap into place. Only then did she look up as he began to speak.

"You're one hell of a shot," he said. "You blew that drone to pieces before I could flip the switch on the mic."

"That was you?" River asked. "We thought it was a security team looking for us. There was really no way for us to know."

"I understand," Cooper said. "You did the right thing. I'm impressed with you both. Hiking through Wyoming in late winter is not easy."

"It was hardly winter," Finn said. "This is a dry year compared to seasons past. It didn't snow at all while we were hiking."

"I've noticed myself," Cooper said. "Do you think Red's polluting the river has something to do with that?"

Finn laughed. "As evil as Red is, he isn't responsible for global warming. The lack of snow is tied to choices made decades ago, but the rivers and their tributaries not freezing, that is probably his doing. He has a lot to answer for."

"The man thinks he's doing God's work," Cooper said. "That makes him dangerous."

"You know he's coming for us, don't you?" River said. "Red. I don't believe for a second that he doesn't care."

"At the moment, Red doesn't know where you are," Cooper said. "But I agree, if he knew, it would double his pleasure. Right now, though, he's focused on trying to pull off this little *coup* of his. Red needs to demonstrate that he's serious enough to carry through with his threat. He's amassed a great following at his compound."

"Or crazy enough," River said. "This is going to end badly."

"Maybe," Cooper said. "It's definitely going to end badly for Red. The question is how much will he get away with before that happens."

"Did they tell you about the poem found outside the presidential compound?" River asked.

"The director showed it to me," Cooper said, nodding. "He said you'd seen it before, translated it as part of your mission-based studies."

"I did," River said. "It makes no sense to find a copy here."

Cooper sighed and pulled out a chair at the table next to her. "We supposedly neutralized that threat when we created the Territories," he said. "The deportations and identification tags are supposed to make the existence of terrorists impossible. I think someone is trying to mess with us. The question is why."

"This all sounds pretty crazy," Finn said. "Why would anyone plant a poem pretending to be a terrorist?"

"To take advantage of the chaos," River said. "To distract us so we look in the wrong place."

"Are you saying there may be more than one person trying to kill my mother?" Finn asked.

"No," Cooper said. "We're just trying to get a handle on the situation. I'll go check in with the Secret Service and FBI. We've already doubled the security at the doors."

River shook her head. "You're looking in the wrong places," she said grimly. "It's going to be something we're not expecting. In my experience, it's the things you can't see that prove to be the deadliest."

THIRTY FIVE

ELIZABETH AND RICHARD walked into the backstage area of the convention center, sidestepping frantic stagehands as they made last-minute preparations. It was a happy sight, she thought, to be the reason for which something exists or happens. Tonight, she felt as if she had a purpose beyond helping keep people safe. That was, of course, an important job, but this evening's speech was something more significant. It was meant to inspire, to reassure–in short, to demonstrate leadership–tasks she'd longed to have on her plate. Of course, she had, but not like this. Not like tonight, when she would ask the audience to celebrate the country's return to its centuries-old tradition of democracy through elections.

She listened intently as the evening's opening act, a local poet from the University of Colorado, began to speak. An expert on the West, she was reading from a work entitled "The Great Migration."

We go by wagon train, horse and foot across the sage grass
Into the unknown for a better life, the dust of the day upon us
Our future as uncertain as the ever-diminishing outlines of our past

The din of the crowd drowned out most other noises, making conversation difficult. Elizabeth smiled and gently grasped Richard's arm to indicate it was time for her to head towards the stage.

"Wait," he said, leaning in close. "Before you go, I feel like I should..."

Elizabeth felt her stomach drop to the floor when she realized he was about to apologize again, trying to clear his conscience on the remote chance he might not see her again. Just in case she was actually stepping in front of a firing squad.

"Don't," she said.

"I can't let you leave..."

"You have to," she yelled over the noise. "We can go over all of this later. *After the speech.*" The emphasis of course was on after, as in *I will return alive and unscathed,* and she gave him a look of certainty, hoping it would quash his urge to revisit his mistakes.

"At least let me tell you I love you," he said.

"And I you," she said. "Now stop. You'll see. It will be fine."

As the President made her way towards the stage, she caught sight of the director pacing off to one side. She acknowledged his presence, mustering another show-must-go-on smile.

"Madam President, everything is going according to plan," Michael said. "There are sharpshooters in every corner and each one has a hidden backup whose identity is known only to me. If one of them goes down, the other will take his place."

"Let's hope it's not needed," she said. "I would hate to die on national television. It would be too much *deja vu* for the audience."

"That's not going to happen on my watch," he said. "I give you my word."

Elizabeth nodded, squeezing his hand to acknowledge his promise, which she knew he meant with every fiber of his being. But she also knew, despite her bravado with Richard seconds before, that no one could promise her safe passage.

She stepped out on to the stage and into the blinding light, gazing at the thousands of people in the audience, some holding signs with her name on it, others waving American flags. Tears welled in her eyes as the intoxicating nature of adoration and celebrity washed over her. *That's it!* The opiate that so many of her colleagues had desired over the years. It would be amazing, she thought, as her brain snapped back into place, if it didn't include the threat of death lurking in the shadows. Undaunted, she stepped up to the podium and waved to the audience, adjusted the microphone, looked over at the teleprompter, and took a deep breath.

Good evening, my fellow Americans.
It's good to be with you here in Denver, the mile-high city, this evening. I'm excited to join you tonight in what marks my first public address in many, many months.
(PAUSE)
The first time I addressed the nation, I was a newly sworn-in President, reeling like all of you at the senseless violence that had taken place, but determined to be a leader and fill the shoes of my predecessor. In the days that followed, we buried our dead—the leaders of our great nation—with immense sorrow and bitterness at the abrupt and unjust taking of their lives.
(PAUSE)
The next time I spoke to the nation was just after an unimaginable attack against our country, one which unmoored us from our past trajectory as a country and sent us on a journey to mend our broken hearts, while protecting the country from further brutality. The task was made more challenging in that the Executive Branch was forced to act without the partnership and guidance of Congress. Over the course of those first, dark days, we made many difficult choices.
(PAUSE)
There is no joy in leadership that requires you to send people from their homes. There is no joy in leadership that restricts public assembly or discourse. To restrain the liberties of this nation and its people, even temporarily, is such a profound sea change—it felt as if we had landed on the moon, or some other distant planet, and were staring down from the heavens, wondering how we managed to travel so very far, far away from our home. The history books tell us our beloved American hero Neil Armstrong felt that his footsteps on the

moon represented great progress for mankind, but our journey was propelled by grief; extreme measures taken to protect our people from further danger.

(PAUSE)

No president wants to face the nation with timidity in their heart. It is our duty to reassure the nation of our safety and well-being, and yet I know that two years ago I could not offer you such blanket assurances—I could only ask for your patience and faith that we as a nation would one day prevail and restore our equilibrium.

(PAUSE, BREATH)

Since that time, I have been on a journey, speaking to you through statements and messages to the nation. But tonight, I am returning to the stage to provide an accounting of our work on behalf of this great nation. We are undeniably a country of before and after. What we were will never be again. But we can and will evolve as a people, adopting new ideas and customs along the way. Just as our ancestors forged ahead into the great unknown of this once uncharted country to make our mighty nation, so too will we reestablish our sense of destiny. We remain a country with a constitution and a devotion to the rule of law, but undeniably, we also remain ambivalent about what freedom means in an era of unrestrained terror and hatred.

(PAUSE, BREATH)

Creating the Territories was a dramatic act designed to ensure an independent United States; a country free of the encumbrances that create vulnerability. We succeeded in our goals, but not without cost. I speak of course of the refugee cities, where some of our fellow citizens sit in limbo, unable to move on from what was meant as a transitional place. We can and must find permanent homes for the remaining inhabitants of the refugee cities. I have been in touch with the governors of several states who have pledged to work with my administration to see that everyone is placed in a new home in the next six months. The deferral government can

and will use the full extent of its resources to see that this
happens.
(PAUSE)

This kind of massive repatriation will require a significant
investment on the part of the government. As President,
once I declared a State of Emergency, and Congress voted
itself into recess, I became the keeper of our National
Treasury. My executive orders set the stage for every action
we've taken. I want to take this moment to thank the
American people for granting me such latitude, knowing
that it goes against the very grain of our nation's founding
principles. There are certainly some among us who would
think me to be in the most envious of positions: a leader,
sworn in rather than elected, and untethered from day-to-
day oversight. I stand here tonight to tell you that there is
no freedom in being disconnected from our country's
traditions and greatest conventions. I am, as I have been
since the moment I assumed office, humbled by the
responsibility bestowed upon me. There has not been one
second of one day that I have not carried the sorrow and
concerns of this nation upon my heart. It is a burden I
gladly carry, for it is nothing compared to what many of you
have experienced. The question we all ask ourselves is how
do we remap our country? How do we reconnect our human
geography and spirit? As I have traveled across our country,
I have learned that this process can only happen organically
as people begin to feel a sense of safety and purpose.
(PAUSE)

I am happy to report that we are mending as a nation,
returning to our more joyous selves. Day by day, the majority
of us have returned to our routines and rhythms of work and
school, taking comfort in the mundaneness of simple things
like shopping for groceries or seeing a movie. Whitman wrote
about this in his inspirational poem "I Hear America
Singing."

I hear America singing, the varied carols I hear,

Those of mechanics, each one singing his as it should be blithe
and strong,
The carpenter singing his as he measures his plank or beam,
The mason singing his as he makes ready for work, or leaves off
work,
The boatman singing what belongs to him in his boat, the
deckhand singing on the steamboat deck,
The shoemaker singing as he sits on his bench, the hatter
singing as he stands,
The wood-cutter's song, the ploughboy's on his way in the
morning, or at noon intermission or at sundown,
The delicious singing of the mother, or of the young wife at
work, or of the girl sewing or washing,
Each singing what belongs to him or her and to none else,
The day what belongs to the day—at night the party of young
fellows, robust, friendly,
Singing with open mouths their strong melodious songs.
**There is no greater sight, no more profound comfort for a
President than to witness the people of this great nation able
to return to the lives unhurried and unscathed.**
(PAUSE)
**Our regained stability brings about the next and most
profound step in our national recovery: the reestablishment of
Congress through national elections. We are, after all, a
country meant to be governed by our peers, representatives
from our own cities and towns, who know us in our daily
lives. Many of you probably know I was once that person,
having been elected to Congress to represent parts of
Wyoming for many years before becoming Secretary of State.
I stand here tonight to urge all of you to participate in the
upcoming elections. I know only too well how toxic the
politics of our country can be, but we cannot shy away from
our obligation to participate in our democracy. It's time for a
new generation of lawmakers to grapple with the issues we
must face as a nation—immigration, national security, energy
independence, and privacy. These are important debates that**

we have tabled during this time of healing and reconciliation, but we cannot put off facing them forever. In the moments of accelerated danger, we unraveled some very old traditions— primarily the assurance that our shores were open and available to everyone. We have instituted national identification programs and other forms of domestic security that should be reexamined from time to time. That is the purpose of Democracy—to challenge our leaders and our laws and put them under harsh scrutiny. Honest debate is the marrow of our country's bones. We must broach difficult topics and speak of uncomfortable things in order to make good laws and policy.

(PAUSE)

Despite all that has happened, the United States remains a powerful idea, a powerful *place*. Our freedoms—such as they are—remain the envy of many and yes, sadly, the rallying cry for a few rogue nations and their followers. But our destiny as a nation has *never* been tied to the opinions of other countries or governments. Indeed, we have always forged our own path and must do so again. Be assured that our country is well prepared to withstand a threat from its enemies. Our military is well-funded and thoroughly prepared to protect us from any threat, foreign or domestic. We have learned from those dark days and stand ready to face any foe. I say to you what President John F. Kennedy said to the public in 1961 as a part of his inaugural address:

"Let the word go forth from this time and place, to friend and foe alike, that the torch has been passed to a new generation of Americans, born in this century, tempered by war, disciplined by a hard and bitter peace, proud of our ancient heritage...Let every nation know, whether it wishes us well or ill, that we shall pay any price, bear any burden, meet any hardship, support any friend, oppose any foe to assure the survival and the success of liberty."

I stand here tonight to assure you that we have survived with our liberty and sense of justice intact. I have nothing but the

utmost confidence in our nation and its people. We have come
so very far from those dark days two years ago. Our future
looks bright, and it will only get better as we commit to
participating in the upcoming elections and restoring our
country's democratic traditions. That will be the final step in
restoring our nation to its full strength. I know I can count on
you to help us reestablish one of our country's most sacred
traditions.
Thank you again for coming tonight to hear me speak.
May God bless you, and may God Bless America.
Good night!

Elizabeth took a step back from the podium, stunned by the roar of
the crowd. The audience was on its feet, clapping and cheering as she
smiled and waved. She looked over at Richard who was standing just
far enough backstage to stay hidden from the audience. He was smiling, his eyes damp. "B-R-A-V-O," he mouthed to her as the crowd
continued to cheer. She turned back to face her audience, waving one
last time before walking off stage, her body vibrating with victory.
She'd done it: sent out a rallying cry, and somehow managed to
survive the evening without being shot. It was turning out to be a good
night.

THIRTY SIX

AN HOUR LATER, after the arena had been emptied of people, the Secret Service loaded Elizabeth into a waiting car. The moment her door shut, an agent whispered something into his wrist monitor, patted the roof of the SUV, and it sped away. Cooper and Richard followed in a second vehicle, leaving River and Finn standing at the curb like tourists lined up at an amusement park, waiting patiently to board the next roller coaster car.

The ride back to the train was noticeably quiet, Finn showing little interest in conversation.

"Your mom made a great speech," River said, trying to break the silence.

"It was good," he offered, but said little else.

"I spoke to some of the agents. They said there were no problems tonight," River said, in another attempt to engage Finn.

"We got lucky," he said, leaning back and closing his eyes.

Even in the dim light, River could make out his shrinking countenance and rigid jaw line. She listened to his long deep breaths, and for a moment was back in Syria with her unit after they'd returned to base from a major incident. Managed emotional retreat was to be expected, she thought to herself, after the stressful night they'd just faced.

River worried there was more behind Finn's silence than exhaustion. Perhaps she'd been too candid with Cooper in front of him. She'd all but said his mother was a dead woman, and in the process, might have scared him away. In retrospect, cleaning her gun had probably been a mistake. Not many normal, well-adjusted men would be interested in a lover who polished her firearm and compared notes with an ex-marine about Muslim martyr poetry and murderous conspiracies. She was also not the type to tremble in Finn's arms and ask him what *he* thought they should do next. She'd been on her own too long to do that. Maybe one day, but in that moment, she was the one with the better grasp of the situation, not him.

River intended to bite her tongue when they got back to their rooms. Feeling Finn's discomfort coming off his body in waves, she had no appetite to add more insult to injury. Somehow though, her empathy curdled into anger. As soon as they cleared the doors, the words come tumbling out of her mouth.

"What is your deal?" she asked. "You haven't said a word since we left the stadium. Is this your way of brushing me off now that you've got what you wanted?"

Finn might as well have been sitting in Montana, his body felt so disconnected from time and space. He couldn't stop thinking about his mom on the stage and the thousands of people, all of them potential killers in the audience. He realized his mother was surrounded by danger all the time, and not the random garden-variety hazards that normally befell parents, like car crashes and food poisoning. It was funny, but he'd never worried about her safety in all the years she was a congresswoman. Even when she was Secretary of State and flying from one war zone to another, the risk seemed minimal. He supposed it was because she wasn't being hunted like a wild animal the way she was now.

"What?" he asked, only half aware of the conversation.

"Great," she said. "Now you're not even listening to me."

"River," Finn said. "Please don't do this. I've had a hard night."

"I don't blame you," River said. "I mean now that you've got your mom and dad back, you can go off and find some debutant to marry and keep the family blood lines intact."

"How can you even think something like that?" Finn asked. "I've never asked you to be anyone but who you are. The fact that I'm being quiet has nothing to do with wanting to end things."

"Then why the silent treatment?" River asked.

Finn froze. He wasn't going to be able to tell her. "It's complicated," he said. "I just need some time."

They say opposites attract, but River didn't think that old chestnut bore out any real results. She and Finn were from two different worlds, one of privilege and one of deprivation and hard truths. They'd had a great adventure and a few glorious nights together, but that was all about to come to a screeching halt. Truth be told, she'd expected it to be a doomed romance from the start, which meant that parting after this mess was resolved would be an easy task. She would go home and pick up the pieces of her life. Ava would have her mother back, and River would get a second chance at living, whatever the hell that meant. She was a horrible liar, especially to herself, but she didn't want to think about how her inclination for unvarnished honesty had turned Finn against her. He was punishing the messenger, and it hurt like hell.

"No problem," River said. "Take all the time you need."

Finn watched River storm out of the room. Working in the wilderness, he'd often been able to avoid difficult situations. Distance and desolation kept him from having to face facts. Tonight though, the truth was inescapable. Finn had come to understand the gravity of it all…the potential for war, death, and destruction. Everything he loved in the world was nearby on the train and he had not the slightest clue how to protect any of it. He wasn't used to being a helpless bystander. There wasn't a situation in the wild he didn't feel ready to conquer, but this was not a class five rapid or a treacherous trail in the wilderness. He knew he couldn't solve this problem through grit and determination. There was a madman trying to kill his mother and irreparably harm the country. Finn was no soldier. He was no killer. He had nothing to offer in this time of crisis except an ability to tie a very good knot or start a fire on a rocky precipice.

And then there was River: brave, smart, and completely equipped for whatever might happen next. It was humbling to watch her with Cooper and see how well she could read the situation. It seemed utterly improbable that she could love a man like him, someone with so little to offer in a moment of crisis. He imagined that after tonight, she would remember him with pity. Remember his fear and ignorance, his inability to see the bigger picture like she and Cooper did. He was ashamed. After a lifetime of avoidance, reality had snuck up on him in a big way. So, he remained mute, a legion of words at his command, but not a damn clue what to say.

Later, as he lay next to River in bed, their bodies rigid with anxiety and anger, he shut his eyes against the night, worried that somehow he had lost his way just as his father had found his way back.

THIRTY SEVEN

THE FIRST THOUGHT that popped into Elizabeth's head as she woke the next morning, one eye open to the sun's rays, was *I'm still alive*. The second thought arrived as a question: *but for how long?* Whatever the answer, she realized, it was a topic best contemplated out of bed. She dressed quietly, leaving Richard sound asleep, and figured the others were also still slumbering, the strain of the last forty-eight hours finally catching up.

Walking three train cars down from her sleeping quarters, she shuffled into the dining compartment, hoping for a cup of black coffee and something warm, preferably a chocolate croissant from the White House pastry chef, but found no refreshments or serving staff when she arrived. Oddly, the train had not yet pulled out for their return to Washington. They must have been taking on supplies, and that was why the staff was absent.

She sat down, content to pass the time gazing out at the snow-dusted Front Range framed by the windows. Years before, she and Richard had visited Boulder with Finn to attend a family friend's graduation from the University of Colorado. They'd walked Pearl Street, the town's charming historic district, and had eaten dinner at one of the better restaurants. Finn had briefly teased that he was forgoing Yale to become a Buff. There were certainly worse things, Richard had joked in mock horror, and then they'd strolled through a few of the used bookstores nearby.

Elizabeth exhaled as she remembered, suddenly wistful for that happy-go-lucky family. She hoped those people would return one day, that they would once again be able to wander and allow desire to be their guide. Wouldn't it be wonderful to live life without the worries of the world on your shoulders, to enjoy the simple pleasure of good food or an evening stroll? The idea was so engrossing that Elizabeth did not hear Red speaking to her until he was looming over her on the couch.

"Are you listening to me?" he asked.

She was listening from that moment forward. Red had not come alone. Standing awkwardly next to him was a sullen-looking young man of eighteen or so, his face riddled with acne. A thin sheen of perspiration glistened off his skin. Scrawny and malnourished, he reeked of abject poverty and misery. He wore a military uniform, but its insignia was not from any branch of the military she was familiar with. Every hair on her body stood on end, and yet her mother's heart immediately went out to him, thinking how difficult it must be, his face so horribly disfigured. There had probably been no prom or dates in high school. Under other circumstances she might have even wondered how he replaced those experiences. What amusements he'd found to fill his evenings when others had been out at the movies, attending parties, or fastening corsages to eager, adolescent wrists. But the answer seemed obvious, given the explosive vest he wore, transformed into a human bomb brought to kill her and everyone in close proximity.

"This is Joshua," Red said. "He's just one of the many who answered my call for patriots. I told you the country wouldn't stand for your idleness."

Elizabeth took a few precious seconds to get steady, trying to tamp down the knot of fear in her belly. Better to be angry than hysterical. "How typical," she said. "You've recruited a young boy to do your dirty work. You're no different than the people you purport to want to stop."

"Those people are savages," Red said. "Joshua is a God-fearing Christian. He comes to me willingly to ensure our country's liberty. When he detonates his explosives, however, everyone will think that that there has been another terrorist attack. The poem I left for the FBI will help confirm their suspicions. I will then be justified in insisting on more Territories, and my army will ensure the last remnants of your weak government don't stand in the way."

"I see," Elizabeth said, thinking of ways to draw out the conversation, on the off-chance her security detail might discover her predicament. "Is the uniform your handiwork?"

Red smiled. He'd created a special feature for the right sleeve: a blue and white variation of the Rebellious Stripes of 1767, a nice tribute to the Sons of Liberty. He was engaged in the same kind of conflict: to remain a free and independent nation.

"Do you like it?" he asked. "There are legions of my soldiers standing by wearing them. One word from me, their leader, and it will begin."

Red paused as if an important memory had interrupted his thoughts, a faraway look in his eyes. For a moment he seemed to be overtaken with some kind of emotion, regret or sorrow perhaps, and then like a shadow, it passed.

"It didn't have to be this way, Elizabeth," he said. "All you had to do was agree to my terms. After everything I did to help you, I expected your loyalty."

Elizabeth rose from the couch. "You're asking for a kind of loyalty that requires betraying everyone else in return," she said. "You're asking for loyalty that is blind to the rule of law. I'm the President of the United States. I owe my loyalty to this country, to its constitution. You...you pretend to fight for liberty, but what you're doing is seditious. You're a tyrant masquerading as a patriot. This has nothing to do with making our country better."

"You seem a little emotional, Elizabeth. Are you on your period?" Red asked. "It doesn't matter, *forget I asked*. The fact is that I am better equipped to do this job than you are. As a man of business and industry, I have the skills and experience that you lack. The people want a President who is capable of bold moves and can anticipate problems and act. After the first battles are over and we have obtained the surrender of your forces, people will see. It's going to be beautiful. The citizens of this nation will see me as an angel of mercy who has come to protect them from a savage government that cared nothing for their way of life. And you, you will be a memory in a textbook. The sad, lonely woman who was a disaster as President, and died at the hands of a terrorist you failed to stop."

Since the moment of her swearing in on the tarmac, Elizabeth understood that she might die. That was the trajectory of elected officials in a post-Caliphate world, and she had tacitly agreed to the terms, mostly because there had been no alternative, but also because she believed in her country. She believed in the idea that one person could make a difference, and more importantly that if you *knew* that you could do something, then you had to try even in the face of great risk. That all had been theory, though. Now the moment of truth had arrived. Somehow, despite all that had happened, she was going to be killed by a zealot and his disciple, just like her colleagues before her. Gun in hand, bomb on board, what did it matter if they spoke Arabic or English? The absurdity of the situation filled her with rage: that she was about to be murdered by a vain maniac with no capacity to understand what he was about to unleash.

She thought of the southern states when they seceded on the eve of Lincoln's Inauguration. Did they really understand the kind of death they were dooming their men and boys to? Six hundred and twenty thousand American souls, when all was said and done, most of the Southerners' hours and days spent walking the land, hungry and shoeless, miles from all that they loved and knew. She knew Red hadn't thought for one moment about the citizens of Pennsylvania, or the soldiers who would be forced to defend the state and the country. He had no care for the families torn apart, the lives irreparably damaged by his hubris. She also knew having a discussion with Red, an impulsive man with no moral compass, was fruitless. Standing there, shaking with fury, she remembered Red's accomplice and wondered whether he, a child not yet worn down by cynicism, could be reasoned with.

"Joshua," Elizabeth said. "Listen to me. You don't have to do this. I

have a son. He's a few years older than you, but I think you two probably have a great deal in common."

"Don't listen to her," Red said. "You and her son are as much alike
as a porcupine and a snail."

"That's not true," Elizabeth said, catching the boy's eye. "Growing
up, my son Finn was painfully shy. He had trouble making friends. He
liked being alone, usually outside in the woods where he could disappear. I used to worry about him. I bet your mom worries, too."

Joshua Brown, the younger of two sons, hailed from central
Kentucky. His mother, a home health aide, had been raising the boys
alone since their father died. A coal miner like his father before him,
Michael Brown passed away after a very slow and painful bout with
lung cancer. Before his dad got sick and died, they lived like most of
the families Josh knew. There might not have been a lot of extras, but
there was enough for new jeans and sneakers, pizza and movies on the
weekends, and even a trip now and then to the lake.

Afterwards, they lived with a kind of scarcity he'd never known
before. His mother worked around the clock to keep a roof over their
heads and as a result they didn't see much of one another. That they all
loved each other was a given, but since his father's passing, life
seemed to have them trapped at near drowning. Joshua decided for
that reason to keep his grief and anger to himself. His problems were
no worse than his brother's or his mother's. He had no right to ask for
anything more than they did, no matter how much he missed his
father, no matter how much his heart was broken.

He let all of his words slip away, thinking if you couldn't say what
you really felt, it was better to say nothing. He became the weird kid,
the quiet one everybody avoided. Once his face began to break out,
there was no end to his misery; someone bigger and stronger lurking
in the halls ready and willing to torment him. He began to fade, first
from school and then from his old life all together. He turned his attention and time to being online, looking for a way to belong to something. Eventually he found what he was searching for in the chat
rooms and forums for other boys and men like him. All the truths he'd
been searching for were there. Overlooked for so long, it was a revela-
tion to find an audience that seemed to know him, understand all of

the indignities he'd suffered. They welcomed Joshua with open arms, never questioning his grievances.

When the call came for volunteers to fight in the rebellion, he'd been only too happy to join. There was no life to leave behind, only a bright future as a member of an elite few. Back at the base, when he tried on his uniform, he felt special, a part of a momentous time in history. But now, standing inside the train car, his body wet with perspiration, the weight of the explosives pulling on him, he felt frightened. Why had he been chosen for this assignment, instead of fighting at the front, which is what he signed up for? He suddenly felt small, once again the victim of a universe hell-bent on his destruction through a series of heartbreaks and humiliations, each one more painful than the previous one.

The President of the United States didn't seem anything like the person he'd been told about. Endless blog posts and broadcasts made her seem like a hapless idiot, but she didn't behave like one. And when she spoke directly to him, it was as if a horrible spell had been broken. He knew she was telling him the truth. Joshua issued a slight nod at her question, his eyes revealing the depths of his amazement that a total stranger, the President no less, could read him so clearly. Then he looked at Red, his face contorted and crimson with anger, and shut down again, looking straight at the wall ahead.

"It's not too late," Elizabeth pleaded, hoping to capture Joshua's attention again. "You can change your mind. I promise no harm will come to you."

Red slapped Elizabeth across the face with enough force to split her lip. "Shut up," he said, pulling a gun from a holster on his hip and pointing it at her head. "I've had enough of you. You know you would *never* have made the cut in a normal election. Voters don't like wimps. They want strong leaders who are not afraid to make tough decisions, like me."

Joshua took a step away from Red, repulsed at the sight of the blood dripping from the President's face.

"Oh, no," Red said, grabbing the boy by the arm. "You are my chosen one, the golden boy who will start the revolution. You were sent to me. This is your destiny."

"You are out of your mind," Elizabeth said, using her sleeve to wipe her mouth, the pain from his blow ringing in her ears. "The people of this country have already sacrificed so much. This boy left his family to come be here with you. What have you done? You won a contract to evict people from their homes to drill oil. That was something you were already good at."

"I gave you the idea to start the Territories," Red said. "Without me you'd be nothing. I made your presidency. I made you a success."

Elizabeth ran her tongue over her lip where a welt had started to form. Red's bravado and lack of self-awareness had always been revolting, but now, as the minutes of her life ticked away, indignation surged through her. The idea that she might die in his company was too much to bear.

"My God, you are truly a soulless bastard," she said. "What do you know about leadership or sacrifice? All you can think of is yourself. I'll tell you what *I know*: this country has no patience for a crybaby. And make no mistake, that is what you are: an insecure man, a child desperate for attention by any means necessary. But you can't actually lead a country with your imbecilic ideas. You can't turn people against each other and achieve greatness."

"Couldn't agree more Madam President!" Cooper said.

He'd been lurking outside, waiting for the right time to enter. He didn't want to spook Red into shooting Elizabeth.

"I've just come from conducting a perimeter check," Cooper said. "Red's mercenaries immobilized the overnight security team and some of the train's staff."

"Tranquilized, if you must know," Red replied. "I didn't want the murder of so many secret service and FBI agents on my hands. *Shoot to kill* would be the standing order every time we have a skirmish if I did that."

Cooper cocked his head to one side. "Skirmish? You're here to kill the President and overthrow the government," he said, raising his gun until it was level with Red's. "I think you should expect 'shoot to kill' to be the order of the day where you're concerned *in perpetuity*. You and this terrorist you've groomed should expect no mercy."

"What gives you the right to judge us?" Red asked. "You're a coward who abandoned his post. You should do us all a favor and turn your gun on yourself. Spare me the trouble of putting you down. As you've mentioned, I've got Russian mercenaries waiting outside. Do you *really* think you can get a shot off before I kill the President? Because you've only got seconds before one of my men takes you out. You picked the wrong side, Cooper. You're going to end up a big fat loser in all of this."

"I don't think so," Cooper said, steel in his voice. "As of five minutes ago, your men were relieved of their posts. We did not use tranquilizers, the price you pay for treason. We're in the process of conducting visual searches car-to-car for any stragglers, but your little coup party has been rounded up."

Cooper turned to face Joshua, whose eyes were as wide as saucers. "The President is right, son," he said. "You don't have to go through with this. Red is about to be arrested."

Undaunted, Red reached out with his free hand and grabbed hold of Joshua. "No, no, no," he said. "We're not quitters. We're going to finish what we started."

Joshua was terribly confused, but also suddenly very clear about what needed to be done. He thought about his father, and what a good man he'd been. How he would have wanted Joshua to do the right thing, even if he started out with bad intentions. He thought about his mother and how she would weep when she heard the story of what happened, wondering why her son would want to kill the President of the United States. In that moment, with Red's fingers crushing his arm, he understood how he could end his suffering and make things right.

Cooper attributed his longevity to a healthy sixth sense for impending danger. It took him only seconds to see the boy had changed his mind about his designated target—Red's sparkling personality once again winning the day. Cooper's task at the moment was to save the President by putting some distance between her and the ensuing explosion. The young boy, mercifully, seemed to read his mind. With all his might, Joshua pulled free of Red, pivoted, and turned back towards the oil tycoon, putting both arms out in front of him. With a great push, he sent the two of them tumbling backwards across the train compartment. Red's face was a mask of shock and indignation, his gun sent flying by the force of the unexpected shove. Cooper grabbed the President and pulled her towards one of the car's exits. The force of the blast knocked them off their feet before they could escape, flaming debris dancing around their heads as they hit the floor.

THIRTY EIGHT

ELIZABETH OPENED HER EYES MOMENTARILY, but had to close them because of the smoke. Sounds were coming through, partially garbled. She thought she heard shouting, maybe even the whine of a fire engine, but couldn't be sure. Aware of something heavy pressing on her legs, she pushed herself up in the darkness. She leaned forward and used her fingers to cautiously feel what was there. She was horrified to make out what felt like an arm or shoulder, and then she remembered. *Cooper!* He'd tried to shield her from the blast.

Unable to move, and unsure if she'd be rescued, Elizabeth began to make peace with the situation. She'd abandoned religion after witnessing the unrestrained carnage at the shopping mall. The violence that day ripped her faith from her. She would not become a hypocrite now by asking for God's mercy at the eleventh hour. She thanked the universe for reuniting her with her son and husband. She was going to die with her family nearby, and with her husband knowing that she loved him. And she knew with *certainty* that he loved her. That was more than many people had at the end. It would have to be enough.

Her mind returned to the moment when she first saw Richard standing at the rear doors of the Convention Center. At the sight of him, her body had begun to quiver like a sixteen-year-old in the back seat of a car at midnight. The moment felt almost as fraught, those seconds between two people unsure how or if they will fit together. She'd plunged in to embrace him. Richard had leaned in, close enough for only her to hear, saying "There are no words that can repair what I have done Lizzie, but poor idiot that I am, I want to come home to my wife whom I love. Can you forgive me?" She did, of course.

The Richard she'd woken up next to the morning after their long separation was older, but by more than the two years they'd been apart. Experience had aged him, like a grape in a barrel, all of his sharpness erased. She knew the situation well, presidential years being like dog years, the wear and tear the equivalent of many lifetimes. One year felt like a decade, especially to someone sleeping four hours a night. That first night, Richard told her stories of his visits to the refugee cities, and of his great shame at walking out. It was an honest conversation, and although she did not apologize for creating the Territories, she did express her desire to try to make things right.

It occurred to her, as she watched the flames licking at her heels, that she might not be able to keep her promise. She also thought about her speech the night before, hoping it would be a catalyst for change, and that there would be elections. And, if there was any cosmic justice, that Red was dead inside the flaming mess before her, his poisonous plans along with him. When she reviewed the facts, the odds seemed good for a favorable outcome, better than she could have hoped for given the people she was dealing with. She let out a breath and lay back down, preparing for what would come next.

RIVER WAS LYING in bed sulking when she heard the explosion. Recognizing the sound, she threw off the covers and rummaged around the room for clothing, a routine she'd performed a half dozen of times before in the Army, when a suicide bomber attacked their compound.

"What is it?" Finn asked, half awake and confused.

"Bomb! You need to get up and find your dad," she said. "Then find Cooper and call the police and FBI."

River heard Finn asking "Where are you going?" but it was too late, she was already out the door, gun in hand. As soon as she got outside, River could see one of the railcars partially engulfed in flames. Guards were moving in all directions, speaking into their radios to try to get a handle on what had happened. The chaos made it easy for her to run towards the train car without being intercepted. She bounded inside, nearly tripping over the President and Cooper. River knelt down to look for a pulse. The President opened her eyes as soon as River grabbed her wrist.

"I should've known you'd be the first one in," Elizabeth said hoarsely.

"Shhh," River said, gingerly checking the President for injuries. "Can you move? I don't want to risk staying in here with the fire."

Elizabeth nodded. "I'm OK," she said, pointing to the body slumped over her legs. "Cooper saved me."

"He's next," River said as she carefully moved Cooper off the President's legs. "Let's get you out of here." She took Elizabeth's hand and picked her up in a fireman's carry. As she emerged from the car, two Secret Service agents were waiting, their guns drawn. "Hold your fire," she yelled. "This is the President. She's alive but needs medical attention. We've got one more inside."

The agents lowered their weapons and allowed River to place Elizabeth on the ground. She laid her down gently, relinquishing her care to them as she ran back inside. Cooper was sitting up when she returned, dazed but coming to his senses. It was then that she noticed the legs of his pants were ragged and charred, the skin below an angry mess.

"Did you get her out?" he yelled.

"Yes sir," she said. "You're next."

"Negative," he said. "I need you to conduct a search and check for other survivors. There was a bomber, a young man, and Red is in here, too."

River raised her eyebrows, but said nothing. Scanning the room, she noticed a large blast hole in the floor at the far end of the car, the scorched gravel and twisted rails below easily visible. Flames were still active in places, making it difficult to conduct a thorough search. She caught sight of a fire extinguisher bolted to the wall, and thinking she could use it to knock down the fire, started towards it, stopping midway when something hit her foot. She looked down to see an arm sticking out of the debris. Bile rose up in her throat as she knelt to get a closer look, remembering too well the gruesomeness of the injuries she'd witnessed in Syria.

She was a hair's breadth away when the battered remains of a man's hand sprung up and grabbed the hand she was using to hold her gun. The ferocity of Red's grip surprised her, his eyes wild with pain, as he rose up like some macabre marionette, his grasp never wavering. She was eye to eye with him, trying not to look at the gaping hole where the lower part of his mouth had been. Wordlessly, Red tried to pull her gun to his own head. She resisted, using all of her strength to keep her arm and the gun low and down at her side. Red was undeterred, fighting with everything he had left to take himself out of this world on his own terms.

The sight of him should have been terrifying; instead, it made her angry. The privileged CEO who'd tried to hunt her down like a dog and kill Finn to protect his empire had no stomach for suffering. He wanted a quick end to his pain; a kindness she knew he would not ever have extended to them. It was also a benevolence life had not extended to her since her father died.

"No," River said, shaking her head. Standing in the wreckage, all the rage she'd been holding onto came rushing forth, hot tears forming at the corners of her eyes as she struggled against her better self to deprive him of the peace he sought. "No," she said again, her arm beginning to shudder from the strain of holding him back. She was about to ask why he deserved any mercy after the things he'd done when she felt a hand on her shoulder.

"I'll do it," Cooper said, standing unsteadily behind her, his face contorted with pain. "Go outside and leave this to me."

River nodded. At the sight of Cooper, Red let go of her hand, allowing her to turn and run for the exit. She did not look back, even when she heard the shot.

THIRTY NINE

COOPER RAISED the back of his hospital bed, pressing the button until his body was upright enough to read comfortably. Damn his legs hurt. He would walk again, but the new skin on his shins would need an extra dose of sunscreen from here on out. He wasn't complaining. The suicide vest the boy had been wearing hadn't fully detonated. If it had, the whole train car would have been incinerated, and there wouldn't have been enough of them left to fill a Dixie Cup. He liked to think it was fate returning a favor for his good deeds, but deep down he knew it was just dumb luck that saved his life.

CEO OF UNIVERSAL INDUSTRIES
DIES IN FIERY CAR CRASH

By Frank Smith, Associated Press
(Houston, TX) -- Redmond Pierce, President and Chief Executive Officer of Universal Industries, the company responsible for managing the United States Energy Territories in conjunction with the US Department of Energy, has died in a car crash near his home, a spokesman for the company said.
Local authorities, who have not released the time or date of his death, cautioned that the accident remains under investigation,

but did confirm that Pierce was behind the wheel when his car hit a tree at high speed and burst into flames, killing him instantly.

Although a national figure, recognized by President of the United States Elizabeth Cunningham for his role in helping establish the Territories, his family has said there will be no public memorial service. A private ceremony is expected in the next few days, but no further information was available at press time.

Cooper set the tablet he'd been reading from on his lap. *This is the way the world ends. Not with a bang, but a whimper,* he reflected, his legs beginning to itch. It seemed incredible to him that after everything, Red should die anonymously, denied both a hero's funeral and a traitor's shame.

"Are you reading about Red?" Elizabeth asked, walking into his room.

"Madam President," Cooper said, looking up as she entered. "I would get up but...."

"That's quite alright."

"It was a smart move," Cooper said, pointing to his iPad. "But no one will ever know what he tried to do."

Elizabeth pulled one of the room's armchairs up to the side of the bed. "It's better that way," she said. "Martyrs are like dry grass and gasoline. One spark of foolish hope on those right-wing radio stations could reignite his rebellion. We did the American people a favor killing Red off in a car accident."

"What about the explosion?"

Elizabeth smiled. "It seems there was a freak propane explosion at the Denver rail yard that damaged a few cars, but no one was injured."

"You've been busy," he said.

"I'm not one for cover-ups and conspiracies, but this was a good use of the government's resources."

"What about the boy?" Cooper asked.

Elizabeth had called Joshua's mother to offer her condolences parent to parent. Joshua had been brave, she told her. His quick thinking had saved lives. Elizabeth could tell by the whoosh of breath over the line as his mother exhaled that she had done the right thing. Although she could never tell anyone, at least the woman would know the truth, although either way his death was senseless.

As for Joshua, Elizabeth hoped that in the last few fleeting moments–and maybe for the first time in his short life–he felt the sense of purpose and usefulness he craved so desperately. It pained her that she was only able to try to deliver such sought-after solace at the end of the boy's life. If only she could repair the broken souls of the people in this country, Elizabeth thought...now that would be something.

"He was killed in a car crash in Denver," Elizabeth said. "We asked the local police to tell the press he'd been in town to look at junior colleges."

"That about ties up all the loose ends," Cooper said.

"I've left a few out there to fix later," she said.

"Hopefully it includes something to keep me busy," Cooper said.

"You can be certain of that," she said. "I didn't come here to talk about work, though. I came here to thank you for saving my life. My injuries were minor thanks to your selflessness. We both know your leg wounds were meant for me."

"You're welcome," Cooper said. "It's not often the President of the United States comes to visit an average Joe like me. And, if we're being honest, I've always wanted to stay in a private room at Walter Reed. I'd like to thank you and the government for the generosity. If I may ask, where's the rest of your security detail?"

"Outside in the hallway," she said. "I told them I wanted to speak with you privately. I appreciate your humor, but all joking aside, if it weren't for you this could have turned out very differently. In addition to saving me, you protected Finn, and helped him and River escape."

"Well, when you describe it like that it does sound important. The doctors tell me I'm healing nicely," Cooper said, pointing at his shins. "Before you know it, I'll be ready to go back to work and get the Territories straightened out for you."

"All in good time," she said. "The job is yours when you're ready. The FBI forensics team is examining what's left of the explosives for some kind of marker, a way to trace it back to the maker. The national security team thinks the supplies will end up being Russian or belonging to one of their satellites, since the materials are restricted in this country."

"It'll be like looking for a needle in a haystack," Cooper said. "But it will also be harder for them to try to interfere in our affairs again."

"I don't know about that," Elizabeth said. "The Russians love disruption. They resent our reputation for infallibility. What I'm still trying to process is Red. How do we explain his actions? He managed to recruit an army to turn against their own country. We're fortunate that his efforts were not discovered. It would be hugely destabilizing, the idea that these right-wing websites can actually help ignite a violent insurrection. These people know nothing about how to govern."

"You're overthinking this," Cooper said. "There was no plan. Red just wanted more Territories and he didn't care who got in the way. He had no idea what he was going to do after he collapsed the government. I'm certain of it. But he also probably believed that whatever happened, he'd handle it," Cooper said. "It's all a game. The responsibility of actual governing is too boring a subject for men like Red."

"My only regret is that I can't prosecute some of the people who helped him," Elizabeth said. "But that would only create more conspiracy stories and animosity and give them the attention they crave."

"I have a feeling there will be other opportunities," Cooper said, his eyelids beginning to grow heavy. "And River? What happened to her after I sent her out of the train car? In the chaos I didn't see her again. Did she tell you about Red? He tried to grab her gun. I found them in a struggle. She did not seem inclined help him end things. My god she is a tough one. I relieved her of the burden before she had to decide."

"Do you blame her?" Elizabeth asked.

"No," he said, his eyelids lowering. "But mercy isn't something we do for them. It's something we do for ourselves."

"You know, for an ex-soldier, you're a deep guy," the President said, watching Cooper fall asleep, his chest rising and falling in a gentle rhythm. "Sleep well. I wish you and I both sweet dreams from here on out."

FORTY

After a marathon Cabinet meeting, Elizabeth climbed the stairs to the White House guest quarters, coming upon Richard and Finn just as dinner was being served.

"You're timing is impeccable," Richard said, rising from his chair. "Sit down and tell us about your day."

Elizabeth sighed. "Long," she said. "It will take some time to recover from Red's mess. Luckily, the public knows nothing of how close we came to open warfare between our own people."

On her call list that morning had been a long overdue discussion with the Russian ambassador, who was "shocked and dismayed" to learn that "unknown rogue agents" had been operating inside the United States. He was only too happy to remove the few survivors and what remained of their hardware, thereby avoiding an international incident.

"What's going to happen to Red's compound?" Richard asked.

"Destroyed. We placed stories in the papers claiming a major industrial accident," she said. "All of the soldiers under Red's command have scattered to the wind on the news that he's dead."

There was more to tell, but Elizabeth doubted she had the energy to relay everything. Scientists, finally able to review Finn's research, were advising the government to amend the policies regarding the Energy

Territories. Elizabeth had already requested new Executive Orders be drawn up that required monitoring all lakes and streams and gave the government the authority to shut down operations as necessary. She was well aware that limited government was a central tenant of the American compact, but the Territories had proven to be an exercise in the *absence* of government, or worse the *abdication* of government. At the time, allowing Universal Industries wide latitude had seemed appropriate, but in hindsight, it was too much independence. She took comfort in the fact that she could fix her mistakes; it was something few Presidents were able to do.

It wasn't the only alteration to the Territories she'd made. With her aides, Elizabeth had also reconfigured Wyoming, restoring half of the state to its normal order. Visitors would once again be allowed inside Yellowstone and the Grand Tetons. And the government would pay for any previous residents to return if they chose to. Since Universal hadn't been drilling on the western side of the state, production numbers would remain level. If the country required more Territories, a list of states with reserves and smaller populations had been identified. In the coming days, residents of those states would be notified that the request to evacuate was possible. Future decisions would be made publicly, with more input. It was infinitely messier, Elizabeth realized, but the benefits were immeasurable. She was also planning to authorize additional cash payments for the refugees to help them finally move out of the cities and relocate, as she'd promised in her speech.

"The movers think they can have our stuff back at the house in Wyoming in about three weeks," Richard said, pulling Elizabeth out of her thoughts. "I'll go back and oversee the unpacking. Maybe you can join me?"

"I'll be there," she said. "And your position at Yale? Are they reinstating you?"

"Baby steps," Richard said. "One class in the fall and a few of my old department head duties to get started."

Despite her fatigue, a wave of contentment washed over Elizabeth. Things were returning to normal. Except for her son, who had remained silent since she'd come in, his head down as he picked at his meal. She looked over at Richard. He shrugged his shoulders, as if to say *he's been that way for days*. Being the mother of a recluse, she'd had little experience over the years with serious girlfriends, but she nevertheless knew the signs of heartbreak looking at her unshaven, sulking son. Finn hadn't seen River since the explosion. She'd arranged for River's immediate private transport back to Idaho for debriefing. At the time, Elizabeth had tried to ask River about Finn, but got no response.

"Finn," Elizabeth said. "Now that the Territories are back in responsible hands, what are your plans?"

"I'm thinking of going up to the River of No Return Wilderness in Idaho for a few weeks," he said, picking at a few stray pasta noodles. "After that I'm not sure. I may ask for a transfer out of Montana."

"You do realize you just said *River of No Return*," Richard said. "At least choose a place that doesn't have her name in it. Or better yet, why don't you call her and find out what's happening? You're both grown adults. This not speaking to one another is ridiculous."

Elizabeth almost choked on her food. "Yes, Richard, you're so right," she said. "That kind of silence is foolish for two people who love one another."

"I'm a glass house, I *know*," Richard said. "But even *I* am capable of learning from my mistakes. Finn, why haven't you tried to reach her?"

Their only son squirmed in his seat a bit before answering. "We met because of the accident," he said. "It was a fluke. If I hadn't washed up near that road, we wouldn't be having this conversation."

"Are you trying to say she doesn't care about you?" Elizabeth asked. "That she hung around and was shot at, and trekked her way through Wyoming, because she felt some sort of misplaced duty to save you?"

"You're making me sound like an idiot," Finn said. "You know it's more complicated than that."

"Is it?" Richard asked.

"Yes," Finn said. "I've spent the last few days with the Secret Service and the FBI, debriefing. Every time I recount a story, River is the one protecting us. She ambushed the guards and helped me escape. She pulled Mom out of a burning train car. Where was I?

Standing around like an idiot, scared to death of losing the people I love. How could she love someone like me? I can't protect her."

"How very *stone age* of you," Elizabeth said. "River doesn't need protection. She needs someone to love her. All of her: the strong parts, the damaged parts, and even a few sides you've probably not seen."

"It's not that simple," Finn said.

"Oh, but it is," Richard said. "I have to tell you something. I hope I'm not causing more trouble between you two, but I saw River once, probably around the same time she found you."

"What?" Finn asked. "Impossible."

"It's true. We were both getting gas at the same time in South Dakota. She was in the lane next to mine. I don't know why, but I had this feeling of being watched. When I walked into the store, I turned around and peered through the glass to see her scrutinizing my stuff through the rear window. When I returned, she pretended like nothing had happened, but looked me straight in the eye as I put gas in the Rover. It made me nervous to be seen so clearly after being so invisible to even myself. I recognized her immediately when you two walked into the kitchen. I'm not superstitious, but honestly, I think it was fate. The two of us out there on the highway and then somehow, we both found our way to you. She brought us back to Elizabeth."

"I agree," Elizabeth said. "It's more than coincidence."

"That doesn't mean you aren't right to be a little afraid," Richard said. "Love is a powerful thing. The pull another human can have on you is profound. But don't let it stop you."

"Why?" Finn asked.

"Because you two are well-matched. You were raised to withstand the worst that Mother Nature can create. You've been alone in the wilderness and learned to endure its silence and respect its power. She's withstood the worst that real life can offer and managed to survive. You're both strong people in different ways, and that's a good thing. If this relationship is meant to last, and I hope it is, you'll come to find that over the years each one of you will be forced to carry the burden of life for the other. That is the nature of things. There will be moments when you are powerless to act, and you have to have confidence in yourself and not see it as a weakness. Trust me. I know a little something about this."

"Your father is right," Elizabeth said. "It's not what you lack that matters, it's what you bring to the relationship. You seem awfully fixated on the past. River was a solider and worked in the Territories. She did what she had to do, but that time is over. I've spoken with River's mother quite a bit since the explosion. What River needs more than anything is a partner, a man who can be a father to her child, a person who can help her find the courage to return to school, to start living again. Someone with a great sense of adventure. Does that sound like anyone you know?"

FORTY ONE

RIVER WALKED into the kitchen just as her mother was pulling a loaf of banana bread from the oven. Tired and hungry, the aroma made her mouth water. It had been a long day, her interviews with the FBI and an entire alphabet of other law enforcement and regulatory agencies a grueling business. She wasn't under investigation, but the last weeks of her life, from the moment she'd seen Finn on the road, to the train explosion, were under a microscope, the authorities trying to understand just what the hell had happened.

"That smells good," River said, rubbing the back of her neck. Her body was stiff from the hard metal chairs at the Hailey Police Station, where they were conducting the conversations. She'd insisted on doing the meetings back in Idaho so she could be with Ava, and no one had objected.

"How did it go?" her mother asked.

"OK," River replied. "They want to talk about everything, every little detail of what happened. Honestly, it all sounds made up, like a script for a movie, but I know it's not."

"I think it's good to talk about it, get it all out," her mother said. "You're a brave woman, River, and you've had to endure a lot."

"I feel a *but* in there somewhere," River said.

Her mother smiled. "*But* the worst is over," she said. "It's time to begin making plans. I understand from Elizabeth that Yale is willing to admit you in the fall."

"*Elizabeth*...you say her name like she's an old friend," River said. "Mom, she's the President of the United States."

"Maybe so, but she's Elizabeth to *me*," Ingrid said. "It doesn't change the fact that it's time to get on with your life."

"And what are you going to do in Connecticut?" River asked.

"I don't know that I'm going," Ingrid said. "You've got a full scholarship with childcare. I may stay here for a while and relax. I'm worn out. Raising a child is for the young."

River opened her mouth to protest, but before she could reply, her mother spoke again. "Oh, I almost forgot, there's someone here to see you," she said, doing her best to sound nonchalant as she sliced the bread.

"Someone?" River asked, her pulse kicking up a notch. "Who is it?"

"It's Finn," her mother said. "He arrived about ten minutes before you and said he would wait outside. Ava is keeping him company."

Finn? They'd been separated since the explosion. As soon as she'd exited the train, she'd been whisked off to the hospital for examination and placed under observation for exposure to biological or chemical weapons. It had been nearly a month since the explosion and during that time, River hadn't heard a peep from Finn. Not that she'd tried to call him. She'd already determined they were doomed the night before the bombing, after the terrible argument they'd had. She'd railed against him and he just stood there, silent as the grave, not even reacting. That was all she needed to know. He didn't love her. She'd told her mother about Finn and his family, insisting that despite their romance, their decision to separate was mutual. She hadn't mentioned him since, but for some reason her mother didn't sound a bit surprised that he was in their backyard.

"River," her mother said sternly. "You need to stop hiding in the past. Marc is dead and his ghost is long since gone. Why aren't you going out there to talk to him?"

"What's the point?" River asked. "He's the son of a president and I'm...."

"You're what?" Ingrid asked. "The daughter of a librarian and a FedEx driver? Are you ashamed of your family?"

"No," River said. "But I didn't attend college."

"True," her mother said. "You joined the Army and served your country. You speak three languages. Do you believe that Finn thinks any less of you?"

"No, it's just that...," River said, unable to finish her sentence.

"Ahh, now I see what the deal is. This isn't about what he thinks," Ingrid said. "This is about what *you* think of yourself. Let it go, honey. You can't change the past. There is a bright future waiting for you. All you have to do is walk through that door."

River crossed the room to embrace her mother. "I'm scared," she whispered in her ear. "What if I can't do this? What if I don't know how to be happy? After all these years, what if I'm broken?"

"Nonsense," Ingrid said. "You're not broken, just scuffed up a bit and lord knows you could use a decent hair cut after the barbers in the Territory."

River sniffled and laughed, a smile breaking out across her face.

"For people like us, being happy is not easy," her mother continued. "Who can blame us after your father and Marc? There's no denying that things were hard for a long while. But you *will* get used to the feeling, and more importantly, you deserve it. After everything you've done for me, for Ava, you deserve to be loved. It's what your father would have wanted. It's what I want for you. That man outside loves you, honey. He wants to make a life with you."

Being happy often seemed like a quaint artifact, a relic of a different time. After her father's death, River learned to prepare for the worst, and all that came to pass confirmed her fears: combat, a loveless marriage, death, and then the desolation of the Territory. Along the way, she became an impervious being. Until Finn. Somehow, he broke through that night on the highway, and since their parting, the void he'd left behind had become a deafening echo inside her heart. What waited beyond her kitchen door felt like the greatest challenge in her life, and yet it also struck her as absurd that she had entered countless villages ahead of her platoon in a war, but couldn't face the man she loved.

"OK," she said, giving her mother's hand a squeeze. "I'll go."

River walked to the door, turned the knob, and stepped into their backyard, the sun's afternoon rays warming her face. She continued towards the end of their property–towards a creek that hugged the edge of their land, shallow and slow moving–where Ava had no doubt led them. It was her daughter's favorite place to play. Walking through the spring grasses and wildflowers, she heard his familiar voice. Finn was standing with her daughter, a fly-fishing rod in one hand, his bright red hair tucked under a baseball cap. He glanced up at River, a smile on his face and a light in his eyes that made her knees wobble.

"Finn," she said. "What are you doing here?"

"There's been a terrible accident," he said.

"An accident?" she repeated, remembering his words from that fateful night.

"Yes, and somehow I was separated from the woman I love," he said. "But, after a short bout of stupidity, I found my way back to her."

"I see," River said, unable to hide her smile. "And this woman, does she love you?"

"I'm not sure," he said. "She keeps her cards pretty close to her chest."

River heard her mother's voice urging her on. "I do love you, Finn," River said. "But I have to get on with my life, go back to school and finish what I started all those years ago. Yale has given me a full scholarship, no doubt thanks to your parents."

"Would you care for some company?" Finn asked.

"You would do that?" she asked. "Leave your job and move across the country?"

Finn nodded, closing the gap between them. Taking her hands in his, he brought them to his mouth and pressed his lips gently against the rough skin of her knuckles. "My life is where you are," he said. "Whatever happens next, we're going to do it together."

"It's not just me," River said, pointing at her daughter. "Are you prepared to take that on, too?"

Finn smiled and turned to face Ava, who stood nearby looking both confused and captivated by the presence of the tall stranger holding her mother's hand. He glanced at the small child almost swallowed up by the grasses, the sun's rays bouncing off her raven-colored hair. Her father was dead. River's father was dead. Someone needed to step into the chasm and love them. Finn knew with certainty that he was that person. After years of self-imposed solitude, he was ready to make messy emotional connections again.

"You bet. The whole package," he said. "In fact, I was just about to teach Ava how to fly fish."

"You were?" River asked. "Is that true?"

"Yes," Ava said. "I don't know how to fish."

"Not yet. But don't worry, it's easy," Finn said, grabbing the girl's hand. "The first step is to try to picture yourself fishing. All you have to do is close your eyes and use your imagination. Picture those fishes coming right up to your line."

River watched them saunter off, Finn's voice still audible as he spoke to her daughter.

"Ava?" he asked. "Can you see them? See those fishes?"

"Yes," she exclaimed. "I see them!"

"That's my girl," he said. "We're on our way now."

THE END

THE END

ACKNOWLEDGMENTS

48 States would not have made it to the finish line without the help of my editor, Cassandra Dunn. (And I owe a big thank you to Berkeley-side founder and non-fiction writer Frances Dinkelspiel for helping me find Cassandra.) When I decided to remain an independent author, I knew I would need help. I want to thank my assistant, Claire Mulcahy, for managing a million tiny details that make a writer's life successful.

I want to acknowledge Rebecca Lown, who designed the book cover, and my publicist, Kourtney Jason. I'm also lucky to be surrounded by friends and colleagues who have been great supporters of my writing. And finally, I'd like to thank my husband, Alec, and my daughter, Stella, for their encouragement and love.